The Living

The Living & The Dead

The Ballad of Nick & Mina

Jonathon Wolfer

ISBN 978-0-9887989-3-9

KELSEYTOWN
PRESS
www.kelseytownpress.com

For my friends

The Living

The Living & the Dead

Chapter 1
China Girl

"Wow, there's stuff in here that I didn't even remember until I read it," laying on her back on Nick's bed, Mina clapped the notebook closed. Then let it fall to her chest.

"Yeah, one of the things that has gotten stronger with my abilities, part reading between the lines and part seeing the actual memories of the story teller," Nick said from his desk chair, squeezing a tennis ball. Four times with one hand then four with the other.

"Wait. Do mean you can see in my head?" Mina sat bolt upright and swung her legs into the floor.

"Not exactly. I see the story in my head but like it's out of the corner of my eye. Ethereal and fuzzy," Nick bounced the ball off the floor into the wall, sending it back into his hand.

"How do you know it's not just what you're imagining?" Mina cocked her head to the side.

"What do you think after reading how I recorded your summer adventures?" Nick bounced the ball again.

"Like you were watching it unfold as I told you about it," Mina narrowed her eyes. "I'm not a fan of your being able to see in my head though."

"It's not all the time, only when you're telling me a story," Nick bounced the ball again.

"Still, that gives me little wiggle room," Mina leaned back on the bed, throwing her feet up onto the pillow.

"Yeah, no lying to me," Nick smiled, then tossed the ball toward the wall again.

But Mina was up and caught it before it had gotten two feet from his hand.

"What did I say about bouncing that ball in the house?" Nick's mother, Trudy, yelled up the stairs.

"I took it away from him, Trudy," Mina yelled back.

"Is that you, Mina? I didn't hear you come in," Trudy yelled back.

"She climbed in through the window again," Nick yelled. He tried to snag the tennis ball out of Mina's hand while her attention was on the stairs but failed. She smiled and shook her head at him.

"Don't be silly, Nicholas. Unless you're pulling a Goldilocks with that mess on your head," Trudy said as she stood on the stars and poked her head up above the hole in the floor and into from Nick's attic bedroom.

"My ninja skills are unparalleled, Trudy," Mina smiled and bounced the ball off of Nick's head, catching it easily.

"Hey," Nick swatted at the ball way too late. "None of that."

"Despite that being hilarious, no bouncing the ball in the house," Trudy smiled as her head disappeared down the steps. "Come get some breakfast before your first day back to school."

At the table Trudy had her New York Times open and was already half way into the crossword puzzle with a pen. Nick and Mina both grabbed plates from the cupboard and piled them high with scrambled eggs, bacon, hash browns and toast. Mina poured herself a cup of coffee and Nick filled a glass with orange juice.

"Thirteen letter word meaning confirmation that some fact or statement is true through the use of documentary evidence, starting with C and the sixth letter a B?" Trudy held the pen in her teeth, picked up her coffee cup and held it out toward Mina. "Top me off please, dear."

After filling Trudy's cup, Mina plopped down at the table next to Nick and dug into her eggs.

"Corroboration," Nick said, his mouth full of eggs, then shoveled hash browns into his face.

"Thank you but I was willing to wait ten seconds for you to swallow your food," Trudy raised an eyebrow.

"He'll only be eating for 35 seconds as it is at that pace," Sue said as she walked into the room and straight to the coffee pot. "Slow down boy. It's dead and can't run away from you."

"I'm afraid Mina is going to steal it actually," Nick smiled.

"Shut up jerk!" Mina said then shoved a piece of toast in her mouth.

"To have the metabolism of a teenager again," Sue sighed as she trotted out of the room.

"We need to get moving as well if we're gonna meet up with Ben to give Penny a sendoff on her first day of school," Mina drained her coffee cup.

"She's never been to school before?" Trudy asked.

"First day of school here, I'm sure she was enrolled somewhere before he adopted her - I hope," Nick stood up.

"I'm sure she'll fit right in either way here, such a sweet child," Trudy smiled. "Have a great start to your sophomore year you two."

Nick and Mina headed out the door. The scooter was parked in its usual spot in the driveway. Mina's Sportster, Tiffany, was parked in the garage at her father's request since it wasn't registered and Mina wasn't old enough to get a license anyway. Mina hopped onto the old scoot, patted the passenger seat and winked at Nick.

"Not fair," Nick said as he got on the back of the scooter. Mina fired it up and opened up the throttle, shooting out onto Main Street. Ten minutes later they were pulling down Hank's driveway. Ben and Penny had been staying there under the ruse of watching his farm while he was away on family business.

The blue Nova was sitting in the driveway in front of the garage. Ben and Penny were loading up.

"What are you guys doing here?" Penny said, her backpack way too big for her.

"We wanted to see you off on your first day of school," Mina smiled as she pulled her helmet off. When she got off the scooter Penny jumped into Mina's arms and hugged her.

"I am so excited, I've always wanted to go to school, never thought it would happen! Do you think they'll like me?" Penny said as she slid back down to her own feet.

"Of course they will," Mina smiled

"I don't know, I'm pretty weird," Penny smiled, but uncertainty filled her eyes.

"I'm pretty weird too, Penny," Nick smiled. "And you have a bit of an advantage over me."

"What advantage?" Penny cocked her head to the side.

"You have a way more bubbly personality than I do," Nick said. "People like that. So just be friendly and everything will be fine."

"Just be yourself," Mina said.

Ben and Nick looked at each other, then to Mina.

"Um, well, be yourself in this form," Mina motioned around the child with her hands.

"I know that," Penny said. "I won't turn into a lizard or anything to show off to anyone."

"I figured you knew what I meant," Mina narrowed her eyes at Nick and Ben. "Hop in the car, and buckle up so Ben can get you two moving."

"Okay," Penny opened the car door, tossed her backpack in the back seat then hopped in. Mina smiled as she closed the door for the little girl.

"Any whispers in the night I should know about?" Ben asked as he walked around to the driver's side of the blue Nova.

"No word," Nick shook his head. "He's not in any of the places you told me to check, at least not when I took a peak."

"One thing our kind is good at is disappearing when we want to," Ben said.

"I just hope he doesn't do anything stupid while he's off being invisible," Nick said. "We should get going before we are late."

"And I promised this little one a donut before her first day," Ben smiled and got in the car. Penny waved from the passenger seat as Ben fired the car up, and headed down the driveway.

"I wanna donut now," Mina walked toward the scooter.

"Of course you do. But we only really have time to hit the Shell station so you'll have to settle for those mini donuts," Nick looked at his watch.

"Then let's move," Mina pulled her helmet on and Nick followed suit.

A few minutes later they were pulling into the gas station down the street from the high school. Nick ran in and grabbed a few packs of the mini donuts, both the powdered and the chocolate, and was back on the scooter a minute later.

At the school, the pair parked near the bay doors to the shop classes. A few other scooters and a motorcycle were parked there too. The parking lot was mostly full already, and Filomena and Holly were getting out of his Mustang.

"Does he have his license yet?" Mina asked as she pulled her helmet off.

Filomena gave Nick a nod, smiling.

"Yeah, he got it and the car on his birthday," Nick nodded back to his friend. "Lucky S.O.B."

"Yes and no, he's old but you're still young and viral," Mina smiled and kissed Nick.

"Did he stay back or something?" Nick asked taking Mina's hand as they headed toward the front of the school.

"Not exactly. He started kindergarten the year before I did but got into an accident the first few weeks of school. His parent's opted to wait and reenroll him when he was 100 percent rather than send him back when he was still dealing with the stress of the accident and school and all," Mina said.

"He never mentioned he was in an accident," Nick said as they walked in the front doors.

"You really think he would talk about his weakness with you? With anyone, for that matter?" Mina said.

"He and I have had a few heavy conversations and I didn't know but somehow you know," Nick said.

"I only know because my father told me, it was a big thing I guess. Got hit by a car, and he was a tiny thing as it was. Doesn't seem to have caused him any problems physically growing up though," Mina said. "Pretty good ball player from what I've seen."

"Yeah, doesn't show at all," Nick looked around the hall for his friend. The story in his head, from hearing those few facts mixed with the conversations he'd had with Filomena made a lot more sense now.

In their respective home rooms, Nick and Mina got their class schedules for the quarter. Mina, having been off fighting in underground supernatural matches, had been assigned her classes by her guidance counselor. Mina easily found Nick at his locker since he was able to get the same one from last year.

"Mr. Crowley signed me up for classes but not a single art class," Mina held her schedule in front of Nick's face. "Where's your schedule?"

Nick handed his to her, "You expected him to care?"

"Yes, he's a guidance counselor and should have known I need to express myself," Mina gave Nick a scowl. "Especially with no breaks between three AP classes."

"I bet if you cry in his office he'll change whatever you want," Nick smiled as he closed the locker.

"I'm not a crier," Mina held their schedules side by side and studied them. "To add insult to injury we don't even have any classes together."

"Then I think you need to put on your best pouty face, do your best impression of someone who does cry and get that changed, cause even I'm in an art class," Nick picked his backpack off the ground and tossed the right strap over his shoulder.

"I think I'll try being a big girl about it first and just demand he change it," Mina handed Nick his schedule and crumpled hers in her right hand.

"Just don't do that to Crowley," Nick pointed to the crumpled schedule sticking out of her clenched fist.

Suddenly, Mina's schedule fell towards the floor and she had a hold of Filomena's fist, which she spun through the air, forcing his body to follow. He came to a sudden stop on his back on the tile next to her schedule.

"Cup check," Filomena wheezed.

Looking to Nick, Mina shrugged and let go of Paul's arm, "Reflex."

"Yeah, like a cat on steroids," Filomena coughed as Nick pulled him to his feet.

Mina narrowed her eyes at Paul.

"Kidding," Filomena put his hands up in surrender and smiled. "Mostly."

"Of course you are, and that's my cue to go take my anger out on Mr. Crowley," Mina feigned tapping Paul where his cup would be and the boy flinched dramatically. Mina smiled and sauntered off down the hall.

"Seems all those late nights you've been spending with Holly are leaving you slow and drained," Nick ran his palm down Filomena's face as though he was petting him.

"Hey," Filomena stepped back and pointed at Nick. "None of that face touching crap."

"What do you have first?" Nick asked.

Pulling his schedule out if his pocket and squinting at it, Paul said, "English with Serenbetz."

"Excellent, same here," Nick said and set off down the hall toward the English wing.

"So we haven't really had a chance to talk since Mina got back and I gotta ask, you okay with everything?" Filomena asked as they meandered through the hall.

"I'm definitely better with her here," Nick didn't look at him. "But some stuff
can't be undone and that's just life."

"Understood," Filomena smiled.

"Are you and Holly all official now," Nick looked over at his friend as they walked into Serenbetz's room.

"Nothing verbal but I am a huge fan of the idea," Filomena said as they sat down side by side in the center of the room.

"She is a sweetheart and you two are like two peas in a pod with how much you talk," Nick laughed. "Like two chickens clucking eight days a week."

"And here I was about to ask if you and Mina wanna go to the movies with Holly and me," Filomena said. "But you'll probably cry cause she and I will talk through the whole thing. Or Mina will gut us."

"Probably both," Nick smiled.

"Seriously, your woman is a brute," Filomena flexed his wrist a few times around. "How are you not broken?"

*****

The lunch room was a madhouse and Mina waited at the doors for Nick even though she hated the noise, the crowd and she was starving.

"Let's grab some food and head over to the art room," Nick smiled as he picked Mina up in a hug.

"Yes, please," she whispered as he brought her gently back down to her feet.

"Any luck on your schedule?" Nick took her hand and led her into the formidable lunch line.

"A little. I was able to switch things around so my gym class is in the afternoon now on two and four days and I picked up a photography class in the morning. So those two study halls on one and three days will be spent on Guided Study in Art. Which means me painting whatever the hell I want," Mina said.

"What period is the gym class?" Nick asked.

"F," Mina frowned.

My Intro to Drawing class is that period," Nick smiled. "We have half a class together now."

Smiling, Mina said, "That will have to do."

******

After school Nick was going to go to the cross country team meeting. He wasn't sure yet if he wanted to join the team or not, but the training sure would help him out on the baseball field. A few of the guys were going and Mina wanted to go see Penny after her first day of school.

Mina had some time to kill since the elementary school didn't get out for a while longer. So she went up to Gert's house to finally take a look around and make sure the place hadn't burned down.

"Yup, still standing," she said to herself, taking off her helmet. The scooter was still running.

Looking around the yard, she noticed the lawn had been cut recently and the bushes in the front of the house had been trimmed.

"Is this where you're hiding out Hank? Right under our noses?" Mina turned the scooter off and hung her helmet off the handlebars.

At the front door she slowly went through her keys until she found the right one, then slid it into the lock. She paused, listened, smelled and felt the air for anything out of place. There was a dull throb and sense of heat she had never noticed coming from inside the house but that could just mean the house needed to be aired out after all this time being empty. Or Hank could be a drunken mess on the couch in a half transformed state between man and werepig. She really didn't want to see him naked again.

When she entered everything was still. The air was stale and it was obvious no one had been inside for weeks. And she couldn't smell Hank, which was a sure sign he wasn't there. Werepig had a very distinct smell, even in his human form- not of pig, or anything like that, just a mixture of hard work, the farm he ran and that sweet caramel scent of magic.

Other than the stagnant air the house was immaculate. But it was very warm inside so she proceeded to open a few windows to let the air through. That dull throb of energy was still there but that could be all the magical items Gert had hidden throughout the place that Mina had never worried about before.

After taking a walk through every room Mina figured that was enough for now and she would come and shut the windows later after seeing how Penny's day went. She pulled into Hanks's driveway just as Ben and Penny were getting out of the blue Nova.

"Hi, Mina!" Penny squealed. The child dropped her enormous backpack and changed into a squirrel. The Penny-squirrel ran up Mina's leg, her side and sat on her shoulder. Then the Penny-squirrel turned back into Penny's normal form - still sitting on Mina's shoulder.

"How was your day, darlin?" Mina asked.

"Awesome," Penny jumped down and turned to face Mina. "Everyone is so nice it's ridiculous. I've got like ten friends already."

"Slow down child," Ben said. "She needs to expend some energy, so we are going to go for a romp through the forest. You're welcome to join us. I would actually prefer it if you do, if you understand me."

"I do, Ben," Mina nodded. "And I could use a run myself. I might have just as much pent up energy as this little one."

"No way, I had to hold back from changing for like eight hours. It's been murder," Penny jumped up and popped into the form of a sparrow and fluttered off toward the woods.

"After you, my lady," Ben smiled and bowed.

Leaping off after Penny, a smile grew across Mina's face. Ben was close behind her when she landed in the woods. He was still in his human form.

Ben smiled as he slammed his fist into a large oak tree, splintering the trunk and sending the tree falling away from him. "Timber!"

Mina laughed and shivered at the same time as she watched the small man run off as the tree fell, leaving the splintered base behind.

"I hope Hank comes back soon, I can keep animals alive, but I can't really help them thrive like he does," Ben said when Mina caught up with him.

"Yeah, he has a way with them, a kinship that can't really be learned," Mina said as she ran up a tree and launched herself into the air. In the sky, she met the Penny-sparrow who looped around on little wings fluttering so fast they were a blur.

When Mina came down Ben was jumping from tree trunk to tree trunk.

"If you ever need too, Mina, I can spar with you," Ben said as he came down on top of a large boulder.

"I'm not sure that is necessary," Mina said.

"The rush of the fight is as hard an addiction to wean yourself of as any I have ever witnessed," Ben jumped into the air disappearing above the tree line.

On foot, Mina raced along the forest floor. Ben came down hard sending leaves and rotting debris into the air around him. When it settled he looked up smiling.

"Feels good to unleash. But it won't calm the storm that comes with the full moon," Ben stood slowly, looking up into the sky above him. "How I envy the two of you."

"When is the next full moon?" Mina asked.

"Soon. I will need you and Nick to take care of Penny for those few days," Ben stepped out of the crater he had created.

"Not a problem, but wouldn't it be better if I go with you?" Mina asked.

"No, I go very deep and the only creature that needs fear me there is the squid," Ben said.

"The squid?" Mina cocked an eyebrow.

"The giant ones love to wrestle and they love lobster," Ben smiled and took off.

The Living

Chapter 2
Oh You Pretty Things

The first few days of school flew by since Labor Day had fall-en on the first of September, making it a short week for Nick and Mina. Holly and Filomena planned a double date for that Friday evening - dinner and a movie.

Mina and Nick met Paul and Holly at 9 East Main to grab some pizza before the movie.

"Our choices for the movie are The Fly or Stand by Me." Filomena said reading his chicken scratch on a scrap piece of paper.

Nick and Mina looked at each other and both said, "Stand by Me."

"Well, my vote is for The Fly. I wanna see something freaky," Filomena said then looked over to Holly. "That means you can either tie it up and Nick and I will have to wrestle for it or you can tip the scales, darlin."

"Um, even though the thought of you and Nick wrestling sounds divine, Stand by Me, easily," Holly said. "Anything based on a Stephen King story trumps some guy puking on Geena Davis."

"Done. The Fly will be for a boy's night out, then," Filomena smacked Nick on the thigh with his open palm then dug his fingers into the muscle.

Nick grimaced but didn't flinch.

"Wait, Stand by Me is based on something King wrote?" Mina asked.

"Yeah, 'The Body'. It's one of the novellas in 'Different Seasons'," Holly smiled. "I'm not huge into horror but that guy can write."

"I never took you for a big reader," Nick said.

"Me either," Mina said. "And I wish I had read the story. I like to read the book before seeing the movie."

"Me too!" Holly squealed. "Have you ever seen anything that

you actually thought was better than the book?"

"I don't think anything like that exists," Mina said.

Nick and Filomena exchange dry smiles.

"Did you see The Shining?" Holly asked. "Or read the book?"

"Both, and I enjoyed the realism Kubrick brought to the whole experience, but the book was still better," Mina said as the pizza they had ordered was set on the table next to them.

"Thank God, I'm starving," Filomena grabbed one of the plates the waitress had left behind. He pulled a piece of the sausage and pepper pizza off the tray and handed it to Holly.

"Thanks, babe," Holly smiled and filled his cup with one of the Grape Foxen Park bottles that was sitting on the table.

Filomena handed two plates to Nick then grabbed two pieces for himself.

Nick smiled at Mina and put two slices on her plate without asking then two on his own.

"So, Mina, where were you the whole summer?" Holly asked after swallowing her first bite.

Mina swallowed and said, "First half of the summer I was cage fighting in Montreal." Then she tore off a big chunk of her slice of pizza.

Nick was in the middle of swallowing his second huge bite and choked a little.

"The rest of it I was in Vegas," Mina smiled.

"There were some crazy rumors like you had joined a biker gang or you became one of those hobos who ride the trains or you had joined the circus," Filomena said.

"The circus one is my favorite," Nick laughed, his mouth full of pizza.

"I think I'm going to go with that one from now on myself," Mina smiled as she chomped down on the crust of her first piece of pizza.

"Come on, where were you really?" Holly said.

Mina looked at Nick, then to her second slice of pizza, "I was looking for family."

"Oh," Holly said. "Any luck? I hope so cause I know how

important family is."

"Not exactly, but I made a really good friend," Mina smiled as a little sparrow landed on the window sill and looked in at her. It flew away before Mina could get a good look at it.

"So did you win any of those cage fights?" Filomena asked as he shoved half of his second slice.

"All of them," Mina said quietly taking a bite of her next slice.

"Pretty sure you could kick the crap out of the two of us at the same time," Paul, with a giant grin on his face, pointed to himself and Nick. "So not too many dudes could stand a chance one-on-one with ya."

"Pretty sure all we'd end up doing is bleeding on her," Nick crunched into his crust.

"Aw gross," Holly said as she bit off the last of the cheesy pizza from the crust. Then she dropped the crust down on her plate.

"You more than me cause I learned a long time ago to run away from her," Filomena grabbed another slice and stuffed half if it in his mouth.

"Smart man," Nick pulled another piece for Mina then the last one for himself.

*****

When they were finished eating the two couples met over at the movie theatre in Madison. Mina and Filomena parked their respective vehicles in the parking lot behind the building. They meandered through the alley between two of the buildings to the sidewalk in front of the theatre and a small diner.

A little bird, a very familiar sparrow, landed on a potted plant near Mina and the scent of Penny was unmistakable. Mina scowled at the Penny-sparrow and motioned her head back toward the ally.

"Nick, I think I left the key in the scooter, I'll be right back," Mina said and spun in her heel.

"A little bird tells me it's in the ignition," Nick grinned.

Mina's face lit up as she and Nick locked eyes. Then she headed back toward the parking lot.

In the ally the little sparrow dropped down into the dark and became Penny in her child form. She smiled, "Hey Mina!"

"What are you doing here?" Mina asked.

"I was bored so I came to say hi," Penny said.

"Where's Ben?" Mina asked.

"He's at Hank's house, he was reading when I left," Penny said.

"You shouldn't be out by yourself, darlin'," Mina knelt down in front of Penny and took her hands.

"I can take care of myself," Penny scowled.

"I know that first hand, sweetie, but I can't help but go all older sister on you and worry," Mina smiled.

"Older sister?" Penny's eyes widened.

"Yeah, we're sisters now. I know I can't tell you what to do, but I do need you to be very careful. After everything that happened in Vegas and New Orleans I don't know what is going to happen with us and we all need to be careful," Mina smiled.

"I know, it's all so mysterious and exciting," Penny said. "It's one of the great things about being like we are."

"That is a good perspective to have," Mina stood up, keeping one of the child's hands.

"You should get back to your date and I want to get back into the sky," Penny looked up.

"You have fun, sweetie," Mina let go of Penny's hand and the child changed into the sparrow once again, and spiraled into the sky above.

Back on the sidewalk, Nick asked, "Find it?"

"The little birdie was right. Gotta stop doing that," Mina took Nick's hand.

"Seriously, you never know who would be a douche and go for a joyride if they saw the keys just sitting there in the ignition," Filomena said. "On a lighter note, we got tickets, now it's time to get snacks."

"Agreed," Holly took Filomena's hand and pulled him toward the door. He hopped ahead and opened the door for her. He held it open for Nick and Mina, bowing slightly as they nodded at him.

At the counter Nick ordered popcorn, Junior Mints, a large soda, and Goobers.

Whispering in his ear, Mina said, "Get some Twizzlers too, please."

Nick kissed her on the cheek and smiled.

*****

After the movie let out, the two couples went their separate ways. Nick and Mina stood next to her scooter in the parking lot and pulled their helmets on as Filomena and Holly peeled out.

"So, home? Or should we do our best to break curfew?" Mina asked.

"I want to go up to Gert's," Nick said.

"What for?" Mina asked.

"I want to check something but I have been hesitant to go into her house alone since you came back, since you told me..." Nick looked down at the ground.

"Since she died," Mina said.

"No, since you told me how she helped make Valen Tine," Nick's eyes shot up to meet Mina's.

"What? Why?" Mina cocked her head to the side.

"Gert has more than one of those Jin up there that I know of - I can feel it every time I'm up there cutting the grass," Nick said.

"That was you taking care of the yard?" Mina said. "I felt it too when I was there the other day."

"Yeah, been doing it all summer. And I know that Gert had spells and charms and all kinds of mumbo jumbo in place protecting her house while she was alive, but I am not sure they are still in place. They may not all be gone, but her magic is breaking down. I think that's why we can feel the heat and the energy growing at the house."

"You want to find the Jin and hide them again?" Mina said.

"Or set up our own charms," Nick said.

"You want to learn magic?" Mina cocked an eyebrow.

"I want to learn more magic," Nick said.

"Learn more magic? Did you get a magic wand you're not

telling me about?" Mina said.

"Let's head up to Gert's. I'll explain more there. I'm pretty sure her phone is still connected, so we can call our parents and tell them we are hanging out with Penny for a bit after her first week of school. I'm sure they won't argue with that."

"Okay then, let's roll," Mina hopped on the scooter. Nick joined and they took off.

At Gert's, Nick and Mina both stood on the front steps and looked at the door.

"To answer your question about getting a magic wand, you were there when we both got one," Nick pulled out the pen.

"What are you talking about?" Mina reached for the door knob.

"Wait," Nick said and held up his pen. "I want to do something with my magic wand."

Mina pulled her hand back and narrowed her eyes at Nick.

Smiling, Nick wrote on the door with the pen, in big sweeping letter, leaving no trace he had just run the point over the surface.

"What did you write? I only caught a few of the letter of your chicken scratch," Mina reached for the door, but her hand stopped an inch from the knob. She pushed harder but the invisible force stopping her hand did not budge. She pulled her hand back, then moved faster than Nick could actually see, but her hand could get no closer to the knob or any part of the door.

Nick shook his head at Mina, then wrapped his fingers around the knob, turned it and opened the door. He smiled and gestured her to go ahead of him, "Ladies first."

"What did you write on the door?" Mina asked as she walked in the house.

"Magic," Nick smiled and followed her inside.

It was much less stuffy since Mina had come by and aired the house out. But it was still warm inside and the pulse of energy was undeniable.

"I don't think the Jin can leave, but they know that Gert is dead, and they are trying to draw someone here to help them get loose or at least wreak some havoc in someone's life like they did hers," Nick said. "So we need to figure out how to stop them from drawing attention to this place any longer."

"Well, Mr. Wizard, how do we do that?" Mina asked as she sat down at the kitchen table.

"First we have to figure out what would be the simplest way to word a spell so that no one will be drawn here by the lure of the Jin," Nick sat down.

"Well, that's easy. Just write that no one can feel them, hear them, see them or be drawn by them to this place," Mina said.

"Then next we need to figure out where to write that. Can't just write it on the wall and expect it to work on the whole property," Nick said.

"You're talking like you already had this figured out, so why don't you just tell me what we do next," Mina leaned on her elbows on the table.

"I sort of have it figured out but we definitely need to work together," Nick smiled. "I need you to jump as high as you can so that I can write over the whole property, in the simplest and most straight forward statement I can, like the one you just said."

"I can do that," Mina smiled.

"And by both of us doing it together, the spell will be much stronger. Not as easily broken like the one on the door. But bear in mind, we need to test that a little more. I think that you could get past my spells with a little force of will because we are connected." Nick stood up. "Let's see how high we need to be to do this right. Oh, but we need to call our folks first.

Outside in the yard, where Mina had spent many hours sweating and bleeding, after calling their parents and getting no resistance on them breaking curfew, they looked up at the stars.

"Are you ready for this?" Mina wrapped her arms around Nick.

"Just try and bring us down gently. Remember, my legs won't heal as quickly as yours if they shatter on impact," Nick smiled, his arms draped over Mina's shoulders.

"Don't worry, sweetie, you won't even touch the ground," Mina shot into the air. The wind whipped past them, and the stars rushed toward them.

In the air, Nick looked down over Mina's shoulder and began moving his arm as though he were painting the letters on a giant canvas. He was about halfway through what he wanted to write as the ground rushed towards them. There was a sudden stop, so quick it barely registered, and then they were sailing toward the stars again. In the air, he knew what he had written and made quick work of finishing the spell, then he smiled. And as they fell back to Earth, he laughed, "You shall not pass!"

On the ground, Nick's feet were gently placed back in the grass.

"Did you quote Gandalf on the way down?" Mina stepped back from him. "You are such a dork."

"You recognized it," Nick smiled, taking her hand. He led her back to the door. They stopped on the steps, and Nick wrote again on the door, then motioned her to open it.

Mina narrowed her eyes at him and reached for the handle. There was no resistance, and the door opened. "What did you write?"

"Nick and Mina only," Nick smiled and walked into the house.

Chapter 3
Sorrow

Sweat poured off of Nick as he hit the sand. He was running more than ever after joining the cross country team and had been pushing himself every day the past week at practice and then pounding the pavement a few more miles at home every night afterwards.

The week had flown by and Nick wanted to jump in the water after all the cardio. He wanted to take advantage of the warm September weather since New England could turn on him at any moment and these cool down sessions he had grown so accustomed too could be lost in the blink of an eye.

On the edge of the water he pulled his sneakers and socks off, then peeled off his sweat soaked shirt and dropped it on top of his shoes. It was only half tide so the water wasn't deep and Nick had to walk out a ways before he could dive in. When he came up for air he rolled into his back and looked up at the stars.

The Summer Triangle was still very visible and would be well into November. The Big Dipper and the Great Bear still stood out in the sky above. But Nick's mind was as tired as his body after a full week of schoolwork and he couldn't recall any of the individual star's names. He was tired and knew treading water, even while floating, was a bad idea. So, he swam back to where his feet could touch and walked back up on the beach.

Picking up his clothes, Nick headed over to the two person swing and sat down. As he stared out over the water, he threw his arm over the back of the bench style swing. The hair on the back of his neck and arms rose slightly, and Nick said, "Hey, Jules, long time no see."

"I've been kinda bummed the past few weeks with Hank being M.I.A." Julie materialized in the seat next to Nick. She leaned back against the swing and Nick could feel the coldness against his arm as her hair passed through his skin.

"I figured you were off with him wherever he's gone on his little walkabout," Nick said.

"No, he didn't even say goodbye. Just poof," Julie disappeared, "He was gone."

"He's dealing with a lot, it had nothing to do with you," Nick said.

Reappearing, Julie said, "I know, Gert was his teacher and mentor and friend for a long time. But I miss him and wish he would let me help him with his grief."

"He always was a loner, Julie. Gert was helping him with that. She was helping him keep to his second chance as well," Nick said. "And that was a lot of work. I just hope all of it wasn't a waste."

"Why would it be a waste?" Julie asked.

"If he goes off the grid and starts doing bad things, he doesn't get another chance," Nick said.

"What do you think he's going to do, Nick?" Julie turned toward him.

"He might hurt or kill someone innocent," Nick said.

"He won't, I know it. He's not a monster, at least not anymore," Julie floated up in front of Nick, fists buried in her hips as she scowled at him.

"Who knows what he is capable of right now, with his mind torn to shreds and the full moon coming," Nick said. "He's proven himself capable of doing very bad things already."

"Like what?" Julie asked.

"He helped kill my uncle and his girlfriend. They were like me and Mina with the pen and the sword. He helped Frank Stone track them down and murder them," Nick said.

"He's not like that," Julie floated a little higher. "Not anymore."

"I hope so, because despite what he did then, I wouldn't want to hunt down a friend," Nick said. "Have you checked out his house in Nantucket?"

"Yeah, that was the first place I checked," Julie floated back down to where her feet almost touched the sand.

"Will you check there again for me every day, just to see if maybe he takes a break from roaming the forests of New England and showers or something," Nick leaned forward, resting his elbows on his knees and lacing his fingers together.

"I can only hope I catch him in the shower," Julie breathed heavily.

"Stop that," Nick looked up at her.

"Prude," Julie said. "But I don't know if I can go every day. It's hard to travel that far often. I've discovered I have to take a break in between jumps like that. If it's just around town I can do it over and over, but the more miles, the more it seems to take out of me."

"Interesting," Nick leaned back on the swing.

"It's annoying, I figured being dead and all I wouldn't get tired," Julie said. "Well, not tired, but drained."

"Still interesting," Nick said.

"Have you figured out anymore of the stuff at the cemetery or the whole being hunted thing?" Julie asked.

"A little, I learned to push the Map Walking and now I can sort of do a little magic," Nick said.

"Map Walking?" Julie raised an eyebrow. "What the hell is that?"

"I can rest the end of the pen on a map and see that place as though I'm actually there," Nick said.

"Just that one spot you're touching? Seems kind of limited." Julie said.

"A little limited, but I can move around the place, go inside of houses or run around as though I'm there just without my body," Nick said.

"Like an astral projection?" Julie asked.

"I hadn't thought about it like that. But yeah, that seems like a pretty apt comparison," Nick said.

"Sounds more like right on the nose to me," Julie said.

"I'm not going to call it that," Nick stood up.

"Like Map Walking is any better?" Julie said as Nick pulled on his shirt. "And boo, you're going?"

"I have practice in the morning and homework to get done tonight. Plus I try and do a little searching for Hank every night with my Map Walking," Nick said, elongating that last part.

"Have you ever tried using that Map Walking to find the people hunting you?" Julie raised an eyebrow.

"I have not, no," Nick said. He shifted from foot to foot, then sat back down. "I really hadn't thought about it. I wouldn't know where to start."

"When you're looking for Hank, where do you look?" Julie asked.

"Places he's talked about, places I've been to with him," Nick pulled on his socks.

"You really think he would go somewhere he's been?" Julie asked.

"It seems to be a common theme among these supernatural beings," Nick pointed at Julie, "to spend time in places that have great meaning to them."

"Touche," Julie said. Then her face lit up. "So, these people hunting you, specifically the Stone guy, what do you know about him?"

"Not much about him, but there is a very famous story based on him. A sci-fi horror novel based on a true story that just might give me a few places to start looking," Nick pulled on his shoes quickly. "You are a wonder that never ceases to amaze me, Julie, thank you. Mind you, I now have twice as much, if not more, work to do."

"Thanks," Julia smiled. "And you're welcome."

"If you want to come haunt my house a little later you're more than welcome and I know that Penny and Ben wouldn't mind if you popped in and said hello to them." Nick stood up.

"I was kind of avoiding Hank's house, so visiting Ben and Penny has been kind of off the list," Julia said. "But I do want to see Penny, that little girl is absolutely adorable and a little spitfire."

"I know she would love to see you," Nick said. "You gotta remember, you're a ghost and can literally disappear. None of us can do that."

"I know," Julia said.

"I understand better than anyone having someone you care about and have spent almost every waking moment with go bub-bye with little to no explanation, and turning to my friends and family was a huge help," Nick said. "You know where I'll be, and you know where Penny and Ben are. Lean on us as much or as little as you need."

"I wish I could hug you so bad right now," Julie said.

"I know you can move things every once in a while, plus I'm not a normal person, so try," Nick said. He held his arms out.

Floating up off the swing, Julie moved into Nick's arms. She wrapped her arms around his neck, and he pulled her into him. For a moment, it was a perfectly executed hug. But she was still a ghost and the facts of the situation could only be ignored for a few seconds and she melted through Nick as easily was he would have cut through fog.

"Thank you," Julie said quietly and faded away.

"You are very welcome, Julie," Nick said. He smiled and shook his head, then took off running for home. He burst through the front door of the old Stanton home, raced up the stairs and up into his attic bedroom. He dropped into his chair, yanked his yellowing and dog-eared copy of Mary Shelley's Frankenstein out of the drawer he had stuffed it in and began combing through the story and making a list of all the places the Monster in the story visits.

*****

"We need to talk, Mija," Mina's father, Rogelio, said as they placed a bowl filled with spaghetti and meatballs on the table in the kitchen.

"Dad, I don't need to have the sex talk, television has relieved you of that particular joy of parenthood," Mina pulled the forked spoon out of the bowl and filled her father's plate, then her own.

Turning around to the oven, Rogelio said as he opened it, "No, Mija, we need to talk about your mother."

"What about her?" Mina filled her plate as her father pulled garlic bread out of the oven and placed it on the stove.

"Well, I have been thinking that with everything that I have learned about you in the past few weeks, the sword and the super powers and the being hunted, that maybe we should take a trip to see your mother's side of the family. Maybe get out of here for a little bit and since you're a whole lot more special than I am her siblings might actually tell you what really happened to her," he said as he piled the pieces of garlic bread on a plate.

"I can't leave right now, Dad," Mina began twirling her fork in her spaghetti. "I left Nick once and I can't do that again. My job is pretty specific, and on top of that, the further I'm away from him the worse I feel physically. Looking back on it I almost didn't get back here to you because my power is tied to him somehow. I heal faster when with him, I feel more powerful than I do sitting here at his side."

"We could bring him with us, since he might be able to help figure out what happened too, he seems to have a gift to get people to talk," Rogelio set the plate of bread down on the table and sat down.

"You want us to go hide?" Mina gasped, then shoved the fork full of spaghetti into her mouth.

"I just want you to be safe, and getting out of Dodge seems like a good way to accomplish that goal," Rogelio grabbed a piece of garlic bread and dipped it into the spaghetti on his plate, scooping up some sauce and noodles, then took a bite.

"It sounds good in practice, Dad, but we can't run, I can't run," Mina said. Her plate was half empty already and she grabbed a piece of bread.

"Why not? There's nothing wrong with being safe," Rogelio looked his daughter in the eye.

"Because Nick and I might be the last chance this world has against some of the most evil creatures that have ever walked the Earth," Mina stared right back into her father's eyes. "And I am well aware of how ridiculous that sounds when said out loud."

"How do you know you're not supposed to just run and protect Nick and your family? That you're not supposed to just grow up to be a teacher or a mother or a senator?" Rogelio said.

"A senator? Really, Dad?" Mina cocked her head to the side.

"Seriously?" he said.

"Would you rather be the father of the woman who becomes a senator or the father of the girl who saves the world?" Mina asked.

"That's not a fair question," Rogelio said.

"Well, as you have said many times to me, life isn't fair," Mina stabbed the last meatball on her plate and shoved it in her mouth. "And after what I saw happen in Vegas and what happened to Gert, I can't just run from them."

"Touché, Mija," Rogelio said. "I'm just afraid for you. And I still don't fully understand this situation or why this Frank Stone is after you."

"Fathers have feared for their daughters for millennia, as you have also said quite a few times before," Mina said. "I'm not stupid. It scares me too, but I'm going to use that fear to be faster and stronger than I thought I could be. And he wants power. He knows what the sword awakened in me and he knows the full capabilities of the pen Nick has. And he wants it all for himself."

"Then why not give it to him? Just be done with this whole supernatural mess and go be a teenager and go to college and get married and make me a grandfather."

"I want to do all those things as well, but I can't give this up to him. I understand now after my summer vacation that it will not go away while I still walk and talk and have a heartbeat, Dad. It's not just a vocation some guidance counselor suggests I go into because I test high in that area. I can do things that no one else on this Earth can do, and whether or not I have the sword in my hand doesn't change that. But it would give this monster an advantage unlike anything else he has ever killed for."

"And he really did kill Nick's Uncle John and his girlfriend Lauren?" he asked. "It wasn't a car accident?"

"Yes, and he had a great deal of help," Mina said.

"How do you know all of this?" Rogelio asked.

"Nick's uncle kept journals, and his ancestors wrote things down in the cemetery on the headstones and at the playground and in a bunch of other weird places. Usually his uncle would have taught him these things or whomever was going to take over for John, but he was killed before being able to pass on the knowledge."

"So you and Nick have been picking this up as you go?" he asked.

"Thrown right into the fire, it seems," Mina filled her plate again. "Hence all the mistakes. Gert taught us what she knew about the pen and the sword, which wasn't much, since Nick's ancestors were pretty tight lipped about what they were really up to."

"Have you two figured out exactly what you're supposed to be doing? Specifically what his role is in this whole thing?" Rogelio used his fork to motion that he meant the whole world.

"Not really," Mina frowned. "We still don't know a whole lot. My powers were pretty obvious. He can remember what he sees down to the last little detail, he can see between the lines when someone is telling a story, like he's seeing their memories as they remember them, he can do this thing where he can see the place on a map as though he is really there--,"

"That's a little dangerous for a teenage boy," Rogelio said.

"I said the same thing," Mina said. "But he also has this gift of being believed when he is telling you the truth. Gert explained it best by saying if Nick saw God and told the world, they would believe whole heartedly."

"Does this gift only work with what he has seen?" Rogelio asked as he sat back in his chair, his plate empty.

"You mean can he lie and be believable?" Mina asked. "He's a teenager so I'm pretty sure he's a pro at that anyway. But what I mean, and what Gert meant, is that he's the line in the sand, the one who is here to see all the bad stuff and to keep the rest of the world fearful of all the stuff that goes bump in the night. If people don't at least have a small idea of all the bad stuff out there in the world, like with horror stories or fairy tales or whatever, they wouldn't be safe. And on the other side of the coin, he and I are here to make sure the supernatural world doesn't get too powerful and just take over the world. We are here to keep a balance. The problem is that Frank Stone is tipping the scales way too far in his direction."

"So you think Stone wants to take over the world?" Rogelio asked.

"I think he wants even more than that," Mina said. "Nick can explain all of this better than I can though. And I think I am going to go bug him once I've finished the dishes."

Mina and her father stood at the same time, "You wash and I will dry, Mija.

"Can you tell me more about the colonies back in the 1600's while we do? Since meeting someone actually from that era my curiosity has been going off the wall about it," Mina picked up the dinner plates and put them in the sink.

"Ah, yes, I keep forgetting that Ben is a three hundred plus year old werelobster," Rogelio picked up the food and began covering it with plastic wrap.

"That also sounds ridiculous when you say it out loud," Mina said as she started on the dishes.

The Living

Chapter 4
I'm Afraid of Americans

"Wake up," Mina sat down in the desk chair in Nick's room.

"No," Nick said. His head buried under his pillow. "Get in here with me."

"Nope, too much to do today. It's already noon and your mother has tried to wake you up twice. They called in reinforcements," Mina pointed at herself with her free hand. Her other hand held a coffee cup. "Your mom invited me apple picking. Your presence is mandatory. Ben and Penny are going to meet us over at Bishop's Orchard, too."

"I didn't go to sleep until the sun came up this morning," Nick kept his head under his pillow. "I am unable to move."

"What on Earth were you doing all night?" Mina sipped the coffee.

"I was exploring Ingolstadt," Nick peeked an eye out from under the pillow. "Is that coffee?'

"It is and where is Ingolstadt?" Mina said. "And why wasn't I invited?"

"It's in Germany. Bavaria to be exact, the southern part of the country on the bank of the Danube River." Nick reached a hand out for the coffee. "And I just got caught up in a project and didn't think to call."

"You can get up and get your own coffee and I would have liked to have seen Ingolstadt. That's where Dr. Frankenstein created his monster, correct?"

"You're a jerk and correct." Nick kicked off his blanket.

"Why were you Map Walking there?" Mina said and held her mug to him.

"I'm following a lead," Nick sat up slowly taking the mug from Mina's hand. He held the cup to his nose and breathed in. "Thank you."

"You're welcome," Mina said. "Stop beating around the bush."

"I'm looking to see if Stone is hanging out in one of the places from the book. I've noticed a pattern with these old creatures like Hank and Ben holding onto places or items from their past. And I am hoping he has some of the same behaviors."

"But the book isn't based on all facts," Mina leaned forward. "So why would he haunt anywhere from the book?"

"I have a feeling Shelley took more liberties with the doctor's story than she did with the monster's," Nick drank down all of the coffee. "I need more of this."

"Put your clothes on and get some more," Mina smiled at Nick. "But put your clothes on slowly."

A few minutes later Nick was draining another cup of coffee. Mina was dipping carrots in hummus and crunching them loudly.

"You two ready?" Sue asked as she walked into the room carrying the mail.

"I am, but he's going to be useless for another hour," Mina covered the hummus and tossed it back in the fridge.

"Works for me cause I don't really need the jackass until the bags are filled with apples," Sue smiled as she walked out of the room.

"I'll take that as the train is leaving," Mina grabbed Nick's hand and pulled him along after Sue. Nick closed the door behind them, and let himself be dragged to the car. He and Mina climbed into the backseat.

"Why were you up so late last night, Nicholas?" Trudy asked.

"Research," Nick said as he leaned his head over the back of the seat.

Mina eyed him suspiciously, specifically for Nick to see.

"I saw all the maps and atlases. What are you working on now?" Trudy asked.

"I'm tracking Frankenstein's monster," Nick smiled at Mina. "I'm compiling a guide book for people who want to visit all the places in the novel, why they are significant, and what might still be in those places that were special to Mary Shelley, the doctor, and the monster."

"That sounds like a lot of fun," Trudy said.

"Sounds like the kind of trip I'd like to take," Sue said. "A literary getaway."

"Are you looking to be the next Arthur Frommer?" Trudy said.

"The Stanton Guide to Literary Adventures," Mina laughed.

"Has a nice ring to it," Trudy said.

"Too much clever banter for me this morning," Nick said.

"Then close your ears, boy," Sue looked in the rear view mirror at Nick and smiled.

"Yes, ma'am. Wake me when you need a donkey," Nick closed his eyes.

The ladies kept up the conversation around him, but Nick drifted off to sleep.

*****

"So you've been doing the Map Walking thing every night, exploring the places from Frankenstein hoping to find Stone hiding out in these places?" Mina dropped two apples from high up in the tree to Nick. He put them into a paper bag.

"Hoping to at least find clues to where he is," Nick said. "You saw him at the arena, which means he does go out into the world for at least special events, but he must live somewhere."

"But what if the novel's locales have no meaning to him? What if lives in a villa on the Rhone? Or a mountainside retreat in the Alps?" Mina asked.

"He very well could but these supes seem to have an affinity for places from their past. Look at Hank and Ben. Prime examples. Ben is also fixated on an artifact from his mortal life," Nick caught another three apples easily transferring them to the bag one after the other. "And he's even got me obsessing over that other stupid hat."

"Even if you do find him at one of these places, what then?" Mina dropped from the tree landing silently next to Nick.

"I want him to come to us," Nick said. He pushed Mina's bangs out of her face and smiled.

"Home field advantage," Mina said.

"And if we must kill him, I want him to die in the same place my uncle did," Nick kissed Mina gently on her forehead.

"That totally made me weak in the knees," Mina shivered as a chill ran up her spine. She shook it off, then picked up two of the apple bags.

"I'm not sure we can kill him, Mina, we won't know that until we stand toe to toe with him," Nick picked up the other two bags. He and Mina cut over into the next row of apple trees where Penny was tossing apples down to Ben.

"Hey, guys," Ben looked over to Nick and Mina smiling. "You two fill your quota for Sue yet?"

"We have," Mina said. She and Nick held up the two bags they were carrying each.

"This one's getting a little over zealous," Ben looked down at all the apples littering the ground around his feet and the trunk of the tree. "Shook that poor tree worse than a nor'easter. Most of these down here are too bruised for anything more than applesauce."

"I didn't do it on purpose!" Penny shrieked as she dropped to the ground next to Mina. "I am so used to landing in trees weighing little more than a sparrow."

"Either a skunk or a raccoon or something will make use of these so no worries, sweetheart," Mina smiled down at Penny.

"So, I overheard you talking about your Map Walking trick and Stone. Have you found anything yet?" Ben asked Nick.

"No, but when I'm there I can feel a pull, like I'm on the right path," Nick said. "Back in the spring, when Gertrude had called us out to Chatfield Hollow after my friends were attacked by a vampire, I felt the same type of draw. It was more pronounced then, with an actual path laid out before me. But the feeling was similar."

"Your kind's tracking abilities are unparalleled," Ben picked up an apple and took a bite.

"My kind?" Nick raised an eyebrow at Ben.

"Tellers or whatever you call yourselves," Ben said.

"The only thing I've found for what we are called was in my uncle's journal that read 'Ego Sum Scriptor' but that was just written on the inside of the cover," Nick said.

"I am a writer?" Penny said. "That's kind of bland."

"You know Latin, too?" Nick looked down at Penny. "How many languages do you know?"

"Lots," Penny said and a grin grew across her face.

"Kid's full of surprises," Ben said picking up two bags of apples in each hand. "Let's bring these bags down to your grandma, Nicholas."

"Not sure I want to know what other surprises are coming," Nick said quietly as he picked up another bag. Penny and Ben laughed as they grabbed the other bags of apples and they all walked down to meet Sue and Trudy.

"Did you enjoy your first trip apple picking, darlin'" Trudy said as Penny came skipping down the orchard.

"It's awesome," Penny said as she came to stop and held out her bag for Trudy.

"Good haul," Trudy said as she took the bag and placed it on the counter with the bags she and Sue had gathered.

*****

The first Cross Country meet was coming up Monday afternoon so Nick had to head to the school when he got home from apple picking. He tried to convince Mina to at least go running with him and the team, but she had no interest in joining the team. She actually had plans with Holly.

"Play nice, please," Nick said as he strapped his helmet to the back of the scooter.

"Of course, my dear," Mina said. "She's actually very nice, and I don't have to talk much cause she never shuts up. I like that."

"What are you two up too?" Nick asked

"Food then painting each other's nails," Mina said.

"Interesting," Nick said.

"That's not code for pillow fight which I know is code for experimenting," Mina narrowed her eyes at Nick.

"I will continue to think you will be having a pillow fight," Nick smiled.

"Go run all that energy off please," Mina shook her head and took off on the scooter.

"Miss you," Nick said smiling then trotted inside to change.

The locker room was full of noise when Nick walked in. Filomena was at his locker next to Nick's.

"So, how long do you think it will take for our respective ladies to break down and have a topless pillow fight this evening?" Filomena sat down on the bench and pulled his shoes on.

"Twenty-seven minutes," Nick smiled as he opened his locker and slipped his sneakers off by stepping on his own heels.

"Seems about right," Filomena stood up. "Hurry up, usual bet is on and I don't have all night to wait for you to change your tampon."

"You can have a head start," Nick said as he pulled off his jeans.

"Crack is wack my friend and it is certainly distorting your world view," Filomena said.

"Time to put your money where your mouth is, friend-o, let's double down this evening," Nick yanked his running shorts on then sat to slide his sneakers back on.

"Oh, well now, Mr. Moneybags, you are on," Filomena's eyes lit up.

Nick stood up and cracked his neck, then his back, then smacked Filomena across the face and said as he took off out the door, "Tag, you're it."

"Oooooooohhhhhhh," Filomena yelled and took off after him.

The boys were out the front door jumping over and weaving between the other kids on the team who were out stretching.

"Wait for the rest of the team you two!" Coach Brucella yelled. He was as intimidating as a cocker spaniel. His hair even resembled the breed's ears. And the boys knew the quiet math teacher/coach wouldn't do much more than yell politely as the pair dashed up the road toward the little log cabin the Boy Scouts had built a few years ago.

The boys covered the distance to Walnut Hill quickly and headed up towards Cow Hill. Nick hadn't run this way since he and

Adam had done so a few months earlier.

The pace was fast, even after the first mile. Nick and Paul were side by side the whole time. But as they came up to Cow Hill, Nick started to turn up his pace, matching how fast his mind was racing. Images of his last run through this section of town bounced around his head, faster and faster. In his head, he raced Adam up the hill, past Chamard Vineyard. In his head Adam's face distorted from the young man he had come to call his friend into the jagged toothed and menacing predator.

Putting on the gas, Nick took the lead by five strides right before the two boys hit the Little Red School House. He was breathing harder than he had in a long time, he was running faster than he could remember ever running, but he knew he wasn't going to outrun the memory of what it had looked like as the monster that used to be his friend had lost his head. He slowed down a bit, shook his head and laughed softly.

"What are you laughing about?" Filomena gulped down air between each word.

"Last time I was running here I ended up laying in that ditch," Nick pointed at the side of the road where he had collapsed after he had run off after Mina cut Adam's head off.

"Oh," Filomena said then put on the gas. Nick shook his head and chuckled again, but easily caught up to Paul. They hooked a right onto Egypt Lane and headed down all the twists and turns of that road.

Neither of them talked again until they reached the end of the road and turned onto Route 81, the road the high school was on. Panting, Paul said, "If you ever need to talk about what happened that night, what really happened, you know I'll listen."

Looking over at his friend, Nick said, "What do you mean what really happened"

"You know what I mean, man," Paul said heavily. "The two of you went hunting what killed Gary and Jason and put Adam in the hospital. Instead it got to finish the job. I can only imagine that's a lot to keep thinking about."

"You are more right than you know," Nick said.

Nothing else was said between the two boys until the high school was in sight.

"Time to earn that green," Filomena said as he put every ounce of strength and energy into his legs. Nick did the same and they were neck and neck as they passed the Boy Scouts' log cabin on their right.

As they veered onto the school's sidewalk the outside wall of the gymnasium seemed to go by Nick on the left in slow motion and it hit Nick like a gut shot from a twelve gauge. What hit him was the one place he needed to look for Stone. The place the monster lost the one thing he wanted more than anything. They place he would go looking for and hoping for something good to happen. The Orkney Islands. This knocked him back a step giving Filomena the upper hand and the win as they pulled past the gym marking the finish line of this race. Paul raised his hands in victory, as he kept jogging. Nick smiled, accepting defeat as the two boys took a cool down lap around the building.

Turning to his friend, Filomena smacked Nick across the face, hard. "That's the first. Remember you double downed and you won't see the second one coming."

"Well done, sir," Nick said as he stretched out his mouth then rubbed his cheek.

When they hit the back of the building, they slowed down, walking to the river that flowed behind the school.

"Are we supposed to call the girls at some point tonight?" Filomena said as he stopped next to the water and started stretching.

"I assume they will track us down when they are done with their pillow fights," Nick said and sat down in the dirt to stretch.

"Let's get some food after we shower," Paul said as he plopped down on the ground.

"Agreed," Nick said and looked up into the trees above him. The sky was starting to darken and his stomach was rumbling.

"Nine East Main?" Filomena suggested.

"Can we do something else? Even Mickey D's or preferably the King," Nick said.

"You want fast food?" Filomena said.

"I've just had my fill of Nine East Main. Hank made me go there almost every day over the summer," Nick said as he stretched.

"Haven't seen him around for a few weeks, where did he disappear to?" Paul stood back up and stretched out his quads.

"Good question. He had some family business to take care of and took off," Nick stood up and did the same.

"What is the deal with that dude anyway? He's pretty weird," Paul said.

"He definitely is a character, has his share of demons, but is a better role model at least financially than my dad ever was," Nick said.

"I think that's the first time I've ever heard you mention your dad," Filomena said.

"Not much to mention," Nick said. "He and I don't see each other much. Never did. He's not really the responsible type."

"Can't choose our parents, sadly," Paul said. "I see my dad maybe for twenty minutes a week with his work schedule. He's a financial genius so I'll never have to worry about money, but I had my first game of catch with Adam and his dad, not my own, so I understand a little how that feels."

"Your mom is pretty awesome though. So hot for an older lady," Nick said.

"How many times do I have to tell you to cut that crap out?" Filomena raised a finger to Nick.

"At least fifty more times," Nick laughed and headed toward the back door of the school.

"Seriously not cool man. For that, and the fact that I'm driving, you're buying," Filomena caught up to Nick as they headed inside.

"Where are we going by the way?" Nick said.

*****

After getting burgers at the diner, Filomena dropped Nick off at home. He called Mina but she wasn't home yet, so he sat down at his desk, pulled out an atlas and the pen and took a deep breath. He turned the page to Great Britain, looked to the northern most part of the British Isles and he found the Orkney Islands.

Placing the tip of the pen right on the city of Kirkwall, Nick closed his eyes. In his head, he could see the streets clearly, but it was still dark. The light of the coming full moon helped and found himself set on a course toward the center of town. Nick knew he was going in the right direction. Someone was trying to hide something here, and the power that he felt made the hairs stand up on the back of his neck and the sent a charge surging up and down his spine. It was unmistakable.

When he got to where he knew the power was coming from, he saw the ruins of two palaces - one on either side of the road. One was little more than a tower with the remnants of a grander structure whittled away by time and wind and water. The other still had the facade of a small castle, but was obscured by tall trees. Even in the darkness it was impressive.

As Nick got closer, his entire body tingled with a static charge. Then, as though crossing an invisible line, he saw the ruins grow and morph. Windows lit up, smoke poured from chimneys and the palace grew before his eyes, bigger, and deeper than the ruins suggested it had ever been. The ruins were merely an illusion, a facade, masking this castle that someone very important wanted hidden.

Hiding behind a tree, Nick looked over the castle. There were no guards on the towers or battlements on the front wall of the building, but he knew there were things lurking in there that were exponentially worse than a man with a gun. He could feel it. Thick in the night air was the smell of lavender. Nick did not doubt the gardens of such a place were magnificent, but he knew better than to go explore right now. In the shadows, all over the castle grounds, vampires stood guard, unseen.

Then Nick laughed, and asked himself, "Why am I hiding behind a tree?" He stepped out from behind the tree and looked over the palace. A drum tower stood on either side of the main wall. Nick could make out what must be the roof of the main hall just past the wall, and the keep beyond that. Two more towers stood black against the night sky beyond the keep.

Walking toward the front gate, Nick strolled right inside the building. There was no moat, or drawbridge and the tall, wide doors were made of oak with bronze reinforcements running in a grid from top to bottom. At the top of the door, the sharp points from the bottom of a portcullis could be seen between the stone of the doorway's arch and the oak doors. While Map Walking, doors no longer stood in his way. But he did usually walk through them rather than a wall simply because it made more sense to go through a door rather than a wall.

The doors opened into a large mud room. Straight ahead was another large oak door, and to the right and left were two smaller doors. Nick headed straight and pushed through the door. Inside was as luxurious and opulent a room as can be imagined. A large hall opened before him - arches rose above Nick's head and held up a vaulted ceiling from which crystal chandeliers hung, lighting the room. Paintings and tapestries lined the walls, while statues stood tall against them, including what looked like Michaelangelo's David. But the most obvious thing in the hall was the dragon.

It was not as large as Nick had expected it to be, about the size of an elephant. It was lying on its stomach mostly curled up into itself breathing slowly and rhythmically, its eyes closed. Nick didn't move, just watched, counting its breaths. On every fifth or sixth exhale, a small burst of fire would come out of one of its nostrils. Short horns grew out of the top of its head, and smaller versions of those stuck out over its eyes, and down its tail. Its wings were tucked in over its back, with small horns sticking out from the joints.

Behind the dragon was a stairwell. Nick knew that's where he needed to head. As he walked past the dragon he looked over every scale he could, memorizing this amazing creature. He had not read anything about them in his uncle's journals or on the headstones in the cemetery. The only person to ever mention one had been Penny and she had barely gotten a good look at it. Hopefully he would be able to come back and see this creature again one day and learn more about it. But he headed up the stairs because he had much more to see in this place.

The smell of lavender was less pungent inside the castle, but it was still very present. Nick didn't feel as though any of the vampire guards were inside, but he laughed a little at the idea of having a security force that also served as air fresheners.

At the top of the stairs was a long hallway leading straight to the back of the castle. This must be the keep - the main living quarters of the castle. It was much darker than it was in the main hall, only small oil lamps high above illuminated more tapestries and suits of armor that lined the walls. The two closest doors to Nick were heavy with large handles with the kind of lock you push down with your thumb. Nick decided to go into the one on the right and found what looked like a study. A large wooden desk sat on the far side of the room with shelves of books lining the wall behind it. A large fireplace sat to Nick's right and in front of it were two leather chairs for relaxing. No fire burned this evening, but the room was lit by the same type of gas lamps in the hall. To the left was an antique onyx globe with gold inlay for the continents resting on a stand of richly stained wood. The legs were carved in the shape of human figures with faces etched in the throes of agony.

On the desk was a lamp, a leather bound journal and a pen. The seat of the high backed leather desk chair was worn from use. On the book shelves directly behind the desk were hundreds of similar journals. The ones sitting on the top shelves looked as though they have been through Hell. Nick reached up instinctively to grab the first journal off the top shelf, but found his hand went right through it, and the rest of him followed.

This wasn't like when he passed through doors or when he walked through a wall. This time images hit him like a ton of bricks. He saw an alley riddled with trash and human waste. He saw what looked like buildings from the movie Young Sherlock Holmes. He saw a man dressed in a very old style black suit slide a brief case across a desk, then a large hand with scars running all over it grabbed the handle. Then he saw a woman's face and heard her scream as her throat was slit, the knife held by the same scared hand. Nick fell backward through the desk. Before he hit the floor his head went through the spot where the journal was sitting he saw a flash of Mina fighting another woman.

Nick laid there on his back for a moment, wondering what the hell it was he just saw. Then he wondered why he could walk through walls and doors and desks but the floor stopped him. But he only questioned that for a second because if he couldn't walk around like in the normal world this whole situation would be even more of a mess. So he focused on what he just saw - Mina grabbing that woman by the head and flipping her around like a rag doll, and he stood up.

Leaning over the desk, looking closer at the journal, Nick said, "Why the hell not?" and stuck his face into the journal. As he did, images poured through his head. The desert, the Las Vegas sign, a banquet hall filled with beings of all kinds, an arena with a Centaur fighting with who looked like Penny until she turned into a huge boulder and crushed the Centaur. Then he saw a mirror, and the face in it was covered in scars and the color of the eyes were unmistakable - one bright blue and the other a deep brown. Then the mirror shattered under the strike of a fist just as scared as the face.

Reeling back, Nick righted himself and whispered, "I did it, I found where he lives."

From the fireplace, a figure came through the wall. It was translucent and muttering in a very thick Scottish accent, "Aye, stupid peasants. You'll see me again."

Nick didn't move a muscle while the ghost did a circle around the room. His head was still swimming with the images he'd just been hit with from the journal, and the idea that he could see inside of a journal or a book when he is doing this little Map Walking trick.

Then the ghost took a sharp left into the desk, passed straight through it and ran right into Nick. The shock of coming into contact with the ghost woke Nick up enough to realize he was falling backwards from the blow. When he hit the floor this time he caught his funny bone against the stone floor and winced in pain.

"God damn it!" Nick yelled. He sat up and rubbed his elbow. Then the pain washed away to fear. "Why did that hurt?"

Nick reached up and grabbed onto the onyx globe and pulled himself up. He patted the globe and could feel the cool stone under his fingers, then he turned to the desk. He picked up the pen, then dropped it. Then he flicked the journal open with his index finger and saw the cursive hand writing inside was elegant and clear. He could easily make out the words, even upside down. He leafed through the pages, slowly at first, then faster and faster until he came to the back page.

Placing both hands on the desk, Nick said, "This can't be good."

Chapter 5
Sound and Vision

An hour passed. The ghost kept on his rant about peasants being stupid, circling the room and Nick read through the first two of the journals on the shelf. Everything Nick had suspected about the monster's story from Frankenstein was true. In the end, Stone couldn't kill himself. The monster tried, but the Arctic Circle was a bad place to burn one's self on a funeral pyre.

Seems being resurrected came with the gift of immortality, or at least the gifts of being nearly invincible, super strong and super-fast. While in the Arctic the monster had tried to freeze himself, drown himself, burn himself, and even disembowel himself. But he always woke up. And after months of trying and failing, fits of insanity and loneliness, the monster decided to join the world again. But what does a nearly invincible, super strong disfigured giant do in 19th century Europe? He becomes a hit man.

The ghost had disappeared, and Nick was getting hungry. He was also beginning to sweat the fact that he was thousands of miles from his home, hiding in the study of his enemy and nothing had come to him concerning how he was going to get home.

Nick stood up and put the two journals back in their place on the shelf. Then he went over what happened when he hit the floor. Standing at the desk, he played over in his mind seeing Mina in the arena, the ghost coming through the wall, then hitting the floor. Then he went over it again, then again, then again. Then he saw it. The ghost hitting him was the difference.

Pulling the pen from his pocket, Nick turned on his heal and stepped over to the globe. He spun it until he found New England. He put the tip of the pen on where he knew Gillette's Castle to be and found himself looking over the Connecticut River. He turned and ran into the house through the attached greenhouse.

"Gillette!" Nick screamed. "Gillette, where are you?"

Running up the stairs, Nick yelled again, "Gillette!"

From a doorway, Gillette floated out casually, "What is all the racket? Oh, hello Nicholas, how have you--."

Nick ran right into the ghost, bounced off and tumbled backwards down the stairs. When he hit the bottom, he yelled, "God damn it, my elbow again!"

"Catch your funny bone, boy?" Gillette chuckled as he floated down the stairs. "And how did you run into me?"

"New trick and funny bone is the stupidest name cause this hurts like hell," Nick said as he rubbed his elbow furiously.

"Stop being a baby and get up and tell me about this new trick," Gillette said and headed over to the couch. "Come sit and chat with me for a minute."

"When I place the tip of my pen on a map, I can see that place as though I am there in my head." Nick said as he slowly walked over to the couch and sat down.

"Like astral projection," Gillette said. "It was all the rage back when I was a younger man. But I've never heard of people running into ghosts while doing it."

"That's the new trick," Nick leaned back into the couch. "When I'm doing my Map Walking trick, I accidently ran into a ghost and got knocked on my ass, found myself stuck in a castle in Northern Scotland for the past few hours. Finally figured out the how, found a globe and tried the trick on you."

"Hence you tumbling down my stairs," Gillette said. "Do you need to call someone for a ride? There's a phone in the office, the museum people put it in a while back."

"Yeah, I'm gonna need to call for a ride," Nick said.

"It is quite late, not sure who you can get out here at this time," Gillette said.

"Damn, I hadn't even thought about that," Nick leaned forward. "What time is it?"

"Almost one in the morning," Gillette floated over the couch.

"Jeez, I didn't think I was gone that long," Nick rubbed his eyes.

"Time flies when you're having fun," Gillette said.

"Or scared out of your mind," Nick laughed.

"What had you on edge, my boy?" Gillette asked.

"I found myself in the home of my enemy. Remember the fella Gert brought us up here to ask you about?" Nick looked at Gillette.

"Ah, yes, the Stone character," Gillette said. "So you and Gert finally tracked him down?"

"I tracked him down," Nick lowered his head. "Gert, Gert's dead. I assumed you would know about that."

"What?" Gillette whispered.

"She was killed when she and Mina ran into that old mosquito, Enoch," Nick looked down at the floor. "I wasn't there, but she and Mina took him out."

"I knew she'd go down swinging," Gillette became more transparent. "You're welcome to sleep on that couch, just be up and gone before the grounds keeper gets here or he'll call the police on you." Gillette disappeared completely.

"Thanks," Nick said. He looked down at the couch and smacked the throw pillow. It was softer than he thought it would be and he lay down.

When he opened his eyes again light was spilling in through the French doors, and the temperature had dropped. Nick was shivering in his t-shirt and jeans. He got up and found the office off of the main room where the phone was. Luckily, hanging off the back of the desk chair was a green hooded sweatshirt. "I'll just borrow this for the foreseeable future," Nick said as he yanked the hoodie off the chair and pulled it on. On the front in big block upper case letters, it read HARTFORD WHALERS. "I'm more of a Rangers fan but this will do."

The phone was on the desk and Nick picked up the receiver. He started dialing Mina's number, but stopped himself on the last digit and hung the phone up with his index finger, then he dialed another number.

"Hello," a groggy Filomena answered.

"Hey douche bag, I need a ride," Nick said.

"I'm not a taxi, call your girlfriend," Filomena said.

"I'm stuck up at Gillette's Castle and I don't think I'll make the meet today if you don't get your ass up here," Nick said, smiling.

"How the hell did you get up there," Filomena picked up his watch, "At 7:20 in the morning by yourself?"

"I'll tell you when you pick me up," Nick said. "And bring coffee."

"Fine, but the front gate is probably closed so meet me down there," Filomena mumbled and hung up the phone.

Gillette was nowhere to be seen, so Nick headed down the drive to the front gate. There was a picnic area and a small pond with ducks milling about, and they didn't seem to be afraid of Nick. They waddled up out of the water toward him quacking for bread. After a minute of following him the ducks figured he was a lost cause and gave up and headed back to the water.

Hunkering down on the cross bar of the gate, Nick stuffed his hands in the front pocket of the Whalers hoodie and waited. It was chilly enough for him to see his breath but the air was warming quickly as the sun took over more of the shadows. Despite the warming air, Nick was forced to stand and pace to keep from shivering. As he was considering some jumping jacks, Filomena came to a screeching halt inches from his legs.

"Come on, jackass, we have a bus to catch," Filomena yelled out the window.

Nick opened the passenger door and slid into the warm car. Filomena handed him a coffee and Nick held it with both hands and took a sip.

"What are you cold or something, fag?" Filomena said then spun the wheels on the mustang sending smoke and rocks into the air behind the car. The back end fishtailed for a few seconds before finding purchase shooting the car off down the road.

"A little," Nick said. "But that's what happens when you wake up on the couch at Gillette's Castle in only a t-shirt and jeans and they haven't turned the heat on for the winter yet."

"How the hell did you end up crashing on the couch at that place?" Filomena hooked his thumb back over his shoulder towards where the entrance of the park was.

"Well, I'm not exactly sure," Nick lied. "But I'm pretty sure alcohol was involved."

"What?" Filomena asked. "I dropped you off at your place at ten o'clock. Who the hell were you drinking with and why when you knew we had a meet today?"

"Must have been a bad idea if you're the voice of reason in this scenario," Nick laughed. "And I was hanging out with Hank, he was back in town for the night and he must have left me there for safe keeping."

"Why not just bring you home or back to his house?" Filomena asked.

"He likes to play pranks when he's drinking," Nick smiled. "Must have broken in there and left me on the couch before he took off."

"That is so not cool that you didn't call me to join in. Sounds a like a blast," Filomena said as they sped down the road.

*****

The bus ride to Montville was quiet and Nick slept most of the way curled up against the window hugging his duffle bag. Filomena woke him up when they got there by elbowing him in the ribs.

"Rise and shine, sweetheart," Paul laughed. "We have some miles to put on our feet."

Nick pushed himself up and shuffled out of the bus behind Filomena. There were a few other schools coming to the first meet of the year and Nick looked around at the other busses unloading their bleary eyed passengers.

"Hope your hangover doesn't kill our chances at taking this meet as a team today," Filomena said over his shoulder in the line to get into the locker rooms.

"I'm pretty sure you're my only real competition here today, douche bag," Nick said looking at the other groups of guys shuffling into the locker room. "Four schools here today, including Montville, right?'

"Yeah, and I'm pretty sure none of them are here just to go

for a leisurely stroll through the woods holding hands so make sure that cockiness of yours is backed up by some wheels," one of the other guys, Jesse Pont, said. "Seriously, you look like crap Stanton. Were you out drinking all night or something?"

Pont's sidekick, Delecke, laughed like a hyena.

"Yes, yes I was," Nick smiled. "And I'm still a little drunk but I'll still leave you choking on my dust."

"Burn," Filomena said and laughed. "Now maybe if you learned how to put down the donuts, Pont, the rest of us would actually get one instead of starving,"

"You snooze you lose, Jackass," Pont smiled.

"Seriously I am so friggen hungry," Nick dropped his shoulders and hung his head back in defeat as he walked through the locker room door.

"I might have a granola bar buried in here," Filomena dropped his bag on the bench and unzipped it. He buried his hand in among the clothes and the towel.

"I'm not sure I want anything that has been sitting at the bottom of your stinky, dirty gym bag with your shorts and socks and crap," Nick sat down.

"You never complain about the stink when I'm tea baggin--" Filomena said, but was cut short by the coach.

"Hustle up, you mongrels, we have a race to win," the coach looked directly at Nick and Paul. "Especially you two. No shenanigans today."

"But that's all I know coach, I'm an old dog and all you have is new tricks," Filomena pulled his sweatshirt off.

Nick shook his head and started changing.

The boys were out the door a minute later, stretched, did a few warm up sprints and were ready at the starting line with the other teams a half hour later. Nick looked over the line of guys to either side of him. He and Paul were right in the middle, and everyone around them looked ready for a battle. Down at the end of the line, there was a boy that stood out to Nick. The kid's eyes kept changing color, and shifting shape.

Searching his memory for anything like that, Nick barely

even registered the gunshot. The crowd of boys raced out ahead of him three or four strides before he was off the line.

"Idiot," Nick muttered to himself, and pumped his legs, pushing himself to make up those lost strides. Filomena took an early lead and the boy with the weird eyes was right on Paul's tail, drafting off of him. Nick was still a few paces behind, but was feeling really good. His adrenaline was surging as he watched this kid run, knowing from the way that his legs moved that he wasn't fully human. In his gut, Nick felt like that the boy was more or less harmless except for the fact that he was faster than both Nick and Filomena and was going to ruin their chance of winning the race today. Whatever this kid was, he was fast and only playing with the rest of the runners. He could easily take off, finish this race, shower and eat and ice cream cone before anyone else crossed the finish line.

Paul knew he was being tail gated and pushed himself harder. He could run harder than he has ever run, run himself to death, but in the end the weird eyed kid would slingshot right past him and cross the finish line first while Paul crumpled over the line dead.

Bunched up with the weird kid behind Filomena were Pont and Richards. With some quick thinking, Nick pulled in on the heels of the weird eyed kid. Pont and Delecke were flanking the kid and Nick was able to silently direct his teammates to stick close to the weird eyed kid while Nick drafted off of him. The weird eyed kid was boxed in and seemed to not even be breaking a sweat. The Kelsey Town boys were pumping their legs as hard as possible, trying to keep pace with Filomena. Pont and Delecke looked over their respective inner shoulders to Nick every so often for new directions.

They ran, in this impromptu formation, for ninety percent of the race. As the finish line grew ahead of them, the weird eyed boy lowered his head and started to pump his legs harder. But at the exact same time, Pont and Delecke pressed in to suffocate his escape.

Startled, the weird eyed boy slowed down, thinking he could pop out behind Pont and Delecke, but Nick was right on his heels, their legs moving in unison a few inches from each other. Nick put an elbow in the weird eyed boys back to let him know he would have to push back or forward or to the left or right to get out. Rubbing is racing, but roughing can get you disqualified. And the weird eyed kid knew he might be faster than these other racers, but didn't want to risk pushing his way out and booted off the course by the judges.

So, the weird eyed kid did the only other thing he could think of doing. He put a hand on Filomena's back and ran harder just before the finish line. This propelled Paul forward over the line first, but it solidified the weird eyed kids spot as second just a few inches ahead of Pont and Delecke.

Nick came in fifth and the rest of the runners poured over the line a few moments later.

Paul, Delecke, Pont and Nick jumped up into each other butt first and yelled, "Hell yeah," as they came down.

The weird eyed kid walked off away from everyone, shaking his head. Nick followed as his teammates fell down on the ground panting.

The weird eyed boy turned to Nick when they were a bit away from the others, "What are you?"

"I'm something that can tell you aren't exactly human," Nick leaned on his knees panting. "What's your name?'

"Alan," he said extending his hand to Nick.

Shaking Alan's hand, Nick kept leaning on his left hand and knee, "Nick. Nice to meet ya man."

"So, what are you?" Alan asked.

"Not exactly sure, but I can see stuff that no one else can and I have a knack for figuring out puzzles," Nick straightened up and put his hands on his head, opening up his lungs. "You?'

"Half incubus," Alan said. "Have you ever met one before?"

"You're my first full or half incubus, Alan," Nick smiled. "But I've met my fair share of interesting folk over the past few months."

"Kelsey Town? Isn't there a werepig down there?" Alan asked.

"Sometimes. Usually he's just a really annoying old guy," Nick laughed.

"I should have seen that little trick of yours coming, but no one has ever been able to beat me in a foot race so I never expected to be tricked into losing. My dad makes me take a dive every so often so

I don't get too much attention," Alan said.

From the other side of the field, a man whistled and waved to Alan - the likeness was unmistakable - it was Alan's father.

"I gotta go, nice to meet ya, man. Hopefully we'll run into each other at another meet. And I won't fall for that trick twice," Alan laughed, turned on his heel and trotted off toward his dad.

"Oh, I've got a few more up my sleeve," Nick quietly smiled.

A few minutes later Nick was inside the building looking for the locker room. He took advantage of the quiet, empty room and showered. His teammates were still outside celebrating and hitting on the girls from the opposing team. When he was finished he dried off, changed and headed out toward the bus with his gear. But he took a wrong turn out of the locker room and found himself wandering down a hall that he did not recognize. He pulled open a random door hoping to find windows at least see what part of the building he was in.

The room must have been a history teacher's - U.S. history, World history, and European history books along with atlases lined the shelves under the windows. Eight by ten portraits of all forty presidents lined the board on the back wall with a biography below each picture, and next to the desk was an old globe on its own heavy, cherry stained stand. Nick reached his hand into his pocket and wrapped his fingers around the pen while staring at the globe.

Pulling the pen out, Nick walked over to the globe. He spun the world on its stand, and watched as the continents and the oceans flew by - round and round and round again. Then, he slapped his left palm down on the globe, stopping its momentum and covering most of North America with his big meat paw. He smiled looking at the outline of the New England coast. Long Island sound was easy to make out and Nick placed the pen tip down roughly where Kelsey Town stood. He closed his eyes and could see the center of town - the Town Green in front of the Congregational Church near his house. Adjusting the pen, the world he saw in his head spun and he was standing outside the high school when everything went still. Smiling, Nick walked inside and headed for the locker room. As he hoped, the always angry ghost janitor was flipping his lid over the mess on and around the benches.

"Why are they such slobs?" the ghost yelled.

"You'd be out of a job if we weren't, that's why," Nick said and smacked the ghost on the back. Nick's ears popped, as though he had just hit ten thousand feet and the fasten seat belt sign had gone off. He fell back onto the bench and shook his head.

The ghost of the old janitor didn't even give him a second look, just whooshed off through the wall ranting and raving unintelligibly.

Nick looked around the empty locker room. He laughed, then opened his locker and tossed his gym bag in. "This is going to be fun to explain. Have to worry about that later." Nick ran out the door and hoofed it home.

Chapter 6
Under Pressure

"That's more like flying, Mina, than jumping," Ben yelled as Mina, Penny and he ran through the Powder Ridge Ski Area in Middlefield, Connecticut. The trees and the rolling hills gave them excellent cover to run as they wished with little chance of being seen by the uninitiated.

"I wish I could fly, that would be so cool," Mina smiled as she landed next to Ben among a growth of Pine trees. Penny circled above them in the form of a sparrow. "And I figured you could jump higher than I can since you're so old and strong."

"Never been much of a jumper," Ben said and leaned up against a tree watching Penny soar through the blue sky. "Lobster's aren't known for their vertical leap."

Laughing, Mina jumped up to the first branch of the tree Ben was leaning against and sat with her legs dangling down. "Now I really want to see if a lobster can jump. Can we make that happen on your next change?"

"If I can remember, maybe," Ben shook his head and chuckled. "But I tend to go all primal and pinchie so I can't promise anything."

Penny the sparrow landed on the branch next to Mina, then turned back into her human form, "Hey guys, have you ever seen a troll?"

Shaking her head, Mina said, "No."

"Yes, why? Do you want to turn into one?" Ben looked up at the two girls sitting on the branch above his head.

"No, I think I just saw one about a half mile ahead of us up the mountain, though," Penny said then fell backward off the branch landing on her feet neatly, smiling up at Ben.

"Let's go check him out," Mina hopped to her feet, then

jumped up into the air. She scanned the area ahead of where they were and found the monster easily - it was even bigger than she pictured.

"Can we Ben?" Penny asked the werelobster.

"Just stay close to me and Mina," Ben smiled and nodded. "And turn into a bear if we run into trouble. Preferably a grizzly."

With a huge smile on her face, Penny popped back into the shape of a sparrow and flew up above the sky above them. Mina came down softly next to Ben, smiled, then launched herself off toward where the troll was sitting in a cluster of rocks and trees. Ben followed her arc and took off running in the same direction.

Mina came down on top of a boulder, silently, behind the troll. Looking at its back, Mina could tell it was eating but couldn't see well enough over its shoulder to tell what it was dining on. Ben climbed up beside her a few seconds later. Penny the sparrow landed on Ben's shoulder, staying quiet.

The troll, hunched over a carcass of some sort, tore it apart - crunching on the bones and slurping at the blood and marrow. Then, the troll tore off a larger piece that was unmistakably a human arm. A wedding band was clearly visible on the ring finger.

With wide eyes, Mina looked to Ben. Ben nodded to Mina knowing what needed to be done. He looked to the little birdie on his shoulder and mouthed the word "bear". The little bird flew over to another boulder, and changed into the biggest grizzly ever seen.

Mina cocked an eyebrow at Ben and mouthed the word, "Really?"

Ben smiled and nodded.

Shaking her head, Mina smiled and dropped off the boulder to the troll's back. The beast reared up, bellowing a low, guttural roar. It swung its arms out, splattering blood from its hands and the limb it held. Mina had to grab onto the troll's long hair to keep from being thrown off because she couldn't get any purchase with her feet. The troll's skin was covered in slime the constancy of cooking oil, and it started to soak into her cloths. After ten seconds of this Mina had the record for troll riding and let go of the bucking monster. Mina came to a stop against the boulder she had jumped off and coughed as she hit it.

Standing off to the side with his arms crossed, Ben shook his head, "Silly girl, trolls are not that easy to catch. Penny, please distract the beast for me."

From the top of a nearby boulder, Penny the grizzly, stood up and roared. The troll turned and answered with a growl, then rushed Penny. Penny the grizzly jumped from the rock feet first and crashed into the troll's chest. The troll stumbled back, but did not lose its footing.

"That thing is tough," Mina said as Penny hit the ground and rolled away.

Ben picked up a rock the size of a basketball and hurled it at the troll's head. The rock connected square with the beast's nose. Blood and snot poured from the creature's face but instead of slowing it down it just looked angrier than it had a moment earlier.

"That they are," Ben walked up next to Mina and pulled her to her feet. "Now would be a good time for you to pull out that little sword of yours."

Glaring at Ben, Mina reached for the sheath hanging around her neck. She wrapped her fingers around the handle of the knife and pulled. As the blade met the sunlight, it grew to its full size and stood the height of a tall man. Mina swung the blade around easily, spinning it through the air in a figure eight around her body as though it weighed nothing, as though it were just an extension of her body.

The troll turned on Mina and Ben, smelled the air and snorted, sending blood and snot from its nose and mouth. It beat its chest and charged at Mina. Ben stepped aside as the troll barreled toward her. The beast was fast, and when Mina brought her sword up to cut the troll in half, it side stepped her and she only clipped its hand, sending a few of its fingers into the dirt around them.

This didn't slow the troll down, though, and it turned on Mina again, spraying her with blood as it reached for her with both hands. Mina jumped through the gap between the troll's legs, and rolled back to her feet behind the creature.

"Are you not going to help me?" Mina yelled at Ben.

Penny the grizzly was leaning against a boulder with her arms crossed, and Ben shrugged his shoulders.

"You're doing fine," Ben said, then pointed behind Mina, "and you might want to turn around."

Spinning on her heel, Mina brought the sword around as fast and hard as she could with the blade parallel to her body. The Troll threw a punch at her back and hit the edge of the sword between its middle and ring finger. The beast's momentum carried it forward through the blade until its fist and forearm were split down the middle to the elbow. This wound caused the troll to step back, and it tried to press the two halves of its hand and forearm together. But it was useless for the troll and it realized this quickly. But not quickly enough.

In those few seconds, Mina brought the sword around and chopped down on the beast's shoulder, severing the damaged arm. The troll screamed and in a rage brought its other hand up, balled its remaining fingers, and brought its fist down like a hammer.

Mina wasn't standing where the troll aimed anymore and when its fist crashed into the ground, sending dirt and dust up all around, she fell from the air, bringing the blade of her sword down through the neck of the monster. She hit the ground so hard that she stopped a foot deeper into the Earth than where all the fallen leaves and pine needles rested.

The troll's head rolled away as the creature's body crumpled to the ground and blood poured from its neck into the dirt and decomposing leaves.

Dropping back down to her normal child size and running up to the decapitated body, Penny said, "That was crazy!"

"Don't get to close, sweetie," Mina stepped between Penny and the troll's body. "Never know if these things might have a magical second wind like a chicken or something."

"Like a chicken?" Penny asked.

"When you cut a chicken's head off its body sometimes runs around for a minute or two afterward," Ben smiled down at the child.

"That's so weird," Penny said and turned toward the troll's head. "That thing was ugly and boy does it stink."

"This thing is going to start attracting some attention. We

should probably bury it or something," Mina looked to Ben.

"Fire is best," Ben said. "But we'll need gasoline so it will burn fast because the fire will be easily seen up here."

"And what about the person it was eating?" Penny asked now looking at the human remains.

"We can just make an anonymous call from town saying we saw something weird out on a hike," Mina said.

"If you can get to work cutting this carcass down to smaller pieces, Penny and I will run and grab a can of gas," Ben said and took off into the woods. Penny turned into a sparrow and flew off after him.

"Seriously, you just take off like that leaving me to carve this thing up? So not fair," Mina set to the task of cutting the troll apart, starting with its legs. Luckily for Mina, it only took Ben and Penny ten or so minutes to get back with a full can of gas.

With the three working together, Penny in the form of the grizzly, the pyre was set up quickly. Doused with five gallons of gas the fire would burn so hot and so fast there would be nothing left of the troll or the fire before anyone could respond to a call about a fire in the mountains. And luckily it wasn't windy or dry so the three did not worry about forest fires. Penny even gave a grizzly thumbs up, approving their departure, and Mina almost peed herself laughing so hard.

"I need a shower after that," Mina said as they got back to the car.

"You certainly do," Ben said as he opened the driver's side door. "You reek of that beast."

"Thanks, Captain Obvious," Mina said. Ben unlocked the passenger door from the inside and Penny climbed in back.

"I wonder what that person's name was." Penny said quietly, looking out the window as they drove home.

"Better to not think about that, Penny. It's sad, but there is nothing to be gained from finding out who they were. It will just raise more questions for you." Ben kept his eyes on the road.

"Do trolls usually eat people?" Penny asked.

"I haven't heard of them doing that very often. They are not hunters, they are scavengers and opportunists. Maybe that hiker got hurt and was easy prey," Ben glanced in the rear view mirror at Penny.

"I've got a question. Are trolls common around here?" Mina asked.

"They can be found anywhere there are forests. Humans tend to overlook them or mistake them for bears. I've only seen them a handful of times and never gotten that close. But I knew you would want to put it down for feeding on a human, so I risked confronting it."

"You would have let it live had I not been with you?" Mina asked.

"Killing that thing won't bring that person back," Ben said, "and on my own, in this form, I am not going to risk being killed."

"Wouldn't you just lobster out if your life was at risk?" Penny asked.

"Most likely," Ben said. "And that would be worse than a troll being on the loose in the woods where only a few hikers might stumble on it."

******

Hunched over an atlas, Nick's body looked as though he were studying hard. But his mind was very far away from the desk, but not lost in the clouds as many teenagers' minds tend to be. His mind was focused on the Orkney Islands, on a castle that looked, for all intents and purposes, abandoned. But magic kept the true palace masked from the mortal world. Nick was inside the study of that palace, burying his mind's eye in the journals of the monster that lived there.

The work was going slowly for Nick. He had to keep an ear out for the ghost that roamed this castle, and he needed to be on the lookout for any others that might knock him out of the map world into the real world. Or was it the ghost world? Nick wasn't sure how the Map Walking trick worked, but on that plane he could touch ghosts as though they were solid. That interaction knocked him into the physical world and he had to be wary of that. Getting stuck somewhere far, far away from his home was not something he looked forward to.

"Ghost Walking sounds way cooler than Map Walking," Nick said to himself as he pulled his head out of a shelf of journals that contained some particularly bloody and chaotic diary entries from the monster Frank Stone. Nick had just spent the last few minutes seeing how Stone had gotten his start in the world of organized crime.

After coming out of the Arctic, where Stone had tried and failed several times to destroy himself, he found himself in need of work. Being a scarred and disfigured giant monster proved a hard sell on the streets of London but stealing came easily and quickly to the monster. So did killing. These activities were noticed by one of the more organized families in the city and they tried to destroy him because they saw him as a rival and he scared the people of London this this family protected. This proved destructive to the family, Stone killed not only the men who came after him, but also tracked down the ones who had sent the killers his way and in doing so he wiped out the entire organization. A rival family watched this happen and took a different approach. They offered Stone a job.

For a very healthy salary, an estate in the country and whatever else he wished, this new crime family only asked that Stone kill whomever they asked of him. Agreeing was an easy choice for Stone. But as he learned more about the business, and began to find other creatures that were not human, an idea began to grow. Why should mortals be in control of these business activities? Why shouldn't he, and others with special abilities, be in control?

The family he worked for had him traveling all through Europe now, killing Counts and Dukes and Princess and Princesses. The deaths always had the look of an accident but gave their loved ones enough doubt to make them cooperate. His travels gave him the opportunity to find more and more supernatural creatures. They all lived in the shadows, not often interacting with each other, not knowing much about each other. Most of them were rich, having lived multiple lifetimes accumulating wealth from their victims or their limited business dealings with the mortal world.

Then Frank Stone met a dragon. The same dragon that now

lived in the main hall of his castle. It was in the forests of Russia that he first saw the beast, and Stone could not help but approach it. As with most wild animals, the dragon ran away, preferring to keep to itself - a characteristic that had helped its species survive. But Stone was mesmerized by the creature's beauty and size, and tracked the animal to its lair. As many stories have already told, dragons have an affinity for gold, only partially because of the metal's color. Gold also has a low melting point and dragons pack the walls of their lairs with the metal along with lead and a few other colored metals. They just happen to prefer gold.

When Stone made his way into the entrance of this dragon's lair he found that every inch of the place was covered in the precious metal. He also discovered the dragon backed into the corner and very unhappy that Stone had the nerve to track it to its lair. The dragon sucked in a huge gulp of air and exhaled a plume of fire so intense the gold walls around Stone melted. This wasn't the first time Stone had burned though. He had tried and failed to burn himself on a funeral pyre multiple times. He wasn't fireproof but only burned on the out-side. His clothes turned to ash, and his skin sizzled and cooked, but when the dragon breathed in again, Stone still stood, starring at the beast.

"I know you are just protecting yourself as your nature deems you to, but I would not do that again or I might get mad," Stone said to the dragon.

This was a surprise to the dragon. It had never failed to burn a man or any other creature to the ground with its fire. Confused, the dragon watched as Stone's skin healed before its eyes. With no other recourse, the dragon inhaled again and Stone knew what was coming.

Faster than the dragon could see, Stone rushed the beast and brought his clubbed fist down on the creature's snout before it could breathe out.

This intruder surprised the dragon for the second time, some-thing that had not happened since it was very young, hundreds of years ago. It closed its snout, shook its head and sat back.

With his hands up in front of him, Stone said, "I do not wish to hurt you, or worse, to destroy you, but I will find a way if you insist on doing that. Hopefully you understand me."

The dragon sat back on its haunches and looked the intruder over.

In his head, Stone saw images that were not from his own memory. Images of gold bars piled high in his arms, and walking away.

Confused, Stone looked up at the dragon who stared right back at him.

"Are you showing me those images?" Stone asked.

The dragon nodded, just once.

"So you can understand me?" Stone said.

The dragon nodded just once again.

"I don't want your gold. I want your help," Stone said.

In his head, Stone saw the dragon burning a village down to the ground with its fire and people running, many of them engulfed in flames.

"One day perhaps, but for now I wish only for you to remember me and when I come back, that you follow my lead," Stone said.

The dragon nodded, once, at a loss for any other action.

That's when Nick heard the door to the study open. He yanked his head out, readying himself to pull the pen off of the map, but waited and hoped that he would be completely invisible to whomever it was coming into the study.

When the door fully opened, he saw a boy walk into the room on crutches and close the door. Nick noticed that the crutches were held in place with bands on the boy's forearms. The boy shook slightly with every step and his face contorted slightly with every movement as he made his way slowly to the desk.

Nick stood still, waiting to be seen. The boy just pulled out the great big leather chair and fell into it. He leaned his crutches against the big desk and took a deep breath. Opening one of the heavy desk drawers, the boy pulled a stack of comics from it and plopped them down on the desk. Nick could see the top one was the first issue of Frank Miller's The Dark Knight Returns.

Smiling, Nick nodded in approval.

Then, from down the hall, a woman yelled, "Nathaniel, are

you in your father's study again reading those comic books?"

"NO!" the boy yelled back, tossing the comics back in the drawer. He pushed himself up to his feet, grabbed his crutches and headed toward the door.

Before the boy was halfway across the study, a tall brunette woman appeared in the door with her arms crossed. "Not in the study, huh?"

Nick held his breath.

"Not fair, Mom, you're super-fast and I'm, I'm, well," Nathaniel held up a crutch, "Fast for a kid on crutches."

"I would have known even if I hadn't walked up here and seen you with my own two eyes, Nathaniel," she pointed at her head, "Mothers have a sixth sense when their children are reading comic books rather than finishing homework. Come on, back to your room and your Latin."

"Why do I have to learn a dead language? It's so boring," the boy said as his mother stepped aside and waved him through the doorway.

"I'm a little behind on my current story lines, but I'm pretty sure Batman studied Latin at some point in his education," the woman said.

"I'm pretty sure I'm never gonna be swinging from grappling hooks, Ma," Nathaniel walked off toward his room.

"Either way, study now, comics later. And I will get them for you. You know your father doesn't like anyone in his office when he isn't here," the woman said as she closed the door.

From the fireplace, a figure came through the wall, translucent and muttering again in its thick Scottish accent, "Aye, stupid peasants. You'll see me again."

Before Nick could react, the ghost turned directly into him. Nick cracked his elbow on the wall and yelled, "Always the elbow!" Surprised at his own stupidity, he covered his mouth with his hands, his pen in his right hand.

As fast as he could Nick ran to the globe, placed the pen on the first place he could make out he knew, and ran through the streets of Nantucket.

After a second of running he jumped to Julie and Holly's family home.

The door of Frank Stone's study started to open. Nick searched the first floor for any of the little kid ghosts, but couldn't find a single one. Then he ran up the stairs and on the second floor landing there stood the ghost of a little boy named Edward.

"Don't move!" Nick yelled as he barreled toward the boy.

"Okay," the little kid ghost said as Nick tackled him.

The door of the study stood fully open, and the woman saw Nick disappear from the study.

"Nathaniel! Have you noticed any new ghosts in the castle lately?" the woman yelled after her son.

"New ones? That's a funny one, Ma," Nathaniel yelled as he walked into his room. "I can't keep track of all the ones we've got littering this place."

Slamming his butt up against the wall, Nick came to a sudden stop and looked up at the ceiling. Edward sat on the floor next to Nick.

"You tackled me," Edward said. "How did you do that?"

"Not sure how it works, but I can travel to different places through maps using this," Nick held up the pen, then flipped over so his back was against the wall. "I put the tip of the pen on the map and I can see the place as though I'm there, but only in my head. But if I touch a ghost, or tackle one, then I transport to that place."

"That's some seriously powerful magic," Edward said.

"Yeah, it's kinda making me nervous, some of the things I can do," Nick said.

Grabbing Nick's arm, Edward said, "I feel different, and I can grab your arm."

But it only lasted a moment and Edward's fingers slipped through Nick's arm right after he uttered the last word. He tried frantically to grab onto Nick again, a look of longing in his eyes.

"Sorry, kid, seems the effects of my 'Ghost Walking' are short lived," Nick said and smiled over at the boy.

"I haven't had contact with a flesh and blood person in over a century!" Edward said

"I'm sorry, I wish I could make it last longer," Nick looked down at the floor.

"Sorry? No need to be sorry, I never thought I would feel the warmth of someone's skin ever again. Thank you for that." Edward started to become more transparent and flicker.

"Well, it was my pleasure. And if I need to make a quick escape in the future I may use that little trick with you again," Nick said.

"Please do!" Edward said and solidified.

Nick pushed himself to his feet. "Now I need to figure out how I'm going to get back to Connecticut."

"Why don't you ask that friend of Julie's and yours, the werepig?" Edward suggested.

"Hank Kelsey? You've seen him?" Nick said

"Yes, he's been sleeping here at night for a while now," Edward said.

"Do you know where he is now?" Nick asked.

"I do not know how he has been spending his days," Edward shook his head.

"Why would he be spending the night here instead of his own house?" Nick said quietly.

"I do not know," Edward said.

"I figured he wouldn't have told you," Nick laughed. The boy just looked at him, confused.

"Wait," Nick said. "I checked his house here, and around town but I would never have thought to check this house. Well played, Hank, well played."

"So he was hiding from you?" Edward said.

"Yup," Nick said and started down the stairs.

Following, Edward asked, "What are you going to do?"

"Scare the crap out of him," Nick laughed as he hit the bottom floor. "What door has he been coming through?"

Pointing, Edward said, "The back door."

"Then we wait near the back door," Nick headed toward the kitchen. "Any food in this place? I'm starving."

Chapter 7
Changes

It was dark when the kitchen door rattled. Nick sat at the table, waiting, with the lights off. The door opened and a large man slipped inside, making no noise.

Holding a flashlight under his chin, Nick flicked the switch illuminating his face, and said, "Boo."

Spinning around, Hank knocked into the counter, sending the dish drain clattering to the floor. Then he crouched into a defensive stance in the corner created by the end of the counter near the door. His hands clenched ion fists and his teeth bared.

"Nick?" He asked. "What the hell are you doing here?"

"Stumbling on you," Nick said as he put the flashlight down on the table with the beam pointing toward the ceiling.

"First, how did you get in here?" Hank said as he reached down to pick up the drain. "And B, you just almost got torn to pieces. I'd be careful who you sneak up on in the future."

"I teleported here," Nick said. "And did I spook the big bad werepig?"

"Teleported here?" Hank pulled one of the other chairs out from the table and sat down. "Like 'beam me up Scotty'?"

"A little more supernatural than that," Nick said and picked up a glass of water and took a drink. "Turns out if I'm doing that little trick of mine with a map and I touch a ghost haunting the place I'm checking out, I appear there."

"How the hell does that work?" Hank stood up and grabbed a glass from the cupboard and filled it from the faucet.

"No idea, but I've done it a few times now, mostly by accident," Nick said.

"I hope it hurts," Hank sat down and drained half of his glass of water.

"What?" Why would you hope it hurts?" Nick said.

"That is way too fancy a gift for you, and I hope you have to pay for it every time you use it," Hank set his glass down.

"That's just mean," Nick said. "And for the record I hit my funny bone twice so far, so sometimes it does hurt."

"Good," Hank said then drained the glass. "Why are you here?"

"I needed a quick escape after accidentally Ghost Walking to a castle in Scotland," Nick said.

"You just think you're the cleverest boy in the world don't you?" Hank grinned.

"What would you call being able to teleport to another place by way of looking through a map with a magical pen and touching a ghost on the other side?" Nick said.

"Let's go with Peter Panning," Hank said.

"That doesn't even make sense," Nick shook his head. "Anyway, I ran into a ghost there, and got stuck for a few hours until I figured out what had happened. Then I went back doing the map trick just to explore some—"

"Why were you exploring this palace in Scotland?" Hank raised a hand motioning Nick to slow down.

"Looking for Stone," Nick said.

"Why did you think he would be there?" Hank said.

"The Orkney Islands were an important location in Shelley's novel. So I figured it would be a logical place for him to hide out. Old creatures like yourself tend to hold on to things from your past," Nick said. "Take your pig farm and Ben's fascination with those hats."

"Fair enough. Did you find anything?" Hank said.

"Maybe," Nick said. "Back to my point. I needed to get out of there quick, found a globe and put the pen on Nantucket and ran into Edward here, and he told me you've been crashing here instead of your own place."

"No one likes a tattletale," Hank said loud enough so anyone eaves dropping could hear.

"You're the one who was hiding from me," Nick said.

"I wasn't hiding from you. I was just hiding in a place I figured you or anyone else wouldn't have looked first or even last. You stumbled on my hideout as you said."

"Well, I found you so this whole running away can end now," Nick said. "I know you're sad but—"

"What do you know about mourning, huh, boy?" Hank stood up and turned his back on Nick.

"I know that Gert isn't the first person you've known who has died," Nick said. "Ten out of ten people die, Hank, even those who call themselves immortal or invincible or supernatural. Some just live a long time before they meet their end."

"That doesn't change how much it hurts to lose someone who changed your life," Hank said over his shoulder.

"Have you stayed on the wagon?" Nick stood up.

"Yes," Hank said. "But, but it's not going well now with Gert gone."

"And you think being off on your own right now is the right road to be on?" Nick said.

"Are you going to help me control this, boy?" Hank laughed.

"I'll do what I can but I think that Mina and Ben and Penny can fill in the gaps," Nick said.

"How the hell is that child going to help?" Hanks turned around.

"Ben said she's pretty powerful," Nick said. "When they went off into the deep ocean, so he could change, she turned into a giant squid and they wrestled, fulfilling his need to fight and destroy and he came back to civilization."

"Sounds like fun, but I don't think play fighting is going to cut it right now," Hank said.

"What about fighting for real, but like in a controlled environment?" Nick said.

"What do you have in mind?" Hank said.

"Do you know of any ghosts in Montreal?" Nick said.

"The city is full of 'em," Hank said. "Do you even know if you can bring someone with you doing that silly Ghost Walking thing?"

"Not yet, but no time like the present to test it out," Nick said. "Hey, Edward, show yourself, kid."

In the doorway to the kitchen the boy appeared, floating a few inches off the ground, "Yes, Nick?"

"Do you know of an atlas or map of North America in the house?" Nick said.

"In the living room on the book shelf," Edward said and disappeared.

"That boy is not very social," Hank said.

"Pot calling the kettle black," Nick said as they walked into the living room.

"I actually enjoyed that about him being here the past few days," Hank said. "He was quiet."

"Unlike Julie and her constant chatter," Nick said as he pulled an atlas off the shelf. "She misses you pretty bad by the way."

"I know, but," Hank looked down at the floor.

"She'll be thrilled if we can make this trick work, I can be certain of that," Nick smiled as he opened the book to a map of Canada.

"What do you mean?" Hank said.

"For a brief moment, while in whatever that plane is called, I can touch a ghost. Real physical contact. And I also want to test if you can touch a ghost," Nick looked Hank in the eye.

Hank's eyes widened.

"It might only be for a second, but you will be able to hold Julie's hand," Nick pulled out his pen and placed it on Montreal, Canada. "But first, let's find a ghost in the great white North."

"It's probably the same temperature there as it is here," Hank said.

"It's just a saying," Nick said. "Now put your hand on my shoulder and let's try and find a ghost."

"It's a stupid expression," Hank placed his hand on Nick's shoulder, and he and the boy were standing on the street looking down the sidewalk. "I forgot how beautiful this city is."

"Can you, by chance, remember any specific place where a ghost hangs out around here?" Nick asked.

"Queen Elizabeth Hotel," Hank said and pointed in the direction of the hotel. "It was always pretty active whenever I stayed there. A few blocks that way on René-Lévesque Blvd. Can you just think yourself there?"

"Sort of," Nick said and they appeared in another part of the city. Now they could see the sign of the Queen Elizabeth Hotel across the top of the face of the building in huge letters.

"Are we on top of a building?" Hank said.

"Why? You afraid of heights?" Nick said and they appeared on the street in front of the hotel. "Cause it's not like you could fall and die until we find a ghost."

"Not a fan of either heights or your humor," Hank said as they walked into the building.

"Heights and crappy jokes, check," Nick said as he looked around the room for anyone that looked like they were out of a different era, or transparent.

"What did you just say?" Hank said scanning the room as well. Then he pointed at an older woman, who looked like she belonged in an old James Bond film.

"Making a list of your weaknesses," Nick smiled as they walked toward the ghost. "Now, when we are within reach, touch the ghost."

"I don't like being your guinea pig, pun intended," Hank said.

"Only room for one crappy comedian on this adventure, so stop it," Nick said as they got next to the ghost who paid them no mind. "Now, grab her."

"Grab her? That was your plan?" Hank said as they stood right next to the ghost woman, who pulled a compact and lipstick out of her clutch, and touched up her lips.

"Whatever, just reach out and try and touch her," Nick said.

The ghost closed the compact and tossed everything back into her little bag, then straightened her coat.

"I think she's leaving, so any day now," Nick looked at his wrist watch.

As the ghost took a step away from them, Hank stuck his hand out and touched her elbow, not even looking at her. Hank's eyes widened in disbelief and his mouth fell open. He squeezed the ghost's arm, and he could feel the coldness on his hand. But that was cut short and he and Nick found themselves on their backs on the floor.

"Why do I always end up on the ground when I do that?" Nick said shaking his head.

"That was different," Hank pushed himself off the ground and reached a hand out to Nick.

"Thanks," Nick said as he pulled himself up.

The ghost was still there, staring at them, completely still.

"Yeah, that just happened, now be on your way," Nick shoed her off with both hands.

The ghost woman gave him a look of disgust then disappeared.

"So, that worked and we're both still alive," Nick said looking himself over for holes or missing parts. "Hope we can find a map, though, so we can get out of here later."

"You didn't bring the atlas with you?" Hank said.

"Seems I can bring the pen and passengers, but not a map or a book. Tried this time and last time, but no luck," Nick said and headed for the door.

"But our clothes came with us." Hanks said and followed.

"I don't know how it works. It's magic," Nick said as they headed out to the street.

"Maybe you should get a tattoo of the world, or at least Kelsey Town, on your arm or chest so you always have a way home," Hanks said.

"That's the most useful idea you have ever had," Nick smiled at Hank. "Now, do you know anyone who will tattoo someone my age with no questions?"

"I can do it," Hank said. "Why are we here, again?"

"Fight Night," Nick said. "This way, I think."

"What do you mean Fight Night?" Hank said as they walked.

"When Mina was off on her little adventure, one of the places she went was Montreal, where she found a bar with supernatural creatures, mostly weres, cage fighting. I figured it will get out some of that blood lust you were complaining about."

"I know the place," Hank said and pointed down the street they were crossing. "It's this way."

"You feeling limber?" Nick said as they headed the direction Hank had pointed.

"No," Hank said. "And this is only a slightly better idea than me accidentally tearing a civilian apart."

"Exactly," Nick said and stopped short in front of an alley. "I'm pretty sure it's this way."

Hank only nodded. His eyes looked wild as the two of them headed toward the only door in the dark alley. Standing in front of the door, Nick could feel the energy coming from inside. He also caught the scent of lavender.

"Mosquitos," Nick said.

Hank nodded.

"How are you feeling towards them these days?" Nick looked up at Hank.

"Not a fan," Hank kept his eyes on the door.

"I figured," Nick smiled as he opened the door and they walked inside.

A crowd was gathered around the cage and watched as two enormous vampires inside traded blows. They moved so fast that it was difficult to make out which one was winning, but Nick had acclimated to seeing creatures move this quickly. Seemed his mind was built to see and hear and smell better than he ever thought and it was finally catching up to everything he was seeing nowadays.

On the other side of the room was a bar and the bartender stared them down.

"Friend of yours?" Nick pointed at the barkeep.

"Far from it. Keep your mouth shut." Hank walked to the bar with Nick close behind.

"Well, well, well, did the big bad wolf blow your house down again, wee little piggy?" The bartender joked, his eyes glowing red. The smell of sulfur permeated the air.

"Have you ever thought about burning a scented candle to cover that horrible scent of rotten eggs?" Hank said. "It truly is rank."

"That's why I let the blood suckers in here," the bartender said. "Not like they spend any money on liquor or food, so might as well benefit from that stupid lavender smell of theirs."

"But they sure do love to overindulge in the third of the holy trinity of vices don't they?" Hank said.

"Aye, and even more so when they can bet against the living," the bartender nodded toward the cage. "The board is short of names that have a heart beat this evening. Not much money exchanging hands right now."

"Shot a Jameson for me and a Shirley Temple for the boy," Hank didn't take his eyes off of the bartender.

The bartender's eyes widened and a smile grew across his face. He turned, poured the shot with one hand and filled a cup with ice, then Sprite with the other. He tipped a bottle of grenadine into the cup for three seconds, then dropped the drinks down on the bar.

Hank looked down at the shot, then to the bartender. Hank wrapped his giant fingers around the shot glass, then tossed the whiskey down his throat, and placed the glass upside down on the bar top.

"I have always wanted to see you fight, little piggy," the bartender said. "Seems to be my lucky day."

"Yours and yours alone," Hank said. "Grab your drink and follow me."

Doing as he was told, Nick kept quiet and followed Hank to the back of the bar and through a door. Small rooms on each side of the hall, like a doctor's office, all housed a table, a sink and a cabinet over the sink. Hank went into the last one on the left.

"Speak quietly," Hank said as he closed the doors. "I'm sure you have a ton of annoying questions."

"You thinking about squishing a mosquito?" Nick said as Hank sat on the table. Nick put his drink down on the sink. "Like in the way that will turn the whole room full of them on us?"

"Possibly," Hank said. "Remember this was your idea."

"Thanks for the reminder," Nick said.

"They'll probably turn on us even if I win though. Not inside, but they'll follow us out or wait for us to leave." Hanks pulled his boots off. "There should be tape in the cabinet. Hand me a roll."

Nick turned and opened the cabinet, grabbed a roll of tap then tossed it to Hank. He leaned back against the sink. "If?"

"What are you scared or something?" Hank wrapped tape

around each of his wrists.

"Not even a little," Nick said and a smile grew across his face. "We have luck on our side."

"Luck is for pansies," Hank said as he slammed his huge right fist into his left palm. The smack echoed through the room. Then he flexed his fingers, "I bet on these."

"Isn't the tape a bit of a laugh since it will just tear off when you change?" Nick asked.

"Don't plan on changing," Hank stood up and took a fighter's stance - knees bent, feet moving and fists up protecting his jaw.

"Then how do you plan on fighting a vampire?" Nick crossed his arms.

"You haven't been paying attention, boy," Hank threw a couple of fast punches at the air. "My power isn't limited to the change."

"Ah," Nick said.

"Yeah," Hank got closer to Nick and tossed a few shots across the boy's brow. Hank's giant fists missed by millimeters.

"What's your plan then?" Nick asked.

"Hit him harder than he hits me," Hank said as his feet shuffled over the floor and he threw punches in the air, bobbing and weaving. Sweat beaded on his skin.

"What if you lose?" Nick said. "What's stopping him from draining you and leaving your carcass for the vultures?"

"The bartender," Hank said.

"The Jinn," Nick said.

"Powerful and crazy bastards," Hank said. "But he runs a tight and honest fight. In here he's the power and it's tap out or knockout in his bar."

"That's comforting," Nick said. "What's this Jinn's name anyway?"

"Jinn don't have names, at least not that they ever tell us," Hank said.

"That's right," Nick stroked his chin as though he had a beard. "I remember reading that somewhere."

"On one of your tombstones no doubt," Hanks said.

"No doubt," Nick said, his eyes widening.

"Mull over what I said about them waiting for us outside," Hank whispered as he threw a series of punches at his shadow. His skin slapped between his arms and chest. "Put that problem solver of yours to use."

"Ten steps ahead of you," Nick said, stroking his chin again. "Well, more like four or five steps ahead of you."

"Right," Hank laughed and stood up straight. "Sounds like I'm up."

"Have fun in there, I'll be rooting for ya," Nick said, picked up his drink and headed out to the bar ahead of Hank.

As he walked he drained the glass. He placed it on the bar and looked the barkeep in the eye. "Another one of these fantastic Shirley Temples please."

The bartender grabbed a glass, poured another drink, and placed it on the counter in front of Nick. Then he took Nick's old glass and washed it in the sink.

Nick took a sip of his drink. "Fantastic once again, sir."

The bartender didn't say anything.

"This is weird but have we met before?" Nick said. "Cause you remind me of someone, I just can't place where I know you from"

"No, I don't forget a face," The bartender grabbed a tooth pick from next to the register and tossed it in his mouth.

"You sure you don't know me?" Nick said pointing at his face and smiling.

"Nope, never met ya, kid," the bartender said, and kept his eyes on the cage across the way, the crowd taking bets among themselves.

Looking over his shoulder, Nick watched Hank walk out and head toward the cage. A young man came out of a shadow and opened up the chain link so Hank could squeeze in. Nick saw they man's face and smiled.

"You keep track of all the money exchanging hands over there? Never get scammed for your cut?" Nick said.

"Never lose track of a dime," the bartender said.

"Really? That's pretty amazing since you're all the way over here and they're all the way over there," Nick said.

"Don't be simple, kid, you know what I am and that this is my place," the bartender said. "And you certainly know that we have never met."

"Okay, okay I see how it is," Nick said. "Since you aren't up for my witty banter, how 'bout I cut to the chase. I know what you are, and I know you are a betting man. Let's say we make a bet."

Crossing his arms, the bartender said, "Go on."

"When Hank wins, we will have a little problem outside with the rest of the clientele. And that's a problem for me since I'm human and they sort of love drinking human blood." Nick said.

"You want to place a bet on how fast they'll drain your weak little body? Seems silly since you'll be dead," the bartender said.

"No, that would be a stupid bet. I want to bet my freedom."

The bartender broke into a full belly laugh, and slapped the bar top, "You'd be better off with the blood suckers in the alley if he loses."

"I'm not joking," Nick said as he looked over at the cage. Hank's opponent, a large, bald and very pale vampire stepped up to the cage. The young man who let Hank in opened the cage it for the mosquito.

"You would really wager your freedom? For what?" The bartender asked, biting back another laugh.

"A wish," Nick said.

A smile grew across the bartender's face, and his eyes looked wild and burned as though someone had stoked the fire in his belly.

"If Hank wins, you owe me one wish. If he loses, I will call you master," Nick held out his hand. "Deal?"

"Aye, we have a deal," the bartender shook Nick's hand firmly, still smiling, as the fight began.

Nick picked up his Shirley Temple, turned, and rested his elbows on the bar behind him to watch.

The two fighters stood facing each other inside the cage. Hank was breathing slowly, but the vampire showed no sign of life.

The vampire took a step toward Hank, then another, slowly, deliberately. Then another. Hank did not move.

When the vampire was face to face with Hank it took a wide,

whirling shot at Hank with its right arm. Hank ducked easily, but the blood sucker was ready for that, and brought its left knee up toward Hank's ribs. Hank was ready as well, and blocked the knee with his right forearm, then threw a quick jab at the vampire with his left. The vampire blocked it with both arms, and Hank took the opportunity to slam his forehead into the vampire's face.

The vampire reeled back, his nose squished, pointed to the right and was much flatter than it had been a second earlier.

Hank struck again as the mosquito left its body wide open to cup its face with both hands. Nick heard the crack of its ribs from the bar, and took a sip from his drink.

The vampire slid backwards from the blow, but did not lose his balance - stopping when his feet met the chain-link fence. It pulled his hands away from his face, revealing that he had gone full monster. Its mouth was wider, all of its teeth were long and sharp, and his eyes showed a fully blacked out pupil. It jumped off the side of the cage, firing off like a bullet at Hank.

Ready for the blow, Hank had his forearms up and pulled in tight to his chest and face. His shoulders were rolled forward and his knees were bent. He absorbed most of the blow from the football-like spearing, but was knocked onto his butt and skidded into the fence behind him.

The vampire was up and pounced again before Hank could get to his feet. Hank was on his back in an open guard position. Hank's legs wrapped around the vampire's torso, and his hands kept the snapping teeth of the blood sucker at bay.

The vampire drew back a fist then brought it down at Hank's chest. It opened its fingers revealing dagger-like claws which it sunk into Hank's exposed skin. The claws dug deep, so deep that Nick winced inside for his friend. Luckily Hank did not waiver as Nick took another sip from his Shirley Temple.

Blood bubbled up around the vampire's fingers and his tongue lashed out of its mouth, spittle dripping from it. Hank's face contorted from the pain, but he didn't make a sound.

Instead, Hank used the fact that the blood sucker's arm was trapped. He locked his feet behind the vampire's back and squeezed.

The blood sucker pulled back, and after four seconds of squeezing Hank released him. But not all the way. The blood sucker's claws were still buried in Hank's chest and Hank grabbed onto the vampire's wrist and locked his fingers together like a vice. Still on his back, Hank relocked his legs around the vampire's arm and neck, squeezing even harder this time.

The vampire panicked and started bucking as Hank slowly pulled the claws from his chest, elongating the blood sucker's arm. The squeezing of his legs and the pulling of the vampire's arm began to separate the shoulder from the torso, and a loud pop and tearing noise came from the cage. Then came a blood curdling scream as the vampire realized his arm was being pulled from the socket.

"Tap," Hank said quietly.

The vampire screamed, and wailed and thrashed but all he did was tighten the grip Hank had on his arm and head.

The vampire lost his footing and fell to the ground. Hank's legs were still wrapped around his arm and head, and this caused the flesh to tear along the back of monster's shoulder - blood oozed out slowly.

"Tap," Hank said quietly.

The vampire's face was feral. Rabid. But he knew he would lose his arm if he did not tap out. He would be a lesser predator for a very long time, until it grew back, but the damage done so far would heal after feeding a few times on smaller prey.

So the vampire tapped twice on Hank's leg with its free hand.

Hank loosened his legs first, then quickly kicked the vampire aside. He slowly pushed himself up, keeping his eyes on the blood sucker, knowing that all the blood suckers in the place had their eyes on him.

There were three beings with heartbeats in the crowd. Nick could feel them there but he had no idea what they were or if they cared that the vampires were pissed. It wasn't their problem, and Nick had a half formed plan that he had pretty high hopes for.

The young man that opened the cage for both combatants appeared once more to let the two creatures out. Hank walked out with his back straight, head high, not looking anyone in the crowd in the eye. The vampire slowly made his way out of the cage, glaring at Hank's back and muttering to himself quietly about how good bacon flavored blood would taste, should they meet again.

"Here's your winnings, pig," the Jinn pulled an envelope of money out from under the bar and dropped it in front of Hank.

"Jameson," Hank said.

The bartender grabbed a rocks glass, some ice and poured a double for Hank.

"What's the plan, Junior?" Hank said and took a sip of his drink. "Cause their plan involves dining on bacon flavored blood in the alley at some point this evening. And fighting one mosquito is very different from fending off twenty or thirty thirsty blood suckers."

"Well, our friend the bartender here is going to help us out of our little jam," Nick smiled and took a sip of his own drink.

"Yeah right," Hank drained his whiskey.

"It seems my duel natured friend doubts me, barkeep," Nick said. "I would like to collect my winnings as well."

"Make your wish then, boy," the bartender smiled.

Hank turned his head slowly to Nick, eyes wide and mouth agape.

"I would like safe passage out of this city with the help of your ward over there," Nick said and pointed at the cage, where the young man was cleaning up the blood from the floor.

"Granted," the Jinn said. Then he looked toward the cage, and yelled, "Charles, get over here."

When Charles got to the bar, Nick stuck out his hand, "Hi Charles. I'm Nick and this is Hank."

"What can I help you with?" Charles shook Nick's hand.

"Get them out of here, the safe and boring way," the bartender said and turned to the sink and got to washing more glasses.

"I guess, follow me, fellas," Charles turned and headed for the door to all the locker rooms. Nick and Hank shrugged at each other and followed. They went to one of the closed doors in the hallway. Charles opened it to reveal a stairwell.

At the bottom of the stairs were rows of empty boxes from

every beer and liquor company one could imagine. There were also two pad locked doors to the right.

"Liquor room is door number one and torture chamber is door number two," Charles said as Nick looked over at the two doors. "And the tunnel leads to one of the Metro lines. You can hop right on a train and be halfway across the city before anyone knows we are gone."

At the end of the tunnel was a large metal door. Charles pulled a key from his pocket. He opened the door and they stepped out into another dark passage. It was light to their right and they saw people on a platform waiting for their trains. The three men walked casually up the steps to the platform

"Where would you guys like to go?" Charles asked.

"To see Bruce," Nick said.

Hank cocked his head to the right.

"So you are THAT Nick and Hank," Charles smiled.

"We are," Nick looked up at Hank then back to Charles. "I owe you a thank you for helping Mina during her adventure."

"Is that what you're calling it?" Charles said. "Cause I would call it a near death experience."

"Well, such is the life we lead," Nick said. "Any chance Bruce is around, though? I have a few questions I'd like to ask him."

"Haven't seen him is a month," Charles said. "He took off into the forest, said that he had spent too long away from what he truly was."

Nick looked at Hank, "Sounds pretty familiar."

Hank just grimaced.

"So, yeah, sadly, I have no idea where he is," Charles said. "I know you were trying to avoid dealing with those vampires in the alley but betting your freedom for a wish was pretty ridiculous."

"What?" Hank said.

"I knew you would win," Nick said. "And if you didn't I would have survived as a slave. That Jinn wouldn't let one of those mosquitos drain his new property."

"He would bleed you daily for something to serve them at fights though," Charles said. A train was pulling up to the platform.

"Should we get in and see where the night takes us?"

"Sure," Nick jumped through the doors of the train as they opened and plopped down in a seat. Hank and Charles stepped on and grabbed onto the bar above their heads to keep their balance as the train doors closed and it lurched forward.

"Since we are trying to get away from mosquitos, I figure we should let a few stops pass before getting off," Charles said. "Are you guys hungry?"

"Very," Nick said.

"Little Italy is a couple of stops away, some great little places to grab some food this late," Charles said.

"I like Italian," Hank said.

"Real Italian, not just mushroom pizza I hope," Nick said.

"Every kind of dish you can think of," Charles said. They all kept quiet for the next couple of stops until Charles motioned toward the door. "This is our stop."

The street was busy for the late hour, and Charles led them over to a small restaurant not far from the subway entrance. Inside was cozy with only ten tables. There were paintings of Roman buildings along one wall, all with heavy, elaborate gold frames.

The Maître d' knew Charles and didn't even ask how many in the party, just grabbed three menus and sat them in the back of the dining room.

"This isn't in English," Hank said as he looked at the menu.

"Italian," Charles said. "You're a vegetarian, correct?"

"Yes," Hank put down the menu.

"Go with the Pasta Primavera," Charles looked over his menu at Hank. "It's excellent. Do you need a suggestion, Nick?"

"Nope," Nick said as he read over the menu. The language easily translated, curtsy of one of his gifts. "I will be going with the Penne alla Vodka con Pollo. One of my favorites and pretty much the same in English as it is in Italian."

"Also and excellent choice. And I will be having the Piccata di Pollo." Charles put down his menu. Nick and Hank placed theirs on top of it and the pile disappeared and a bread basket appeared with a bowl of garlic olive oil next to it.

"Interesting." Nick said.

"This restaurant is run by folks in our world," Charles said. "We will not be bothered by any questions or curious ears. But if you would like something to drink other than water, just say it out loud."

"A beer?" Nick said.

"No," Hank said. "But I'll take a Yuengling."

"Fine. A water and an iced tea," Nick said.

"Water all around then," Charles said. The Maître d' sat another table in the front of the restaurant near the window. An ordinary looking couple with eyes only for each other. The Maître d' walked in back and then came back out with two waters and bread for the other table.

"Can they see us?" Nick asked.

"No," Charles said. "Only the staff can see us here. Even a vampire wouldn't know we were here. If it were inclined to eat at a place like this, it would only see an empty table in the back of the dining room."

"Do they tack on 20% to the bill from the start for that kind of service?" Hank said.

"It's gratis for me and my employer," Charles said.

"Employer? That's being pretty liberal. Figured that living fart would remove every title you could call him from your vocabulary other than master," Hank said.

"He's softened a bit on that front," Charles said. The drinks appeared on the table.

"Did he get bored of torturing you?" Hank said and took a sip from his beer.

"Luckily for me he is easily distracted and easily bored," Charles said.

"He tortured you?" Nick picked up his tea. "Why?'

"To test his power," Hank said. "Jinn like to play pranks. And when they have a slave, they can make that slave immortal, more or less. And they enjoy torturing their slaves with tricks and outlandish wishes."

"Can you kill a Jinn?" Nick asked.

Both Hank and Charles said, "What?"

"Can you destroy a Jinn?" Nick asked. "Seems like this one has crossed the line and you said yourself, Hank, that nothing is truly immortal. So, can one kill a Jinn?'

"It has been common practice for most of history that the truly devilish and demented Jinn are imprisoned in objects like oil lamps," Charles said.

"Or knives," Nick looked directly at Hank.

"Small weapons, easily hidden or carried, have been practical choices over the centuries as well," Charles said.

"And it's long been said that your kind are the only ones who can trick and trap a Jinn," Hank said, then drained his beer. When he placed it down it filled once again and he smiled.

"My kind, huh?" Nick said. "Still a little confused on what I am and all."

"You and me both," Hank said and took another gulp of beer. The food appeared on the table and the aroma from the dishes hit the three men like a sledge hammer.

"Oh, wow does that smell good," Nick looked over his plate.

"Best Italian food in North America," Charles said picking up his fork and knife.

"We'll see about that," Hank said as he dug into his dish with his fork.

"Anyway," Nick said and took a bite of his food. "So Jinn can't be destroyed. But they can be imprisoned. And it's something that my kind can supposedly do. If your employer were to be imprisoned in a lamp or woopie cushion what would that mean for you?"

"He would be set free," Hank said with a mouth full of pasta and vegetables.

"Really?" Nick said, and took another bite of his food.

"Yes," Charles said taking a bite of chicken.

"You have enough to deal with right now," Hank said. "Don't make promises that you can't keep cause you might be dead soon."

"I promise nothing," Nick said. "But I do enjoy a challenge."

"You would help me like that?" Charles asked.

"It seems my number one job is to protect people from the supernatural world. It's reiterated over and over again in the lessons my ancestors left behind. When a creature becomes too powerful or exercises too much leverage on the mortal world it's my job to stop that. And your Jinn has crossed that line. But I need to figure out how to help you first, so, like Hank said, no promises."

"I said no promises because you already have a quest that involves you being hunted," Hank said.

"I have a plan for that actually," Nick said. "Frank Stone has a son."

Hank stopped chewing his food and his mouth fell open.

The Living

Chapter 8
Loving the Alien

"Hello," Mr. Medellin said after picking up the ringing phone.

"Hey, Roger, it's Trudy," she said. "I was wondering if my son is on your couch."

"He is not," Roger said. "Haven't seen him for a few days now, sadly. Everything okay?"

"I just haven't seen him since yesterday morning, trying to track the boy down," Trudy said. "It's like hunting bigfoot sometimes."

"Hold on a sec and I'll run up and ask Mina. Might take a moment for an answer since waking her these days is like disturbing a hibernating bear," Roger said as he walked up the stairs with the portable phone.

"Ah, the joys of having a teenage daughter," Trudy said.

"I'm told I'll miss the drama when she goes off to college," Roger said as he went to Mina's door. He knocked, then said. "Mina? Are you up yet?"

"Sort of," Mina yelled. "Please tell me you brought coffee?"

"I did not, can I open the door?" Roger said away from the phone.

"Yes," Mina said.

Opening the door, Roger found Mina half in bed with her feet on the floor. "Trudy is looking for Nick. Do you have any idea where he might be?"

"Nope. I was hanging out with Holly and Julie last night. Never caught up with the boy," Mina said, her head still under the covers.

"Holly and Julie?" Roger raised an eyebrow.

Flipping the cover down, Mina said wide eyed, "I can't shake referring to them as a pair. Holly is running me ragged doing girly things."

"Ah," Roger said and closed the door. Then he put the phone back to his ear. "Sorry Trudy, seems she was out late with her friend Holly and didn't catch up with Nick last night."

"He's probably at Filomena's house," Trudy said. "No one ever answers the phone over there though."

"Most likely crashed out on the couch there," Roger said.

"My son, the four time Olympic gold medalist couch surfer," Trudy said. "Well, thanks, Roger. I'll talk to you later."

"Bye Trudy," Roger laughed as he walked down the stairs. He went to the kitchen and put the phone back on its cradle.

Mina came stumbling down the stairs a few minutes later and Roger handed her a cup of black coffee. "I made eggs and tortillas. I need to head into the Town Hall though, and get a couple things squared away for my trip on Monday."

"Okay, I'll see ya later. I think I'm heading to the Roger Williams Zoo for the day with Penny and Ben." Mina smelled the coffee, breathing in deeply, then took a big gulp.

"Oh, that sounds like fun. Has Penny ever been to the zoo?" Roger asked.

"Nope," Mina grabbed the skillet filled with eggs and sat down at the table.

"That should be a hoot," Roger said then kissed Mina on the top of her head. "Have fun and tell them I said hello.'

"Will do," Mina grabbed the tortilla warmer and pulled out four of them. "Have a good day, Dad."

Roger smiled and headed out the door to the garage.

Stuffing her face, Mina sat there for a moment. She took another swig from her coffee then jumped up and grabbed the phone. She dialed Hank's phone number.

Ben answered, "Hello."

"Ben, it's Mina," She said.

"Good morning," Ben said. "Ready for a road trip to the zoo? I have a cooler stuffed and ready with snacks."

"I am," Mina said. "Except Nick is M.I.A."

"What do you mean?" Ben said.

"His mom just called here looking for him, and he's not here," Mina said. "So, he's missing."

"Maybe he's out with his buddy, what's his name?" Ben said.

"Paul Filomena," Mina said. "I'm going to head over there and check right now."

"Don't get worked up, Mina," Ben said. "He's a teenage boy and he might just be passed out on a couch over there."

"He better be," Mina said. "Could you go over to Gert's quick and check to see if he's there for me and I'll meet you at your house in a half hour?"

"I'll take a run over there right now with Penny," Ben said. "See you in half an hour."

Mina dropped the phone on its cradle, shoveled another egg filled tortilla into her mouth, changed and was on the scooter three minutes later. She was at Filomena's door in another five.

The door opened as Mina was slamming her fist against it, and Paul stood there shirtless, "What the hell is the deal?"

"Is Nick here?" Mina said pushing past Filomena looking around, smelling and listening.

"No, haven't seen him since the meet yesterday," Paul said. "No one else is even here."

"Did anything weird happen when you saw him?" Mina turned on the boy looking him in the eye.

"Not when I saw him," Filomena said. "But, he did have me pick him up at Gillette's Castle. Said he'd been out partying with that weirdo Kelsey the night before and they had broken into the castle."

"Hank Kelsey?" Mina asked.

"Yeah," Paul said. "They crashed there, but Hank left him there and Nick needed a ride to the meet."

"Anything else?" Mina said.

"No," Paul pointed at the door. "Can you leave now?"

Mina walked out the door, right over to her scooter.

"Were you raised in a barn?" Filomena yelled as he slammed the door shut.

Mina pulled on her helmet, hopped on the scooter and headed to Hank's house.

When she walked into the house, Ben was in the kitchen eating breakfast.

"No sign of him at Gert's," Ben said. "Did you have better luck? Penny is still out flying around burning off some energy."

"He wasn't at his friend's house," Mina sat down at the table and grabbed a handful of breakfast sausages. "But Filomena said that Nick saw Hank on Friday night. And that they supposedly got hammered, broke into Gillette's Castle and then Hank took off again."

"Sounds plausible," Ben said.

"Yes," Mina ate a sausage. "But where are they now? Specifically Nick?"

"He had a Cross Country meet right?" Ben asked.

"Maybe they met up after that and have been out blowing off steam again," Ben said.

"Why wouldn't Hank have come back to his place if he was around?" Mina said.

"Hank has more than one property around here," Ben said. "And with everything that has happened he may have only wanted to make contact with Nick. They did spend the whole summer together and got very close."

"But they hated each other when I left," Mina said.

"A summer at one another's side could easily bond two men into friendship," Ben said. "Hank never had a son and from what I've learned about Nick, they are very much alike. And Nick doesn't have his dad around and it seems to me that they found in each other what they were missing, despite their stubbornness."

"I hadn't thought about it that way," Mina said. "But if Nick is with Hank, he would have called and told me."

"Are you sure he would have if Hank asked him not to?" Ben said. "What if by telling Filomena that was his way of getting you that info?"

"That just seems far too complicated," Mina ate the last of the sausage she had in her hand.

"The surface of that boy's ability to scheme has only been scratched. The Teller's I've known in the past have all been master strategists," Ben said.

"So, I'm supposed to just hope that this was Nick's way of telling me that he is out causing trouble with Hank?" Mina said.

Penny came running into the kitchen yelling and hugged Mina, "We're going to the zoo!"

"That and go to the zoo," Ben smiled as he stood up. He grabbed a plate and put some eggs and sausage on it. "Sit and eat, Penny."

"I'm too excited to eat, let's hit the road!" Penny said, pulling on Mina's hand.

"Eat first, please," Ben said. "And as for the other thing, best we can do is hope and most likely we will find him in town when we get back. You disappeared for how long? Like three months without calling? It's been only a little over a day since you last spoke to Nick? I'm sure he's just out being a teenage boy."

Penny didn't even sit, she just hoovered up the eggs and sausage standing at the table.

"The zoo it is," Mina said.

"Shot gun," Penny yelled as she dropped her fork and ran out the door.

They were on the road a few minutes later, headed toward Providence. Ben had picked up a used Jeep Grand Wagoneer a few days before. It was blue with the faux wood paneling on the sides.

"What do you have to listen to in this beast?" Mina asked from the back seat. She looked up at the dashboard and was relieved to see it had a radio and tape deck.

"Nothing more than the radio," Ben said. "Been meaning to pick up a few tapes but I have no idea what I should be listening to these days."

"Luckily for you I have my favorite mix tape in my Walkman," Mina fished in her bag, pulling the mix tape from her Walkman, and handed it to Penny.

On the side was written, 'The Ballad of Nick and Mina'.

"Is this gonna be all depressing music like you usually put on?" Penny asked.

"Not all of it," Mina smiled as Penny slowly slid the tape into the car stereo.

Ben looked in the rearview at Mina as the static of the tape came through the speakers, then Freddie Mercury's voice flowed from the speakers of the Wagoneer, "Here we are, born to be kings, we're the princes of the universe." A smile spread across Ben's face.

Over the next hour, Mina, Ben and Penny snacked on chips, veggies, hummus, and rocked out to the likes of the Beastie Boys, David Bowie, Queen, The Cure, INXS, Kenny Loggins, The Ramones, Prince and Depeche Mode.

It was only an hour drive and they pulled into the Roger Williams Zoo parking lot with most of the day still ahead of them.

"What would you like to see first, Penny?" Ben asked.

With her eyes wide and a huge smile on her face, Penny said, "I wanna see a lion. And the giraffes. Oh and llamas."

"Can we skip the llamas, please?" Mina said.

"Um, no," Penny said as she ran toward the entrance.

"Did you have a bad experience with a llama?" Ben laughed.

"Yeah, of the were variety," Mina said as they walked up to the entrance.

"Very phlegmy from what I've heard," Ben said as he bought three tickets.

"To say the least," Mina said as they walked into the zoo.

Penny ran squealing from enclosure to enclosure. Ben and Mina let her just run ahead, giving her a lot of freedom. Unlike other children her age, she could never fall victim to a kidnapping - she could easily turn into a bird and fly away or into a bear and tear a bad guy to pieces. And now she has the visual reference for every big cat that the zoo had on exhibit making her that much more prepared and dangerous.

"Anyone hungry?" Ben asked.

"Yes," Penny and Mina said in unison.

"Jinx," Penny said. "You owe me a root beer."

At a concession stand, they got a few sandwiches, some French fries and three root beers. After that they hit the Farmyard exhibits - which included llamas and alpacas along with rare varieties of cows, chickens and sheep.

The ride home was quiet. Penny fell asleep in the back seat while Ben and Mina listened to the radio quietly - changing from station to station as they lost the signal.

When they pulled into the driveway at Hank's house, Ben said. "Let's make some calls before you rush off to look for Nick. We can narrow the search down that way."

Mina snarled.

"We're home already?" Penny said as Ben turned the truck off.

"That we are," Ben said. "Are you hungry again?"

"Very," Penny said.

"Let's make some food and some phone calls," Ben smiled as he got out of the truck.

Penny grabbed Mina's and Ben's hands, standing between them and said, "Thanks for today."

Mina and Ben looked at each other, then to Penny.

"It was our pleasure, sweetie," Mina said.

Ben just smiled down at the child. She smiled back then let go of their hands, turned into a chimpanzee and climbed up the side of the house. She went in through an unlocked window.

Chapter 9
Fame

Nick woke up at dawn the next morning. Charles had procured them a room at the Queen Elizabeth Hotel. Standing in the window of his room of the suite, Nick looked out over the city as the sun chased away the darkness.

"Sleep well?" Charles asked, leaning against the doorframe with his arms crossed.

"I can sleep anywhere," Nick said.

"I remember Mina mentioning how heavy of a sleeper you were," Charles said. "Said you're biggest talent was falling asleep on couches."

"Did she talk about me a lot?" Nick asked, not looking away from the window.

"More than she should have considering the situation she was in," Charles said.

"Understood," Nick turned and smiled at Charles.

"Want me to order some breakfast?" Charles asked.

"That would be awesome," Nick sat down on the end of the bed. "Can I ask you something, Charles?"

"Sure," He said.

"Have you ever been in love?" Nick asked.

"Yes, but it's new to me so I'm not the best to ask for advice," Charles said.

"It's pretty new to me as well," Nick said. "Where is this love of yours? Geographically speaking?"

"I do not know where he is right now," Charles said.

"I know that feeling well," Nick said. "Is he a slave as well?"

"Yes," Charles said.

"What's his name?" Nick asked.

"Ishmael," Charles said.

"I knew it," Nick smiled.

"Knew it?" Charles asked.

"I saw it when Mina told me her story from the summer. In my head, when you tell me a story, I see everything, very clearly, almost as though I'm looking at the memory," Nick said.

"Almost?" Charles looked Nick in the eye.

"Mostly," Nick laughed. "I knew you from what I saw in Mina's telling of her adventures over the summer, when I saw you open the cage for Hank."

"Ah," Charles said. "Very interesting ability. Quite a pair you and Mina make."

"That we do," Nick said. "Quite unique."

"To say the least," Charles said.

From the other room, Godzilla-like footsteps were heard, then stopped. In its place the sound of someone taking a leak filled the silence.

"Hank's awake," Nick said, the urine still flowing from the other side of the suite.

"How much does his bladder hold?" Charles asked.

"A lot," Nick stood up. Charles turned and walked out into the main room, Nick followed. Hank's door was also open and he came out a few seconds later, stretching.

"I need food," Hank said.

"Just about to call down to put an order in," Charles picked up the phone.

"Did it seem like a really easy getaway to anyone else last night?" Hank scratched himself. "I've never known that Jinn jackass not to toy with people."

"I think that's the trick," Nick said.

Charles was speaking quietly into the phone placing their order.

"That is a stupid trick," Hank said.

"It's got you second guessing the whole situation," Nick said.

Charles hung up the phone, and said. "Food will be up shortly. And I think that Nick is being modest."

"What are you talking about?" Hank said. "And is there any

aspirin in this place?"

"No, and I think that one of Nick's gifts is that the Jinn cannot trick him," Charles said. "I was wondering about this all night, waiting for the other shoe to drop. After I was told to help you, I kept expecting something crazy to pop up. Instead, we got out quickly and easily, had a nice dinner and got a good night's sleep. Seems a little coincidental that the only time I've ever seen a wish not go haywire is when someone like you asked it."

"I call bull. Can you call back down and ask them to bring some up?" Hank asked.

"Sure," Charles said. "I still thank that Nick is something different to the Jinn, he can make a wish and it comes out exactly as he asked, and why his kind can imprison them."

"The kid is high enough on himself as it is without any more smoke blown up is crack," Hank looked at Nick.

"Look, I don't know why it was so easy, but I do like the fact that I got a nice little vacation out of the whole thing," Nick said. "But I do need to get home, I'm supposed to do something for my mom in like an hour. Move furniture or something."

"There's no way you can drive back to Connecticut in an hour," Charles said.

"I don't plan on driving," Nick said. "I need a map or an atlas. Two, if possible."

"I'll call down to the front desk and ask if they have that along with the aspirin," Charles said.

Ten minutes later, Hank had eaten half the bottle of aspirin and all of them were stuffing their faces with eggs, pancakes and coffee. Charles had left bacon and even Canadian bacon off of the order.

"I can't thank you enough for your help, Charles," Nick said as he dropped his napkin on his plate.

"It was my pleasure," Charles said. "I just wish that Mina had been along for the evening. I miss her."

"Why don't you come back with us and visit? Could you do that?" Nick asked.

"I would have to make a deal with the bartender," Charles said. "And I don't exactly get the best rates with him, if you know what I mean."

"Well, I will look into that and see what I can do. I could really use your and Bruce's help when everything goes down." Nick stood up and grabbed the two maps off of the serving cart. He stuffed one in his pocket, and opened the other. It was a map of New England and southeast Canada.

"I will get a message to Bruce as soon as I can," Charles said. "Now, how does this trick with the map work?"

"I have no idea, but I'll have to ask you what it looks like from this end if it works," Nick put out his hand to Charles.

Shaking his hand Charles said, "If it works?"

"I don't expect this magic stuff to work the same way, or at all, every time," Nick said. "That would just make sense."

"It's smart to expect the unexpected when it comes to magic," Charles let go of Nick's hand. "Well, I look forward to crossing paths again."

"It was real and it was fun, Charles," Hank shook the man's hand. "But it wasn't real fun."

"Have a good one, Hank," Charles smiled and shook his head.

Nick put the pen down on the shoreline of Connecticut.

"Where are we going to pop up this time?" Hank said as he stood up and grabbed Nick's shoulder.

"The high school," Nick said as he wandered into the building in his head. The ghost janitor wasn't in the locker room, but Nick could hear him rambling about the gym teacher's office in the back of the locker room. He headed back there and right towards the ghost janitor. "I hope."

Hank crashed into a bookcase full of physiology books and binders full of different team building games and exercises. The particle board gave way under his weight and broke into thousands of pieces, sending books all over the room. Nick slammed gut first into the desk. The ghost janitor gave them a dirty look, mumbled something under his breath and then took off through the wall.

Still trying to catch his breath, Nick reached into his pocket and pulled out the spare map. "Sweet, I can carry a map with me."

Pushing himself up, Hanks said, "A tattoo would be way more efficient. Always handy and just plain cooler than carrying a map around with you in your pocket like a nerd."

"Still underage," Nick said gulping air as he fell back against the wall.

"I said I can do it for you," Hank opened the office door.

"You'd probably draw something like Ronnie James Dio's portrait," Nick followed Hank out into the locker room. "Instead of a map."

"Sounds like an awesome tattoo," Hank kept on walking right out into the lobby. "But you'd be able to see what I was doing if it was on your chest or forearm."

"Have to be chest since I need to be able to hide it from my ma and grandma," Nick said as they walked out of the front door of the building. "You gonna stick around or head back out into the wild?"

"Be at Gert's at 3:15 and maybe I'll see ya there," Hank said. "And thanks for bringing me on this adventure with you. I certainly feel more in control than I did while I was avoiding contact with people all together."

"Just stick around and we can keep working the program," Nick smiled.

"You look like you want to hug, so I'm gonna walk away now," Hank turned on his heel and trotted off toward his farm.

"If I go all the way up to Gert's and you're not there I'm gonna be pissed," Nick yelled.

*****

When Ben and Mina walked in the front door of Hank's house, they both stopped dead in their tracks looking at the two occupants of the living room.

"How was the zoo?" Nick asked from the recliner.

"Seriously?" Mina said. "That's what you lead with after disappearing for most of the weekend?"

"Technically I only disappeared for a few seconds. The rest of the time I was at a Cross Country meet or with him," Nick pointed at Hank.

"Hello," Hank said from the couch.

"And you, where the hell have you been?" Mina glared down at Hank.

"Around," Hank said.

"That isn't an answer," Mina said.

"How are you my old friend?" Ben asked as he sat down in the living room.

"I'm doing alright," Hank said. "Thank you for asking."

A sparrow flittered down the stairs, landing in the shape of Penny next to the chair Ben was sitting in. "Hank! Nick! You're both back safe and sound!"

"Of course we are. Why wouldn't we be?" Nick said.

"Mina was so worried about you Nick, she was stressing bad cause she hasn't seen or talked to you since Friday," Penny said.

"Really? How 'bout them apples?" Nick smiled at Mina. She scowled at him.

"And well, we haven't seen you in a long, long, loooonnnng time Hank," Penny said.

"I needed a vacation," Hank said.

"Don't we all," Ben said. "And I hope you spoke with your mother today, Nick. She was also trying to track you down."

"I did. Had to help her and my grandma move some furniture this morning."

"Seriously, where have you been all weekend?" Mina asked.

"I had the Cross Country meet yesterday morning, then stumbled into Hank, and we found ourselves in Montreal. We met your friend Charles —" Nick said.

"You met Charles?" Mina said. "How did you get to Montreal?"

Nick looked at Hank, and Hank nodded.

"Magic," Nick said. "I'll show you later."

"Why later?" Mina said.

"It takes some work, and I don't have all the kinks worked out yet," Nick said.

"So, you can fly now or something?" Mina asked.

"No, I can teleport," Nick smiled. "It's an extension of the Map Walking."

"No way!" Mina said.

"Yes way," Nick said.

"What's teleporting?" Penny asked.

"Like in that Star Trek show when they beam down for an away mission," Ben said.

"Oh, and the red shirt guys don't make it back," Penny laughed.

"I never noticed that," Ben said.

"You only started watching the reruns last month so you're excused," Hank said.

"So, you can teleport?" Mina said. "That's not magic."

"I don't use a computer or a machine to do it, so it's magic," Nick said.

"How do you do it then?" Mina said.

"I'll show you soon," Nick said. "It's hard to explain. And I'm really tired after."

"Fine," Mina stood up and walked into the kitchen. "I'm hungry anyway."

"Me too!" Penny said and followed Mina into the kitchen.

"I could use a sandwich, too," Hank yelled.

Chapter 10
The Man Who Sold the World

"Thank you," Hank said as he touched Julie hand.

Julie didn't say anything, but a slight gasp escaped her lips as Hank's finger tips touched hers. Hank was ready this time for the shock and kept his balance. This gave him a chance to press his whole hand against Julie, who now pushed back as hard as she could.

"This can't be real," Julie whispered.

"It's real and I fell on a rock," Nick said from his butt in the sand. "Should have done this inside, next to a couch or a bed."

Hank and Julie kept their hands together for a few more seconds. But as they were used to, Julie's hand slipped through Hank's.

"No, no, no, no, no," Julie said as she grabbed at Hank, but her hands and arms went right through him.

Hank smiled bigger than Nick had ever seen him smile.

"That might be the first genuine smile I have ever seen on your face," Nick pushed himself back to his feet, then brushed his hands off on his jeans.

"Do it again?" Julie looked to Nick.

"We will, sweetheart," Hank said. "But it isn't easy on him."

"Yeah, kinda rough on my posterior and funny bone," Nick said.

"When can we do it again?" Julie said, trying again to touch Hank's hand.

"We can test some other ideas I have tomorrow," Nick said.

"What ideas?" Hank asked.

"On the next trip I want you to lead with your lips," Nick said and started walking toward the parking lot.

"That is a fantastic idea!" Julie said as she appeared at Nick's side.

"Thought you'd like that one," Nick smiled as Julie vanished from his side, and appeared back with Hank.

The familiar putt, putt, putt of Mina's scooter came from the bridge over the marsh into the beach parking lot. She was pulling off her helmet as Nick's feet met the asphalt, and he planted a big kiss on her lips. Mina let her hand holding the helmet fall to the side, and slid the fingers of her other hand up into Nick's hair. She kissed him back, hard.

"Nice to see you too, darlin," Mina said.

Nick smiled and said, "How was your run with Ben and Penny?"

"It was good," Mina said. "How did everything go here?"

"It went well," Nick said. "But I don' think it will ever last more than a few seconds."

"Having the ghost right next to you didn't help?" Mina said. "Really thought that would give you more time or something."

"Me too," Nick said.

"Am I still giving you a ride home?" Mina asked.

"Yes please," Nick said. He turned toward the beach and yelled to Hank, "I'm heading out."

"Good," Hank yelled back not taking his eyes off of Julie.

Shaking his head, Nick pulled his helmet from where it hung off the side of the scooter and strapped it to his head.

A few minutes later Nick was at his desk and Mina was sprawled out on his bed.

"I have something I want you to read," Nick said as he pulled a notebook out of his desk.

"Are you finally gonna show me the notes from when you figured out how to ghost walk?" Mina made the international sign of quotes with her fingers when she said ghost walk.

"No," Nick said. "But it does involve the Map Walking trick."

"Gimmie, gimmie, gimmie," Mina reached for the notebook. "How many of these do you have hidden from me?"

"Just this one," Nick said.

"I don't believe you for a second," Mina leaned back on the bed and cracked open the notebook.

"Feel free to search me," Nick smiled.

"I may just have to do that," Mina said. "After I read this."

Nick stood up and walked down to the kitchen. He grabbed a bag of chips and a glass of ice tea. He went out to the porch and sat down on one of the chairs.

A few chips into the bag, Nick heard Mina yell, "NO WAY!" Then he heard the clomp, clomp, clomp of Mina's boots down the stairs. She burst out onto the porch through the screen door.

"Want some chips?" Nick offered.

Grabbing the bag of chips, Mina said, "Yes, and take me to meet my cousins."

"We can go see them," Nick said and took a sip from his ice tea.

"No, I want to use the Ghost Walking thing to go there and meet them," Mina said.

"Maybe," Nick said.

"Why maybe?" Mina put her free hand on her hip.

"Gotta find a ghost there first so we can get there," Nick said.

"You really think that would be very difficult?" Mina sat down. "Everywhere we go we run into a new one."

"True," Nick said and took the bag of chips back.

"So," Mina said.

"So, what?" Nick said.

"Let's go," Mina said.

"Maybe you should contact them first, and start a dialogue," Nick said.

"Why?" Mina asked.

"Not everyone likes surprises," Nick said. "Especially those who have something to hide."

"What do they have to hide?" Mina took the bag of chips back.

"Oh, maybe the fact that the family is full of shapeshifters?" Nick said.

"Right," Mina stuffed her mouth full of chips. "I'll call my grandmother tomorrow around lunch then. It's too late there now."

"Just try and be subtle," Nick said.

"You don't want me to blurt out that I have super powers to

my grandma over an international phone call?" Mina said. "But she'd be so proud."

"Just think how much more impressed she will be when she sees it in person." Nick said.

"I wonder if she's a shapeshifter too." Mina said.

"You'll have to ask her," Nick said. "I only saw your cousins."

"Okay, now I'm getting way too excited. I haven't seen my mom's side of the family since her funeral." Mina jumped up.

"When was the last time you talked to any of them?" Nick asked.

"Before my little adventure," Mina said.

"Really? You're a horrible granddaughter," Nick said.

Mina smacked Nick on the shoulder, knocking him off the chair.

"Uncalled for," Nick said from his back.

"Totally warranted, jerk," Mina pulled him to his feet. "I can't believe you said that."

"Okay, maybe I was a little too quick with that comment," Nick said. "Sorry."

"Of course you are," Mina said. "I almost broke you."

"Not even close," Nick pulled Mina into him and kissed her.

"You're not totally forgiven yet," Mina said. "But thank you for sharing that bit about my family."

"You are very welcome," Nick smiled.

"I have to run," Mina said. "My dad wanted me to swing by the Town Hall and help him with something."

"I bet he needs something heavy moved," Nick laughed.

"I will not be betting against you," Mina scowled and headed to the driveway.

"I'll leave my window open later if you want to swing by," Nick right the chair and sat back down.

"Maybe," Mina said as she pulled on her helmet. She fired up the scooter and took off out of the driveway.

Chapter 11
Space Oddity

"How are you doing these days, sweetie?" Trudy asked as Mina sat down at the table. "And thanks for volunteering to help me make all these breads for the fundraiser. Nick's no help these days with Cross Country and whatever else he's been up too."

"The pleasure is all mine, Trudy," Mina said. "To be honest I am in need of a good dose of maternal guidance these days."

"What's on your mind?" Trudy said as she pulled mixing bowls from the cabinet and placed them on the table.

"A lot," Mina laughed. "But most importantly, I've been thinking about my mom. Like a lot."

"That's understandable with how everything is changing and you're doing that whole growing up thing." Trudy pulled flour and sugar out of the pantry.

"I'm having some issues with this whole growing up thing," Mina said.

"You and me both," Trudy pulled the baking soda and a brown bunch of bananas out of the fridge. She dropped those on the table and turned to the dish drain and grabbed a large wooden spoon.

"I'm sure Nick isn't making it any easier on you," Mina pealed the bananas and placed them in one of the bowls. Trudy placed the wooden spoon next to the bowl.

There were measuring cups and spoons on the table already along with vanilla extract, salt and butter.

"My mother might actually be worse than him when it comes to the ridiculous behavior," Trudy laughed. "But yes, he has been extra moody lately."

"Has he talked to his dad at all?" Mina asked as she picked up the wooden spoon and mashed the bananas.

"I'm not sure actually," Trudy said as she measured out flour into a mixing bowl.

"I wish he would talk to him more," Mina said. "I can't understand why he wouldn't try and at least talk with him since he's still alive."

"That is partially my fault," Trudy measured the sugar and poured it with the flour. "I was so mad at him for a very long time and Nick hated seeing how miserable I was. I've tried to get him to look past that, cause I have, and just talk and learn about each other."

"Why were you so angry with him?" Mina asked, still mashing the bananas.

"It was very complicated," Trudy went to the fridge and grabbed the eggs. "Nick's father was married when we met."

"No way!" Mina looked up from the bowl of mashed bananas.

"Crack six of these into the sugar and flour," Trudy handed Mina the carton of eggs. "But when I met him at a David Bowie concert he didn't tell me he was married."

"You like Bowie?" Mina asked.

"Very much so," Trudy grabbed the bread pans from the counter and sat down. "It was my first time seeing Bowie, I was studying abroad in London and my friends surprised me with tickets for my birthday. And we met these guys who were a few years older than us. Nick's dad was one of them. They were in London on business and decided to go to this concert. I ended up having whirlwind romance with Nick's father that week while he was in town and had no intentions of having it go any further."

"But you got pregnant with Nick." Mina said as she folded the eggs into the flour with the wooden spoon.

"No," Trudy greased the pans with the butter. "I went to school at NYU and when I moved back to the city I ran into Nick's father at a bar. I knew he worked in the city, but I never expected to run into him, not in a city of millions. And we picked up where we left off in London. I had only one semester left, was already working at a literary agency as an assistant and knew I wanted to continue on to be an agent so I stayed in the city when I graduated. And I thought that Nick's father was going to be the one."

"Then you found out he was married?" Mina was finished mixing the eggs and flour and sugar and picked up the bowl of mashed bananas.

"No, I got pregnant," Trudy stood up and turned the oven on to preheat it. "I told him about Nick, he freaked out and went on a rant about how I had to keep it because he was Catholic. I was planning on keeping Nick even without the lecture and that's when he confessed to being married."

"Wow," Mina said. "What did you do after that?"

"I demanded an explanation," Trudy grabbed a package of walnuts and sat down. "Turns out he and his wife had been having a great deal of trouble in their marriage, but they were catholic and didn't believe in divorce. So, he could leave her but never marry me legally."

"Did that matter?" Mina asked.

"Yes and no," Trudy said. She stood up again and grabbed the meat tenderizing mallet from the jug that held spatulas and spoons next to the oven. "I didn't care about the marriage part but I wasn't going to continue in a relationship with someone who was still legally married to another woman."

"Understandable," Mina started filling the bread pans with the banana mixture.

"Not long after all of that I lost my brother," Trudy said.

"You were pregnant when your brother passed?" Mina asked.

"I was," Trudy said.

"That's intense," Mina said.

"Very," Trudy said. "So, Nick was born, I was promoted to junior agent after my maternity leave and I tried to have a business-like parenting relationship with Nick's father. But that went up and down as he dealt with his guilt over how he treated his wife and me. He started drinking more and more - becoming unreliable and I didn't trust him with Nick. Luckily, I had a lot of help from my mother who didn't mind coming down to the city. She was happy to get some space from this place after what happened to my brother."

"I'm not anywhere near being a mother but I can't even imagine how horrible it could be to lose a kid," Mina said.

"She is the strongest women I have ever known," Trudy said. "I may be biased being her daughter, but that woman has been through a lot and always kept truckin' along."

"I think you're both at the top of that list of strongest women," Mina said.

"Luckily for me there's strength in numbers, and I'm surrounded by such strong women, including you Mina," Trudy said. "Your mother would be very proud of you, just as I am."

"I just wish I could have had all the stupid moments mothers and daughter have - even the fights," Mina said. "Would be nice to hear her voice again, even if it were her screaming at me to do the laundry or something."

Chapter 12
Boys Keep Swinging

The fire was enormous at the bonfire up in the power lines this time around. Mark was home for the weekend from college, and had hauled a bunch of wood pallets out in his truck and they had lit all of them on fire all at once. Well, Filomena had doused the stack with lighter fluid and tossed a book of matches on it while no one was looking.

The fall air wasn't holding the warmth from the sun during the day anymore so the temperature was down in the forties. The fire was burning so hot though, everyone was at least ten feet away from the pit they had dug.

"This seems to go against everything Smokey the Bear taught me," Mina said staring into the giant fire.

Filomena looked around from the log he was leaning against. About three dozen other kids were hanging around, drinking beer, talking, laughing and playing music from the back of the '78 Mustang convertible that seemed to be at every party. Billy Idol song about dancing with himself blared from the car's speakers and Paul said, "Half the people at this party are volunteer firemen, so we're safer than if Smokey himself was here."

"I don't know about that, kiddies, since the reason they volunteer is cause they like to watch stuff burn," Mark whispered over his red plastic cup from his seat on a round log.

"Don't spread rumors, Mark, that's not nice," Holly said from where she leaned up against Paul.

"Swear to God, most firemen do the job cause they're pyromaniacs. That and the rush of running into a fire when everyone else is running away from it," Mark said.

"Aren't you a Kelsey Town Volunteer Fire Fighter, Mark? Are you confessing to these fine people your sins, my friend?" Nick said choking back a laugh. Mina was leaned up against him where they sat on the ground with their back against a long log.

Touching his nose, Mark said, "Ding, ding, ding, right on the nose sir. I'm the textbook case. You, Filomena, you're just a nut job. Seriously, that was like ten pallets at once. You're such a dumb ass."

"Hey, it's warm isn't it?" Paul shrugged.

"Very," Holly, Mark, Mina, and Nick said at the same time.

"Whatever. I didn't think it would be that tall," Paul said.

Everyone laughed.

Their laughter was cut short by a yell over near the keg, "Seriously, this thing is kicked already? You guys suck at everything in this town, especially hospitality."

Looking over his shoulder Nick could see who was running their mouth.

"That's the meathead who cracked you across the face, Nick," Filomena said.

Mina started to push herself off the ground but Nick held her back as best he could. She stopped before anyone noticed she had tried to stand and looked Nick in the eye. Nick shook his head no.

"I'll take care of this," Mark placed his cup on the ground and stood up. His fists balled up.

"No, man, let it go. He's just a jackass and he'll leave since there's no more beer," Nick said.

"What the hell?" A smaller guy named Thompson yelled when the meathead pushed him near the keg.

"No letting that go," Mark didn't wait for any protest from Nick this time.

Nick and Filomena jumped to their feet.

Nick looked down at Mina and smiled, "We got this, sweetheart."

Holly didn't move from her seat up against the log and rolled her eyes, "Boys."

Paul and Nick followed Mark over to the keg. There were three football players from Madison including the meathead jackass who had hit Nick over the summer. All of them lacking the same amount of neck.

"I think you guys should leave," Mark said.

The mouthpiece of the group turned and looked at Mark, "Oh really, big shot? Why is that?"

"No more beer. Party's over," Mark said.

"Luckily for us, seems this guy plans ahead and just told me he has a cooler full of beer in his trunk, isn't that right little fella?" The meathead said.

"Yeah, but —" Thompson said, but was cut short by Mark.

"Don't care what he has in his trunk, party's over for you," Mark said.

"Are you and your little friends gonna bounce us outta here?" The football player said. He friends all puffed up as big as they could be. "I've already put the fear of God into that one over there, didn't I, buddy?" He pointed at Nick.

"No fear, friend-o, just pity," Nick stepped forward. "There's only three of you, and there's like a dozen guys here on our side, so you've lost already. Stop trying to look cool and go on your way."

Mina was on her feet watching carefully.

"This kid thinks we're scared of all these losers here," the meathead said.

Nick looked over his shoulder at Mark, then to Paul. Nick shook his head and his friends knew to wait but be ready.

"If we're such losers then why do you want to hang out here with us?" Filomena asked. "That doesn't even make sense."

"We're here to show your girls what real men are like," the meathead smiled.

"Real men begin with manners," Nick said.

The fist came fast, but Nick was ready and ducked enough so the meathead's arm flew over his head. Nick slammed a fist into the meathead's groin and stood as fast as he could, driving a head-butt into the football player's chin. The meathead dropped to the ground, unconscious.

"What the hell?" One of the other football players yelped, but neither of them moved.

"Holy shit!" Filomena yelled.

"Pick him up and bring him home," Nick said. "If you guys

can find some manners, the two of you are welcome to crash our parties but he's not welcome."

"Ok," one of the football players mumbled and the two of them picked up the unconscious meathead, dragging him away to their truck.

Grabbing Nick's shoulders and roughly massaging them, Mark said, "Where did that come from, Bruce Lee?"

"Lots of practice," Nick said looking over at Mina. She smiled and shook her head at him.

"That was awesome!" Filomena bounced as they walked back over to their seats.

"Is that what you and Hank were doing while I was away? He was teaching you how to fight?" Mina whispered in Nick's ear.

"Yup," Nick said. "I'm not just a pretty face anymore."

"You never were a pretty face," Filomena said. "But seriously, you need to teach me how to move like that."

"I learned from my buddy Hank," Nick said. "He might consider giving you a few lessons if you buy him a couple of mushroom pizzas."

"He taught you how to fight?" Mark asked.

"Yeah, helped pass the time over the summer," Nick said. "Figured it would be good to know after my first encounter with that meathead, too."

"Good use of your head," Mina said and smoothed out the hair on top of Nick's head. He winced a little, but only enough for Mina to notice. She checked her hand for blood quickly, faster than anyone else could see, and was happy to find it clean.

"Now I don't know which one is tougher, Nick or Mina," Filomena said with a huge grin on his face.

"She's tougher," Holly said.

"Definitely," Mark said.

"But I fight dirty," Nick said. "Only advice my father ever gave me that I won't write off. There are no rules in a fight. Fight to win, whatever it takes. Bite, scratch —"

"Punch someone in the nuts," Filomena said.

"Whatever it takes," Mina said.

"Did you even feel anything there when you cracked him in the sac?" Mark picked up his cup and took a sip. "Dude's gotta be on 'roids so they can't be any bigger than marbles by now."

"Honestly, I think I might have popped one of them," Nick grimaced, and so did the other guys. "Like, have you ever smashed a grape with your fist?"

"That's disgusting," Holly said. "And horrible. Maybe you should have told them to bring that guy to the hospital."

"He'll wake up in the back seat of the car on the ride home and he'll know if he needs to go to the E.R. or not," Nick said.

"Seriously, thinking about popping one of them makes me feel sick," Filomena jumped up and ran off beyond the reach of the light of the fire and yacked.

"Really? That is your line in the sand?" Mina yelled. "Didn't figure him for having a weak stomach."

"Can't fault him," Mark said. "Thinking about that is kinda making me queasy too."

"Testicles are so frickin' weird," Holly said. She and Mina broke out laughing.

The Living

Chapter 13
1984

"Never really registered with me that Yale is this close to Kelsey Town," Nick said as they got off the bus in front of the Yale Art Gallery. The architecture of the buildings ranged from gothic archways to Greek inspired columns to modern glass edifices all packed nicely along Chapel Street in the Elm City. "I never knew New Haven was this pretty."

"Only Yale is pretty. The rest of the city is a dump," Julie said as she floated off the bus followed by Mina, Holly and Filomena.

"Only the Yale area is this nice. Most of the city is run down and kinda sketchy," Filomena echoed.

"The most annoying part of being dead is people saying the exact same thing you said because they couldn't hear you," Julie frowned and floated away and out of sight through the wall of the building.

Nick and Mina exchanged glances and rolled their eyes.

"Okay, everyone," Mr. Yoho, the art teacher, said to the group of forty teenagers riddling the sidewalk. "You have two hours to roam the gallery. We meet back on the front steps right there at noon. And be as courteous and cautious as I have instructed you while inside. That means no touching, Paul."

"Why single me out?" Filomena balked.

"You know why," Mr. Brucella narrowed his eyes at Paul and Nick. "And no horsing around inside."

"Of course not, Coach," Nick and Paul said in unison.

"We will be floating around so feel free to ask us or the staff here any questions you might have on the pieces in the collection," Mr. Yoho said. "Now go get some culture."

The students filed up the steps through the front door. Inside the lobby on the left there was a donations box. The gallery was free to the public but accepted donations

Filomena pulled a ten out of his pocket and dropped it in, "That should cover all of us."

No one said anything, but Mina cocked her head at Paul's generosity.

"Let's head to the fourth floor and work our way down," Mina said. "Since everyone else seems to be starting down here, it'll give us a little more room not being clustered together with everyone else."

"Agreed," Nick said and they headed for the door to the stairs. The staircase was a wide spiral and they hoofed it up the four flights and found themselves surrounded by pieces from modern artists such as Lichtenstein, Close, Pollock and Picasso.

"We're gonna go this way," Paul said pointing to the right with his chin. "Give you kids some privacy to enjoy these masterpieces."

"You just want to find a quiet corner to make out in," Holly said and smacked him on the shoulder.

"Several actually," Filomena smiled as he and Holly headed off to the left.

Hand in hand, Nick and Mina headed right and walked slowly past each piece, not saying a word, just looking over every inch of the works of art. The floor was mostly open space with partitions making small three sided rooms.

Then Nick stopped in front of a large Jackson Pollock Drip Painting. It was chaotic, as his pieces tended to be, and it was very dark.

"I'm a much bigger fan of Impressionism than Modern Art, myself," Mina said.

"I've always really liked Pollock's stuff. I like the chaos I guess. But there's something different about this piece. Now I feel as though there has always been something different about his pieces that I've seen in person," Nick said getting closer to it, examining the jumble of thick white lines of paint over black lines and black wash. The sign next to the piece read, 'Artist: Jackson Pollock, American, 1912–1956. Number 13A: Arabesque.'

"What do you mean?" Mina said. "Looks like a jumble of lines to me. It looks like every other Jackson Pollock I've seen pictures of."

"Do you think these things have alarms on them?" Nick stepped a few feet back taking in the whole image.

"Probably. What do you see?" Mina crossed her arms next to Nick.

"It's like I see an image inside of an image," Nick said.

"It's not a far-fetched idea," Mina said. "Painters were always painting over their works, and stuff sometimes shows through. Do you want to touch it with the pen to see if stuff pops up like at the cemetery?"

"Yes," Nick said pulling the pen from his pocket. "Really quickly. Keep an eye out for me."

"This is a horrible idea," Mina said looking over her shoulder. "There's probably cameras looking at us right now."

"Are you scared or something?" Nick smiled at her as he inched toward the painting.

"Not, I just don't want you to mess up the painting," Mina said.

"I not even going to open it," Nick said. "I can do it with the cap on. Just need to touch it real quick."

"Then get to it, the security guard just went around the corner," Mina said.

Nick was already touching the corner of the canvas with the pen, but nothing happened.

"Anything?" Mina said looking around.

"Nope," Nick stepped back. No alarms went off and no one came running.

"Maybe you have to use the actual pen tip?" Mina suggested.

"I haven't had to do that in months. It's more sensitive than that now," Nick said.

"Or you're just more powerful than when you first figured that trick out," Mina said.

"Not sure powerful is the right word since it's just a trick," Nick said walking up and down the length of the painting.

"What about the other trick when Map Walking? The one when you can see inside of a book?" Mina said. "Wish I had that ability, would make reading books so much easier and cooler, to be able to see the story happen like a movie but without a bunch of producers and directors screwing the whole thing up."

"Maybe," Nick said. "Things do look a little different on the ghost plane. Maybe that's what I'm picking up here."

"Do you have a map with you?" Mina asked. "If not, will a map of the gallery work?"

"I do not, and it might," Nick said. "They had the pamphlets downstairs with each floor laid out in them, didn't they?"

"Yeah, near the front desk," Mina said grabbing Nick's hand as they headed toward the stairs. They raced down and Mina grabbed one of the pamphlets with her free hand. Nick smiled at the woman working the front desk, then they ran back up the stairs.

"Let's sit down on the bench for this," Nick sat down on a narrow bench in the middle of the gallery not far from the Pollock. Mina sat down next to him, her eyes wide and a huge grin on her face.

With the map open on his lap, Nick placed the pen on where they were sitting and closed his eyes. Mina had her hand on his shoulder and closed her eyes as well.

"What is that buzzing noise?" Mina said as they looked around the room.

"Pretty sure it's coming from that Jackson Pollock painting," Nick said. "Does it look a little different to you on this plane?"

"It looks like when there's static on the T.V. screen," Mina said. "Touch it."

"You touch it," Nick said looking over the painting, not getting to close.

"This is your super power, not mine," Mina said. "So go to it."

"Give me a second to think things over," Nick said.

"What's there to think over, it looks out of place even in this plane, as you call it, and it wants you to touch it," Mina smiled. "Just do it."

Reaching out slowly, a bolt of static electricity arched between his fingers and the painting. It didn't hurt but he could feel it through his whole body. He kept his fingers a few centimeters from the painting.

"That is a new sensation," Mina said.

Nick quickly looked out of the corner of his eye at Mina then back to his fingers. Then he pressed his hand forward and his fingers disappeared into the canvas. Then his hand. Then his wrist.

Looking again to Mina, he said really fast, "1, 2, 3 go!" And he jumped into the painting.

"Seriously, you could have just said you were going to do that and walked in," Mina said.

They were standing in an art studio, built in what looked like an old barn. Piles of crumpled canvases littered the corners of the room and paint was splattered on every inch of floor.

"You were the one who was like 'touch it, just do it.' So I went for it." Nick looked around. A man stood looking at Nick and Mina. "Whoa."

"Interesting," Mina said looking from Nick to the man . "You're Jackson Pollock."

"Hello. And you are?" Pollock said.

"I'm Mina and this is Nick," Mina pointed at her boyfriend.

"What is this?" Nick asked.

"This is a message I worked into my paintings for people," Pollock said. "I met a man a few years ago who pulled back the curtain for me, so to speak. He showed me the supernatural world and he blew open the doors to my imagination."

"What was this man's name?" Nick asked.

"Ray Stanton," Pollock said.

"Like the one who gave your Uncle John the pen?" Mina asked.

"Probably. It was sort of his trademark, that pen of his. A trademark of his family it seems," Pollock pointed at Nick's hand holding the pen.

"So, what's the message?" Nick asked. "And why did you paint it into your work?"

"The message is that monsters are everywhere, that all those ghost stories, and folktales and myths and legends are based on something real. There is something lurking in the shadows, and it can hurt you. And you are better off aware of them. Our acceptance of their existence helps keep the balance between the two worlds." Pollock said.

"I'm pretty sure that only someone like me could come in here and see this message," Nick said. "So what's the point?"

"You can come in here, but most people get the impression that there is something off about my work, that there's more to it than just a jumble of lines. It evokes emotion and sets off alarms inside one's mind," Pollock pointed at his head. "That was what Ray helped me put into my work."

"So, Ray was your muse?" Mina asked.

"Yes," Pollock said. "And there are thousands of other works of art, books, movies, plays, and songs that men like Ray have influenced over millennia that in one way or another have a similar message as mine."

"Like?" Mina asked.

"Frankenstein," Nick said.

"Exactly," Pollock said. "Ray had mentioned many times that he was working on making the end of that book a reality. He pointed out that we never really do see the monster die on his own funeral pyre."

"No, we didn't," Mina said quietly. "And Shelley was a bit more forward and obvious with her message than you are."

"I was an abstract expressionist, she was a gothic romanticist. I'm not into hand holding like they were," Pollock said.

"What are you guys doing?" Filomena's voice floated through the air like it come from far way.

"We gotta go," Nick said.

"Have a good one," Pollock said as Nick opened his eyes to see Filomena's hand waving in front of his face.

"Earth to Stanton," Paul snapped his fingers.

Slapping his hand away, Nick said, "Cut it out."

"What are you two doing?" Filomena asked.

"What does it look like?" Nick stood up and waived the map at his friend.

"Day dreaming," Holly said.

"Exactly," Mina said.

"We're gonna head down to the third floor. You coming or do you wanna have some more time with your map?" Paul said.

"We're done here for now," Nick looked to Mina. "We'll have to find out how much farther this rabbit hole goes down later."

"I think it's all just one really deep rabbit hole for us, Nicholas," Mina said quietly as the four of them walked to the stairs.

*****

"Are you ready?" Nick asked. He had the atlas open to Greece on his desk. His pen was resting on the map right outside the city where Mina's mother was from.

"Yes," Mina said. "You know that Homer mentions Trikala in the Iliad?"

"He wrote that they supplied ships for the Trojan War," Nick said. "Remember, do everything just like when we did this with Julie."

"I got it," Mina said. "You worry about not hitting your funny bone this time."

"I think it's just part of the penance I have to pay for this ability that I have to get used to," Nick smiled. "Close your eyes."

Looking over the grass and rocky outcroppings reaching toward the sky, Mina said, "My memory doesn't do this place any justice."

They were quiet as they made their way to the place where Mina's grandmother said they would find a ghost. The ancient Roman Baths were easy to find. So were the ghosts.

"Your grandmother undersold this place," Nick said counting slowly in his head. Transparent forms of men of varying ages littered the old stones that formerly housed the baths. "There are over thirty ghosts here."

"I wonder if any of them are like Julie?" Mina said as they approached the closest one to them. "Hey, are you on repeat or can you understand me?"

The ghost didn't respond, he just looked around, then disappeared.

"We should get this part over with. We don't have a lot of time," Nick said. "We can bug them another day."

"Okay," Mina said and smacked the ghost that got within reach. The old man had on a toga, and looked startled, but disappeared as Nick and Mina filled their lungs with Greek air.

Still on their feet, Mina said, "Look, you didn't crash and burn this time."

"Yeah, this time. We need to go this way." Nick headed northeast, picking the pace up to a run. Mina was right next to him as they found the little road leading out to the horse farm where her grandmother lived. They were quiet for the two and half mile jog, and ran through the front gates a little over twenty minutes after appearing in Greece.

"I'm really nervous," Mina said as they walked up the steps to the front door of the house.

As they hit the top step, the front door flew open, and a little Greek woman yelled as she wrapped her arms around Mina faster than most people could move, "Oh my God, look at you. You're a woman!"

Tears filled Mina's eyes, "I have missed you so much, Nana."

"And I you, sweetie, and I you," she said. "I can't believe you are here. I've wished for this for so long."

"Luckily for us, I met Nick and was able to get here so easily," Mina said.

"This is the Nicholas?" Mina's grandmother kept her arms around Mina but looked over at Nick.

"Nice to meet you, ma'am," Nick said smiling.

"Call me Nana," she said. "We have a lot to discuss, so please come in."

Inside, the house smelled of spices and roasting meat. A table in the kitchen was set with four plates.

"Sit, sit. One of your cousins will be joining us," Nana said. "Sadly, this was so last minute that your other cousins weren't able to get back from University to see you so it will only be Damara with us today. And her parents are actually on holiday in Paris. I talked to them last night and they wish they were here for your visit."

"Well, luckily, visiting won't be much of a problem anymore," Nick leaned back into his chair.

"I have to say that my curiosity was piqued by how quickly you got here, and the questions Mina asked me on the phone about there being a haunted place nearby," Nana said.

"Well, I will answer any questions you have. I only ask that you do the same," Nick said.

"Nana, I know that my mother was a shapeshifter," Mina said.

"I wondered how long it would take for you to figure that out," Nana sat down.

The kitchen door opened and a girl that looked exactly like Mina walked in. Her eyes widened as she looked at everyone sitting around the table.

Nick stood up.

"Oh, just in time for dinner, Damara," Nana said standing up.

"Hello," Damara said.

"Hey, cuz," Mina stood up, stepped toward Damara and wrapped her arms around her. Damara hesitated at first, but then returned the hug just as fiercely.

"We could seriously be twins," Mina said.

"The pictures your dad sent were always a little weird to look at because of how much we resembled each other," Damara said.

"I made papoutsakia stuffed with ground beef," Nana said bringing the dish over to the table.

Damara washed her hands in the sink and brought the water pitcher over to the table when she sat down.

"So, now that the cat is out of the bag, how did you two get here?" Nana said as she piled each plate with the stuffed eggplant.

"Ghost Walking," Nick said.

"Still sounds silly to me," Mina said.

"What is Ghost Walking?" Damara asked as she dug into her food.

"I can see through a map to the place, in my head, and if I touch a ghost in that place, I appear there," Nick said and took his first bite.

During the rest of the meal, Nick and Mina explained everything that had happened to them, most of what they could do and some of what they were afraid of.

When they all dropped their napkins Damara stood and cleared the plates off the table. Mina followed her cousin's lead. Nick stood and picked up his plate but Nana shook her head.

Standing, Nana said. "Come outside with me for a moment, Nicholas. Talk with me."

Nick followed the old woman out the door into the backyard. To the right a barn stood and a paddock spread out beyond into the rocky terrain off on the horizon. The sun began to set.

"I was hoping that this world would have passed Mina by," Nana said. "But it seems that it has landed hard on her shoulders."

"That it has," Nick said.

"You can't hide from this world," Nana said. "You understand that, right?"

"I know that," Nick said.

"Are you going to do everything you can to keep her alive?" Nana asked.

"We are going to do everything we can to keep each other alive," Nick said.

"Good answer," Nana smiled, then yelled. "Damara, Mina, come outside please."

The two girls came out laughing and said, "Yes, Nana?"

"Damara, we need to show your cousin and Nicholas what we can do," Nana said and turned into a horse.

Damara smiled, jumped up and turned into a bird. She fluttered around Nick and Mina, then landed on the back of Nana the horse.

"Excellent," Nick said.

"My turn," Mina smiled then launched herself into the air. Her cousin the bird flew into the air behind her.

Nana the horse snorted at Nick, then looked at her back.

"Oh, no, I'm quite all right watching," Nick said.

She nudged him with her head, then looked at her back again and nodded.

"Fine,' Nick said, then jumped up on Nana the horse's back. She took off into the field toward where Mina came down. Damara fluttered around as the horse galloped by with Nick on her back. When Mina jumped, her cousin the bird followed. For the next hour, Nick saw the Greek country side by horseback while Mina and her cousin jumped and flew through the air.

The Living

Chapter 14
We Are the Dead

"Hey buddy," Mina said walking through the waterfall. "Long time no see."

"Don't sneak up on me like that!" Conan jumped and sent the coins he was counting into the water around him.

"What's going on, amigo?" Nick said as he walked in behind Mina.

"Ah, Nick," Conan righted himself. "I have some business to discuss with you."

"Business?" Mina said. "How is business going?"

"Very, very well," Conan reached down into the water to gather the coins.

"Good to hear," Nick said and placed a pair of children's pants on the rocks behind where Conan was fishing for coins. "Brought you some new pants too. I still find it so odd that a creature as wealthy as you can't go buy his own clothes. Somehow."

"He can't exactly walk into Sears and browse the children's section, now can he?" Mina sat down on one of the rocks.

"No, I can't," Conan said. "Plus I don't like spending my own money."

"That seems a lot more likely," Nick said. "So, where do we stand with the next deposit?"

"Next deposit?" Mina asked.

"Well, I have half of the winnings here right now from side bets," Conan looked around behind him. "I can have it in your accounts by the end of the week. But there is still the matter of the problem at the tournament."

"I don't care about that money, I told you that was yours to do with as you wish," Nick said. "It was your payment for helping me set all those accounts up for the Stanton House and my family."

"But if she wins we will be rich beyond our wildest dreams!" Conan's eyes lit up as he pointed at Mina.

"Wait, if I win the tournament?" Mina said. "What are you talking about?"

"Where I saw you, in the desert," Conan tossed the coins he had in his hands into his pot of gold.

"I know where I was and what I was in but explain what you get if I win?" Mina said.

"The tournament isn't over," Conan said. "There was no clear winner, and a bunch of clear losers. So, none of the final bets have paid out."

"Tine isn't dead?" Mina asked.

"No, and that shapeshifter you saved is also still breathing," Conan said.

"Well, that's not going to change, so it seems you're never going to see those winnings again," Nick said. "You should have invested more wisely."

Pointing at Mina, Conan said, "Have you ever seen her fight? She was the safest bet in the world! Except for her whole maternal instinct kicking in making her save that child."

"Her name is Penny," Mina said.

"What?" Conan sat down next to his pot of gold. "Oh, the child. Doesn't matter, I still have my gold here."

"More than you have ever had, thanks to us," Nick said. "Don't forget that."

"I would never forget that," Conan said. "I enjoy knowing you. Not so much her though, because she's usually so rough."

"You grow to love that," Nick smiled at Mina.

"Just to keep things straight, you don't know if Valen Tine is dead or alive?" Mina asked.

"Well no," Conan looked down at the water. "It could just be you and the shapeshifter—,"

"Penny," Mina said.

"It could be down to just you and Penny," Conan said. "The arena was a mess after what you did. It was chaos."

"You leave a wake of destruction everywhere you go," Nick

laughed.

"It's not funny," Mina said. "You don't know how bad it was there. I didn't think Penny and I would survive, and I didn't know if Bruce and Charles were alive until you told me about running into Charles in Montreal on your little outing with Hank."

"I didn't think I was going to make it out of there either," Conan said. "It was a mad house. You broke so many old magical spells keeping not only the fighters in check but all the other creatures inside the arena. Saw the Minotaur get obliterated by a hundred claws, luckily he regenerates back in the Cretan Labyrinth. Crazy bull enters the tournament every time. One of my favorite side bets is how long he lasts."

"So he doesn't die? Thought that was against the whole idea of the tournament being to the death," Nick said.

"He gets a pass since he does die but gets resurrected in the labyrinth a few months later," Conan said. "His curse is tied to the labyrinth itself. Magic and science make for strange and dangerous monsters."

"So if the labyrinth was destroyed he would not come back?" Nick said.

"Right, but he has tried that many times and it never works. Just don't go in there and you don't have to worry about him," Conan said.

"Unless you're in the tournament, " Mina said. "Or were a virgin back under the rule of King Minos."

"Yes, but he doesn't go out beyond that," Conan said. "And he was starved back in those days into killing those young boys and girls."

"He doesn't hunt people down, so he is still in balance with the whole supernatural world and mortal world," Nick said quietly. "But I might need to talk with him. He helped you escape for a reason, Mina, and I'd like to know why."

"That's easy to figure out. Daedalus created not only the labyrinth but the arena you fought in, Mina," Conan said.

"He saw you break the spells holding everyone there. You shredded the rule book," Nick said.

"He thinks I might be able to help him break the bonds that tie him to the labyrinth," Mina said.

"Or destroy the labyrinth all together." Conan hopped to his feet and looked out of the water flowing down over the entrance of the cave. "I need to go hunt down some food, so if you don't mind, I will take my leave."

"Happy hunting," Mina said as Conan disappeared. She looked to Nick who was staring at the water pooled at the bottom of the cave. Mina watched him for a few moments then asked, "Hey, where are you?"

Shaking his head, Nick said, "I need to find out if the Minotaur has regenerated back at the labyrinth. We might have another ally."

"You're gonna have to fill me in on this plan you're hatching one of these days," Mina stood up and headed out of the cave.

Laughing, Nick stood and said, "You think I have a plan?"

*****

Nick was at his desk writing in a journal when Mina appeared in his window.

"Gonna be too cold for me to leave that window open soon," Nick flipped the notebook closed and turned toward his bed. "You'll be forced to use the door one hundred percent of the time instead of just five."

"I suggest you just leave it unlocked and nothing changes," Mina said as she lay down on the bed. "Come over here and cuddle with me, I need a recharge."

Sliding from the chair into the bed next to Mina, Nick said, "What have you been up to?"

"I'll tell only if you tell me what you've been up to," Mina said as she rested her head on his chest. "All of what you've been up too."

Wrapping his arms around Mina, Nick said, "The 'I'll show you mine if you show me yours' trick."

"Exactly," Mina hugged him back with the arm she had thrown over his body. The color rushed back to her face as she melted into him.

"I think I found Stone," Nick said. "And his family."

Raising her head off of Nick's chest, Mina said, "Say that one more time, I may have ruptured both my ear drums earlier and I don't think they healed yet."

"I found Stone and his family," Nick said.

"First time you used the words 'I think'- which is it?" Mina looked him in the eye.

"Oh, I thought your ear drums hadn't healed yet after whatever you were doing," Nick said.

"Seriously, what do you mean about Stone and a family?" Mina said.

"He wasn't there any of the times I've gone, but I've seen Valen Tine and their son a few times."

"Let's start with where this place is," Mina asked.

"Orkney Islands, Scotland," Nick said.

"How did you find this place?" Mina asked.

"Map Walking and deduction," Nick said.

"And why were you Map Walking in Scotland?" Mina said.

"I was exploring all the places mentioned in Shelley's book," Nick said.

"Still hard to believe that her book is true," Mina said.

"Well, sort of true. The basis for the story was true. A scientist resurrected a monster and Shelley found out about it," Nick said.

"Now, the million dollar question, how did she find out about all of that? It screams 'Stanton was here' to me," Mina said.

"Yup," Nick said.

"Imagine all the other great writers your family may have influenced. Wait, there was something in one of your uncle's journals about telling a young writer about some of the stuff he saw. Remember?" Mina jumped up fast, and was looking through the pile of John's journals that sat on top of the book pile next to the desk.

"Vaguely," Nick said as he sat up on the bed and put his feet on the floor.

On the third journal she picked up, she smacked her index finger down on the page and said, "Here. 'Found myself in Maine talking to a young man named Steve at a diner near one of the universities up there. He was going to school for English and was a writer. He was reading a collection of stories by H.P. Lovecraft. My uncle whispered to me that one of our ancestors had been very close friends with Lovecraft. I asked this young man about the book and we ended up talking for hours and I told him all these stories about things I have seen. He was really interested in the town of vampires my uncle and his wife brought Lauren and me to. After destroying the younger vampires who could walk in the day, we burned the town to the ground to finish the job.' You know who he's taking about, don't you?"

"Sounds a bit like the plot to Salem's Lot," Nick said.

"A bit?" Mina dropped the journal back on the pile, and walked over to Nick.

Wrapping his arms around her waist, Nick pulled Mina into him and pressed his ear into her belly, "Want me to show you where they live?"

"The vampires?" Mina asked.

Pulling his back to look up at her, Nick said, "No."

"I know what you mean and yes," Mina smiled down at him.

"No time like the present," Nick stood up and walked over to the desk. He pulled out the atlas he has been using from the desk drawer and picked up his pen. Mina stepped behind him and put her hand on his shoulder.

Having been there a few times now he knew what to expect and when he closed his eyes, Nick and Mina saw the remains of the small castle.

"What is that feeling I'm getting off this place?" Mina said.

"Take a step forward," Nick said, stepping forward through the static field that wrapped the area like a cloak. He pulled Mina with him and before their eyes the place changed and grew from a roofless ruin to an estate fit for a king.

"Awesome," Mina whispered.

"Wait until you see what's inside," Nick said as they walked to the front door.

Nick sped them through into the main chamber of the palace. In the center of the room sat the dragon.

"No way!" Mina's eyes widened. "Is that real?"

"As far as I can tell," Nick said. "Not that I've ever tried to pet it though."

"Are you chicken?" Mina said.

"Yes," Nick said. "It's loyal to Stone."

"How do you know?" Mina asked.

"The journals in the study upstairs," Nick said.

"Show me," Mina said and they headed up to the study.

"Be on the lookout for a really annoying Scottish ghost. He's the one who knocked me into this place the first time," Nick said, then peaked his head through the door to see if the room was empty. "Coast is clear."

"Would that really matter?" Mina asked as they walked through the door. Most of the room sat in darkness but the glow from the desk lamp left the desk bathed in low light.

"If that stupid ghost was in here we would have waited," Nick said. The large desk sat before them with the leather journals lining the book shelves behind it.

"And you've read all of those?" Mina pointed up at the journals.

"I've leafed through most of them, one way or another," Nick said.

"How many times have you been here?" Mina asked looking around the room.

"Half a dozen times," Nick said.

"What else is hidden in this place?" Mina asked quietly.

"I really haven't explored much. Found all of this and kinda get sucked into it every time, then get disturbed and/or almost caught," Nick said.

"Well, no time like the present to do some more in-depth exploring. Maybe we can find Stone's weakness and be done with this whole mess," Mina said.

"Just keep your eye out for any ghosts," Nick said.

"On it," Mina said, and put on her most serious face as they moved back or into the hallway.

"Let's just look in every room before going crazy snooping around," Nick said.

Inside the next door down they found the room in complete darkness.

"Can't you see in the dark or something?" Nick asked.

"A bit, but all I can make out is a bed against one wall and a dresser against the other wall," Mina said. "Don't you have some magic that can turn the lights on or something?"

"That would be extremely useful, but no," Nick said. "But if we get knocked into this place by a ghost I will happily risk turning on every lamp to keep exploring."

"On to the next room then," Mina said as they backtracked slowly in the dark.

"The door was right behind us, right?" Nick said then shook his head. "Like that matters when I can just walk through walls anyway."

"I was waiting to see how long that would take you to figure out" Mina laughed.

"Hey, sometimes I'm not that quick, jerk," Nick said as they passed though the wall into the hallway. This time, the hallway wasn't empty.

"Tine?" Mina whispered. At the end of the hall, Valen Tine was cradling a boy who was convulsing violently.

Trying to sooth the boy, Tine whispered in his ear, "It will pass, baby. Just relax, I've got you. Everything will be okay. I promise. Just let it pass."

"Yes, and that's her son," Nick said quietly. The boy's crutches were tossed aside, one against each wall of the hallway.

"And you think he is also Stone's son?" Mina asked.

"Pretty sure, yeah," Nick said.

"Why?" Mina asked.

"Tine said that the boy's father would be upset if he was found reading comics in the father's study," Nick said. "And that study is definitely Stone's."

Tine kept a hold of her son on the floor, whispering quietly in the boy's ear.

"What's wrong with him?" Mina asked.

"He's having a seizure. And with the crutches I think he has--," Nick was cut short as his body was slammed left into the wall. The angry Scottish ghost ranted and raved off through the hall as Nick grabbed his left elbow and yelled out in pain, "God damn it! Not my elbow again!"

Tine was on her feet, blocking her son from view, "Who are you?"

While Nick was pushing himself off the floor, Mina growled from her feet, "Oh, great."

"Melia?" Tine said. "Is that you?"

The boy was on the floor, his body still tense but the spasms had stopped.

"Hello, Valen, long time no see," Mina said.

Moving fast, Valen Tine grabbed a lance from the suit of armor on her right, and pointed it at Nick and Mina. Tine yelled as she charged, "What are you doing here?"

"Arts and crafts," Nick said as he pulled the extra map he had in his pocket and Mina unleashed her sword from the sheath hanging from her neck.

Tine's first blow glanced off to the right and Mina came around with the sword. Tine blocked most of the blow with the shaft of the lance, but the force of the hit snapped the wooden portion off from the metal.

Flipping back, Tine grabbed a mace from the suit of armor on her left.

"A plan would be good right about now," Mina yelled as Valen Tine came around with a blow from the mace.

"I am going to kill both of you for coming into my home," Valen Tine screamed.

"We aren't here to hurt you, lady," Nick yelled.

Tine and Mina were trading blows with their respected weapons now, back and forth.

"I don't think she cares," Mina yelled.

Nick had the map spread on the floor, the pen resting on Cow Hill Road in Kelsey Town. His eyes were closed.

"When I'm done with you, I'm going to hunt down the little shapeshifter and finish this," Tine yelled. "You should have just stayed in Vegas and accepted your fate then."

"Step back toward me so I can get a hold of you," Nick yelled, reaching his hand out for Mina.

Tine came down with a brutally fast hard blow, pushing Mina down to her knees and sliding her backwards. Nick grabbed her ankle. Tumbling backwards, Nick and Mina crashed into the hutch in the dining room. Plates, big and small, on and around them, clattered, fell and shattered on the wood floor.

"Ow," Nick said.

Looking around at the broken china, Mina said, "My dad is gonna be so pissed."

Chapter 15
Teenage Wildlife

"I can't believe it's October," Nick said. He was on the couch with Mina leaned into him.

"I can't believe the Mets or the Expo's are on a T.V in my house, let alone both of them at the same time," Filomena said as he sat down on the floor in front of Holly. He leaned back between her legs and hung his arms over her knees.

It was the bottom of the tenth and the Mets had the lead 6-4.

"Seriously, we should be watching the Sox destroy the Orioles," Holly said.

"You should have picked a better horse," Nick said. He dug into a bowl of potato chips that was on the end table. "You lost fair and square, so we watch the Mets. Gonna go all the way this year!"

"The Mets, really?" Paul said. "Not likely."

"They are on fire, and you can't deny that," Nick said. "They are stacked on the field and at the plate."

"Doesn't matter, they have no chance against the best of the American League in the end," Paul said. "Strawberry struck out three times tonight."

"Exactly, even if they square off against the Red Sox in the end they won't have a chance," Holly said.

"Struck out three times but crushed the first out of the park," Nick said.

"That's still only a .250 average," Paul said. "Not good enough to take it all."

"The Red Sox have to make it there before you make claims like that," Mina said. "Both teams have to win like seven or eight more games before they can claim either the National or the American League let alone play in the World Series."

Nick, Holly and Paul turned their heads slowly toward Mina.

"What? Not like it's super-secret knowledge. I do know how to read you know," Mina said.

"Well, okay then. I guess we'll just watch the game," Paul said.

"A little logic cancels out your trash talking skills that easily, Paul?" Nick said. "Gonna have to remember that for later bets."

"I just wanna see if the Mets can put their money where their mouth is," Filomena said. "And not choke on these last few plays."

"What was this bet anyway?" Holly asked.

"Paul seemed to think that Hank would win in an eating contest against Mina," Nick smiled.

"That is a tough call to make," Holly said. "I probably would have put my money on Mina, cause I've seen here put away a whole pizza—"

"Don't judge me!" Mina said.

"Not judging at all. You're in better shape than I am and can eat whatever the hell you want. And you work out more than these guys do." Holly pointed at Nick and Paul.

"I don't know about that," Paul said. "Now that I'm training with Hank, I'm pretty sure Nick and I have you beat."

"Dude, you've worked out with him twice," Nick said. "When you've been at it for a month you can call it training."

"Oh, you doubt that I'll stick with it?" Filomena said as he stood up. The game was over and the Mets had beaten the Expos.

"Can you get me another soda while you're up?" Mina called.

"Maybe," Paul said and headed for the kitchen. "I ain't no bum, Mick. I ain't no bum."

"Did he just get the last word in by quoting Rocky?" Mina asked.

"I don't think he's bringing you back a soda, I think that's our cue that he's going to bed. I'll go check and report back." Holly jumped to her feet and followed Paul's trail.

"And they all called me odd for so many years," Mina said.

"Neither of them are coming back, so what now?" Nick said.

"Wanna blow this pop stand and see what kind of trouble we can get ourselves into?" Mina gave Nick a quick peck on the lips.

"I think after our little run in with Valen Tine, we should stay as far away from trouble as we can for a few more days," Nick said.

The teens stood up and stretched.

"So, do you just wanna go back to your barn and make out?" Mina asked.

"Sounds like a good plan, but I might get the wrong idea about you." Nick smiled taking Mina's hand.

Squeezing his hand hard, Nick whined in pain as Mina said, "And what idea would that be?"

"Ow, ow, ow, ow not fair," Nick said.

Releasing some of the pressure on his hand Mina said, "Hopefully the pain will work as a good substitute for a cold shower."

"You were the one who suggested making out in my barn," Nick said as they walked toward the door.

"A PG-13 activity," Mina said as she opened the door.

"I'm a guy and no matter how much pain you put me in, my mind is gonna end up in the gutter every five minutes or so," Nick said as they walked to Mina's scooter.

"Is your mind in the gutter right now?" Mina asked.

Smiling as he picked up his helmet from the scooter, Nick said, "Yes."

"How do boys get anything done thinking like that all the time?" Mina said as she fired up the scooter and threw her leg over the seat.

"We are excellent multitaskers," Nick said as he slid onto the seat behind her. He wrapped his arms around her waist.

Mina shook her head, smiling, then opened up the throttle and took off down the driveway.

Chapter 16
Golden Years

"That rain is really coming down," Sue said as she walked into the kitchen.

From his spot at the table doing homework, Nick said, "I was hoping it would let up so I can take a run."

"You might have to just brave the wet panties for a workout today," Sue said as she filled her coffee cup.

"Panties, Grandma? Really?" Nick said.

"Sorry, briefs," she said as she sat down across from Nick at the table. "With your grandfather and uncle being gone so long, some words have slipped from my vocabulary."

"I will accept that answer," Nick said.

"You look a lot like your grandfather and uncle," Sue said. "Stanton genes run pretty strong."

"I wish I had met them," Nick said.

"I do too," Sue said. "And you're great Uncle Ray, or great, great uncle actually. You all have the same air about you. Especially you and Ray. Ray was only a few years older than your granddad. They were basically raised together."

"What was Granddad's name?" Nick asked. "No one ever references him as anything other than Granddad."

"You're named after him, Nicholas," Sue laughed. "Didn't you know that?"

"I might have. But it gets lost up here," Nick pointed at his head, "Since I never got to meet him."

"That's understandable," Sue said and took a sip of her coffee. "You would have had a good time with them."

"Were they all pretty rowdy?" Nick asked.

"Bonkers, the whole lot of 'em," Sue laughed. "They all loved their midnight adventures just like you do."

"What do you mean?" Nick shifted in his seat.

"You're mother and I aren't oblivious, Nicholas," Sue stood up and patted him on the head.

"Oh," Nick said.

"That's interesting, you and your great, great Uncle Ray have the same hand writing."

"Wait, really?" Nick said. "How do you remember what his hand writing looked like?"

"There's a book that belonged to him on the shelf in the living room called The Hero with a Thousand Faces, filled with his notes," Sue said as she walked out of the room.

For a moment, Nick sat motionless, holding his breath. Then he was a blur and ran into the living room. He scanned over the books on the shelves, almost all of them were old and most of them didn't even have titles on the spines. Just worn canvas or leather covers.

But on the bottom shelf, there it was a very faded hardcover of Joseph Campbell's The Hero with a Thousand Faces. On the inside cover there was an inscription:

> \- Raymond -
> We, the Tellers,
> are the spark
> that lit the fire
> that shows the way.
> Spread the fire
> As far as you can
> Fan the flames
> So it burns hot
> But keep it
> From burning wild
> Tend it, share it
> And stay warm.
>
> John Robert Stanton
> 1949

The handwriting of the inscription was not like his, but his great, great uncle had received it as a gift. Most likely from a keeper of the pen, a Teller.

Thumbing through the pages, there wasn't anything else written until about halfway through the book. That first handwritten note looked eerily similar to Nick's horrible chicken scratch and read, "The first Teller was the son of the muses. This boy grew and introduced storytelling to humanity, this simple idea made it so, as a species, we could learn from our mistakes and our triumphs. Collective knowledge, passed down and shared, keeps our species alive."

"Teller," Nick said softly. He looked up out the window at the rain and smiled, remembering the first time he met Ben on that beach in Nantucket. "There's one question answered."

He ran upstairs to his room, sat on the bed with his back against the wall next to the window and read for the rest of the day. The premise of The Hero with a Thousand Faces was that all the stories that have survived for thousands of years, from all over the world, share common themes and patterns. This shared pattern is called the monomyth.

About twenty or so pages into The Hero with a Thousand Faces, Nick read, "A hero ventures forth from the world of common day into a region of supernatural wonder: fabulous forces are there encountered and a decisive victory is won: the hero comes back from this mysterious adventure with the power to bestow boons on his fellow man."

There were three main stages of the journey - Departure, Initiation and Return. Each of those were broken up into multiple stages, and some of the most famous stories, from Buddha to Odysseus to Moses to Jesus all share many of these stages and themes. But the notes in the margins were even more interesting. They weren't notes about the text, but rather ideas and information that applied to Nick's world directly.

The first note from Ray read, "The Tellers were the first to notice the things that were not like us, the dead walking among the living, the monsters that began to feed off of us, and those that were once us but no longer had the spark or had the spark of many. All of these were dangerous to humanity."

A few pages after that note, Nick found another. He grabbed a notebook from the desk and started copying them down. "A Teller sought out the fiercest warriors in the world, and found the Amazons. This Teller and the most skilled Amazon fell in love creating a bond that enhanced their natural abilities tenfold."

"The Teller and the Amazon traveled the world, finding more and more that looked different to them, discovering that the supernatural world had grown along with the natural world, balanced. A little bit of supernatural wonder went a long way, and it took a great deal more of natural wonder to even the scales. In some places, the natural world was over taking the supernatural world and vice versa. Some places were far too dark and some places far too light."

Thinking about that for a moment, Frank Stone came to Nick's mind. Stone's life was about changing this balance or destroying it all together.

"The bond created by the Teller and the Amazon will echo throughout eternity, and their kind will seek each other out. They created the first incarnation of the pen and the sword to help their successors tap into their natural abilities. This channeling of power destroyed them, but they knew this would happen, and did it so their successors would profit from their knowledge."

"So that's where this 'to the death' crap started," Nick said.

"The Teller's ability is passed down through the males of the family. The physical power is found in females with Amazonian blood. These women are inherently stronger and faster, and possess a thirst for knowledge and adventure that needs to be satisfied. The Teller's abilities compliment this well and create a bond that makes them both infinitely stronger together than they could ever be apart."

Scanning through the rest of the book, Nick wrote down the last few notes. If he had known about this book earlier he would have known about the Map Walking trick and the added bonus of what happened when he ran into ghosts. Ray called it 'Projecting.' Nick also found notes about being able to see inside of books while 'Projecting' and how this can also be applied to paintings marked by Tellers.

"Why couldn't I have found this months ago," Nick shook his head and looked out the window. The rain had let up and rays of sunshine were breaking through the clouds in a few places. He set the book and notepad aside, stood and stretched. He grabbed his sweats, changed and ran down stairs.

"Looks like your undies will stay dry after all," Sue said as Nick hit the bottom of the stairs.

"Undies doesn't work either, Grandma," Nick stopped in his tracks in front of the entry way to the living room.

"Fine, underpants," Sue looked up from her crocheting.

"Not much better," Nick said as he headed out the front door on his run.

*****

"So, we were destined to be together?" Mina swooned in Nick's arms.

The tide was coming in and the surf was up a bit as the waves crashed on the beach a few feet away from them.

"And to die together it seems," Nick said.

"Like you said about life, none of us get out alive," Mina kissed Nick on the cheek as they walked along the sand. It was cold on their bare feet, but the sun was warm on their faces.

"Yeah, I'm a realist," Nick smiled. "Yay."

"As long as you're not a glass half empty kinda guy, I'll keep you around," Mina said.

"I'm more concerned with the fact that you're an opportunist and will most likely drink the water when I'm not looking," Nick said. "Just like you steal half of every meal we eat together."

"You look well-fed despite that fact," Mina smiled.

"Luckily I can cook," Nick said.

"Even more of a reason to keep you around," Mina said.

"So it's not destiny then, it's just my informal grooming," Nick said.

"You were destined to be raised by two amazing women who would teach you the lessons you needed to succeed with a girl like me," Mina said and stepped away from Nick, but keeping his hand.

"Oh really?" Nick said.

"Yup," Mina stepped back toward Nick. He pulled her against him and kissed her.

"I don't mind my destiny sometimes," Nick said as he opened his eyes.

Smacking him softly on the cheek, Mina said, "So, what are we destined for next?"

"I'm hoping that cheeseburgers and fries come next," Nick said.

"I think that can be arranged," Mina said. "But I was thinking a little more long term. Maybe like the next six months? Maybe, how are we going to end this little hunt we are a part of?"

"A part of? I guess we can't exactly call ourselves the hunted any longer," Nick said as they walked back toward the scooter and their shoes. "Not when we know where Stone and his family live."

"Have you seen him there yet?" Mina asked.

"No, just Tine and the boy."

"Do you know what's wrong with their son? Is he an epileptic or something?" Mina asked.

"I think it's more than that, he also relies on crutches and seems stiff whenever I see him. I looked up those symptoms and something called Cerebral Palsy shares all of them."

"Could that be a result of what Stone is or from how Tine was created?" Mina asked as they sat down on the ground next to the scooter.

Brushing the sand off of his feet, Nick said, "Not sure. Anything is possible when someone who was resurrected from the dead has a kid with someone who tricked a Jinn into making them Supergirl."

"Do you know if any of your ancestors' protector's had kids?" Mina asked. "Seems with everything I've read a nephew or great nephew gets the pen in your family."

"My great-great uncle and his wife had a daughter, but she's buried next to them at Indian River Cemetery. She never had any children of her own."

"How did she die?" Mina asked.

"Drunk driver," Nick said.

"Oh," Mina said and stood up.

"You were worried that our kind can't have kids, weren't you?" Nick asked.

"I know we're still kids but I would like to be a mom one day," Mina pulled Nick to his feet. "A long way down the road. When I'm way older. Like twenty five or twenty six."

"Understood," Nick said. "We need to survive the next few weeks first though."

"That would help," Mina said.

"My plan could get us killed," Nick said.

"I'm well aware of the 'to the death' clause. I just wish you would lay out all the details so that I can come up with contingency plans that might up our chances of survival," Mina said.

"There are only two possible outcomes, Mina," Nick said. "And death is part of both equations."

"Just tell me what you have cooked up," Mina said through her teeth.

"I can't take it back if I say it out loud," Nick said. "And thinking it makes me feel like a horrible person."

"We gonna pour sugar in his gas tank?" Mina smiled.

"Much worse than that," Nick looked down at the ground.

"What's worse than killing him like we have already talked about umpteen times?" Mina said.

"Killing his son first," Nick said.

They looked at each other quietly for a few moments. The wheels turning behind Mina's eyes.

"Yeah, that's pretty messed up," Mina said and fired up the scooter.

*****

"You have got to be joking," Hank yelled. "That is the worst idea I have ever heard, and I've killed children before."

"It will send him into a frenzy, he will lose control, and he will be so overwhelmed with grief and in such a rage he will be vulnerable," Nick said as they sat around a fire in Hank's backyard. "And no one likes a tattletale, Mina."

Penny was roasting a marshmallow over the flames.

"You really think I was going to be the one to slit the kid's throat?" Mina said slowly turning a stick with a hotdog on the end of it in the fire. "I'll happily carve Stone a new one, but kill a handicapped little kid? That's not something I think I can do. As chance would have it though, we know a child killer or two."

"Hey," Ben said. "I have been on the wagon for many moons now."

"And we're all very proud of you kemo sabe," Hanks said. "And it's a horrible idea, you suicidal idiot."

"What about killing Tine? That should knock him off his rocker and make him vulnerable," Mina pulled her hotdog out of the fire and bit into it.

"He loves her, but she doesn't mean anything to him compared to that child. If we took them both out, that would break him down so much it would make him lose control of all of his power. It would let us get close enough that we could tear him apart and spread him across the globe," Nick said.

"That is a very graphic," Ben said.

"I don't really enjoy thinking about doing any of these things, but from everything I have seen of the monster, our only shot at stopping him is first getting him to lose control of his power. That means overwhelming him with anger and grief and sadness and pain. All at once. Taking away his family seems like the only way we can make all of that happen. And all that will leave him open to dismembering him. Because, sadly, he can heal as fast, if not faster, than Mina."

"Why don't we just kidnap them?" Hank said.

"That would give him time to plan, and rally help," Nick said. "We have to hit him with everything so fast he can't plan or think his way out of it. He's not just powerful, he's smart. That's how he's gotten so much power." Nick grabbed a marshmallow from the bag and picked up a stick. He stabbed it into the marshmallow then held it over the fire.

"If it were even possible, not a single piece could go wrong," Ben said. "Or we would all die."

"What if we just tricked him into thinking his son was in danger?" Penny said.

"He's too smart for us to bluff," Nick said. "He would have to see his son broken and dead to believe it."

"Then we show him his son being killed. You do know a shape shifter who can pretend to have a broken neck." Penny stood up, put a hand on her chin and with a shove spun her head around as though she had no vertebrae. Her head flopped to the side, then snapped back into place. "See, as long as I know that is what is going to happen I can just think my neck broken."

Everyone was quiet, only the crackling of the flames broke the cold night air.

"That's brilliant, actually," Hank said. "Way better idea than murdering a crippled kid."

"Are you sure you would want to do something like this, Penny? It will be very dangerous," Mina asked.

"I was already planning on helping you fight when the time comes, Mina. Family fights side by side. And you're my sister now," Penny smiled.

"It's great idea, but remember it adds another layer of risk," Nick said. "We will have to sell it that much more now. I think we are gonna have to kidnap the boy, and leave a really clear trail to our doorstep so that he doesn't hesitate to follow."

"Make the plans, Nick," Ben said. "And make them so that we can execute the whole thing in only a few hours. Plan everything you possibly can. I mean even where Hank and I stand so that we can control as much as possible when he comes for us. What little chance we have will come and go fast."

"I know," Nick said.

"If you can make your plans work around Chatfield Hollow, that would be great," Hank said.

"Why there?" Mina asked.

"I like that place and wouldn't mind dying there," Hank said as he stood. He turned around and walked off into the darkness of the forest.

The Living

Chapter 17
Drive In Saturday

"I know where the hat is," Hank said to Nick. They were sitting at a table at 9 East Main. "And I already ordered a mushroom pizza since you were late."

"Whatever. Where is it?" Nick asked. Two bottles of Foxen Park grape soda were on the table. He grabbed one and filled his glass with it.

"Probably in the oven still," Hank grabbed the other bottle and drank straight from it.

"No, the hat," Nick shook his head.

"A collector out in Japan has it," Hank said.

"Did you see if he is willing to sell it?" Nick asked.

"He did not accept my offer," Hank said.

"How much more does he want for it?" Nick asked.

"More than I can pay," Hank said.

"How much?" Nick asked.

"You don't understand, it's not money he is after, he is a collector," Hank said.

"What does he want then?" Nick said as Fern walked over with their pizza.

"Here ya go, boys," Fern said as she placed the pie down on the table. "Anything else ya need?"

"We're good," Nick smiled at her as he pulled a piece of pizza from the pie.

"Be back over in a few to check on ya," she said as she turned and walked away.

Hank pulled two pieces off of the pie and dropped them onto his plate. "He wants a Jinn."

"We have a bunch of those," Nick said. "I've found seven so far at Gert's."

"But we can't give him one, who knows what ridiculous wish he is going to ask, and what kind of crazy trick the Jinn will pull. Gert spent her life tracking those down so they wouldn't fall into the wrong hands." Hank bit the crust of his first piece in half.

"And? If he's rich and has his mind set on finding one, he'll find one. Gert didn't have all of them and there are free ones that I want to put into a nice little prison, maybe a whoopee cushion or a VHS of Footloose." Nick took a sip of his soda. "And why shouldn't we profit from the deal?"

"Why Footloose?" Hanks asked between bites.

"That movie was horrible. Why didn't they just go to the next town over and dance and listen to music?" Nick said. "I want those two hours of my life back."

"I thought it was okay," Hank shrugged.

"You also grew up in a time where women couldn't show any ankle," Nick said.

"It was a very different time," Hank said. "And I will never understand your taste in movies. You love Top Gun and that movie was ridiculous. It was just propaganda to get kids to join the military."

"It would be so cool to be a fighter pilot though," Nick said.

"Exactly," Hank said. "Back to the point, even if you could go and trap that piece of trash Jinn bartender, I wouldn't allow you to give it to this collector - or any other Jinn on hand. Not after all that Gert went through to hide them."

"So our other option is to steal the hat?" Nick said. "Kinda dangerous since the dude knows someone wants to buy it."

"My thoughts exactly," Hank said.

"What if we made it look like it was destroyed?" Nick said.

"Oh, that is an interesting idea," Hank said.

There were only two pieces of the pizza left, and Fern appeared next to the table.

"How you fellas doing?" She asked.

"Great," Hank said.

"You guys gonna need anything else?" Fern asked.

"We're just gonna do the one pie today, thanks," Hank said.

"Just one?" Fern laughed. "Can't remember the last time you

boys split only one pie between you."

"We're trying to get the big guy's cholesterol down," Nick laughed.

"Well, cutting down a pizza at a sitting is a start, but I wouldn't expect someone as young as you to be worrying about cholesterol," Fern said.

"Don't let the smooth face fool ya," Nick said. "He's no spring chicken."

"You're no more than thirty-five, thirty-six max," Fern said, scrutinizing Hank's face.

"He moisturizes," Nick laughed. "Daily."

"And I use sunblock too," Hank said.

"Well, if you're any older than that, I'm gonna double my daily moisturizing routine," Fern said and headed back to the kitchen.

"How do you suggest we make it look like it was destroyed?" Hank asked.

"Find a new hat that looks like it, burn it to a crisp, and leave it in the place of the other one when we take it," Nick said.

"That might work, or at the least make him look a different direction than me when it happens," Hank said.

"Does this guy know who you are?" Nick asked.

"Not directly, but I'm sure if he tried he could find out," Hank said.

"Is he-still feels weird asking this-supernatural?" Nick said.

"No, but he is obviously aware of it," Hank said.

"See, now that's an interesting twist," Nick said. "How does he know? How much can he see of that world?"

"He's not like you, but the more he explores the supernatural the more the curtain opens," Hank said. "And a Jinn in his hands would only compound the problem that creates."

"Well, it's a risk but if it will get Ben to shut up about the hat, then I want to take it," Nick said. "And there's no time like the present. Any chance you have a beaver hat handy that we can burn?"

"Actually, yes," Hank said.

*****

"This is a lot more fun than I thought it was going to be," Holly said as she and Mina took apart the carburetor from the '75 Sportster. Holly's hands were dirty and she had a smudge of grease on her face. "And what will this do for the bike? Seemed to be working fine before when you took me for a ride around the block."

"I am cleaning it, and putting in larger jets to go with the filter and bigger pipes I am putting on. More air means more fuel needed means more exhaust that needs to be expelled." Mina's hands were covered in grease as she screwed the last of the new jets into place, then backed it out a turn so it was seated properly.

"Will that make it go faster?" Holly asked.

"It will be more powerful, but it may only go a little faster. I'm more interested in being able to speed up quicker to highway speeds or to get out of the way of problem situations. And she will be louder," Mina smiled and picked the carburetor up off the workbench.

"Louder?" Holly said. "I didn't think that was possible. Why do you want it louder?"

"Loud pipes save lives," Mina said as she fit the unit back between the jugs on the Sportster. "Hold this in place while I secure the bolts."

"How is that?" Holly asked as she held the carburetor in place.

"Bikes are much smaller than cars, and harder to see, but if you can hear mine, then there's a better chance you will give me the proper room on the road," Mina said as she tightened down the bolts with a wrench. She had become used to using only her fingers but had to concentrate on at least faking the last bit of tightening down the bolts and nuts with the tools.

"Okay, I see. Engaging another sense to make up for the lack of info from the others," Holly smile

"Exactly," Mina said as she finished the last of the tightening. "All done with that part."

The roar of a Mustang's engine could be heard pulling into the driveway.

"Sounds like Paul's here," Mina said and handed Holly a rag.

"You've got some grease on your cheek."

"Ha ha, really?" Holly took the rag and wiped her cheek off.

"You can go wash up inside of you need to," Mina said.

"Nah, I need to stop home and change before dinner with Paul's mom," Holly said.

"Is this seriously the first time you're meeting her?" Mina asked as a honk blared through the garage door from the mustang. "How rude."

"Yes, pretty weird but their family isn't exactly nuclear," Holly said. "Thanks for showing me this."

"Thanks for giving me a hand," Mina said.

"I'll call ya later and tell you what his mom is like," Holly said.

"I am curious what the woman that gave birth to him is like," Mina said. "Have fun."

"Bye," Holly said tossing the rag down on the bench and walked out the door.

Mina grabbed onto the nuts that held the exhaust pipes and started unscrewing them with her fingers. She got all four off the manifold, then two out the four holding the pipes to the frame. She placed the pipes to the side and went about putting on the new straight pipes. When she had all the nuts on, she picked up the new air filter and secured that in place.

She wiped her hands off on a rag then slid the key into the ignition. She flipped the kick starter out and was about to slam it down when there was a knock on the garage door. She looked over her shoulder saw Charles's smiling face through the little window.

"What the hell?" Mina yelled and ran to the door, yanking it open.

"Hey, lady," Charles said.

"What are you doing down here?" Mina asked as she threw her arms around his neck.

"Came to say hello," Charles said.

"You tracked me down just to say hello?" Mina released her friend. "Come inside, are you hungry or anything?"

"A little," he said as he followed Mina into the house.

"My dad made chili last night, hope you don't mind it a little spicy," Mina said as they walked into the house and headed to the kitchen.

"Sounds fantastic," Charles said as he sat down at the table.

"So, how did you get away from that Jinn of yours?" Mina asked as she pulled a bowl out of the dish drain.

"He asked me to track down Bruce," Charles said.

"Water, soda, iced tea or orange juice?" Mina said as she opened the fridge.

"Iced tea, please," Charles said as Mina pulled a large container of chili out of the fridge.

"Do you think Bruce is down here somewhere?" Mina said as she pulled the iced tea out of the fridge and poured a glass for Charles.

"I followed a lead down this way," Charles said as Mina placed the iced tea on the table.

"Why would he be down here?" Mina asked as she placed the bowl filled with chili in the microwave.

"He left me a note about coming to spread Gert's ashes, as you asked," Charles said. "So, all I have to do is wait."

"Did he say he was going to get me first to do all of that?" Mina pulled a few flour tortillas out of the fridge.

"No, but I expect his intentions are to contact you first, to plan a memorial of sorts, and spread her ashes," Charles said then took a sip of his tea.

Wrapping the tortillas in a paper towel, Mina tossed them in the microwave with twenty seconds left to cook. "Why wouldn't he just tell you that he was going to do this?"

"He went a little wild after Gert was killed. When we got back to Montreal, he tore off his suit and disappeared into the wilderness," Charles said.

"Sounds familiar," Mina said as she pulled the chili and tortillas out of the microwave.

"Pardon?" Charles said.

"Hank did something similar," Mina put the food down on the table, then grabbed Charles a spoon and sat down. "When I told him she was dead he took off. Nick tracked him down and convinced him to come back."

"Ah yes, they told me a little about that when I met them after the fight," Charles said and spooned some chili into his mouth.

"That's right, I forgot about that little adventure Nick took without me," Mina said.

"Nice kid," Charles said as he spooned up more chili. "This is amazing."

"My dad's old family recipe," Mina said. "Did you walk here or take a magic carpet ride?"

"Rental," Charles smiled and pulled the keys out of his pocket. "Lucked out too. All they had left was the luxury sedan."

"Do we have to wait here for Bruce to show up, cause I'm sure Penny would love to see you," Mina said.

"Penny's here with you?" Charles said through a mouthful of chili.

"She's staying with my friend Ben, up at Hank's." Mina said.

"I'm certain Bruce will be able to find us wherever we are in this little town," Charles said.

"Ok, I'm gonna clean up while you finish eating. Cool?" Mina stood up.

With his mouthful of chili again, he gave a thumbs up.

"I'll be back," Mina said as she raced up stairs.

*****

"Thanks," Nick said as Ben pulled him to his feet. He had suffered another rough landing after Ghost Walking. Turned out the collector in Japan had quite a few ghosts in his compound. It only took Nick, Ben, Hank and Penny a few minutes to find the place, get inside and run into a ghost accidentally.

"You really need to work on your balance, boy," Ben said.

"If I was as strong as ten men I'd land on my feet more often, too," Nick said.

"Penny had no problem with the landing," Hank said.

"She came through in the form of a bird," Nick said. "But

whatever. Where do we go next? I was hoping we would have had more time to search around before we tripped into this place."

"Could have done at least a little reconnaissance of this place," Hank said.

"That's your fault," Nick said.

"How is it my fault?" Hank said. "You're the leader in your little Map Walking trick."

"Will you two stop," Ben said. "We need to find the hat and get out of here before someone finds us."

"Too late," Penny said as she turned back into her little girl self. A pair of Rottweilers were looking at them with bared teeth. The dogs made no noise.

"Oh fun," Nick said. "Just what we need."

"You're worried about a couple of puppies?" Hank said.

"I'm worried that they will alert someone who will be a problem," Nick said.

"I'll take care of it," Penny said and turned into a Jack Russell Terrier.

"Huh, I would have gone bigger," Hank said.

Penny the dog walked slowly up to the larger dogs. She cocked her head to the side and barked. The bigger dogs looked at her, then sat down.

"I think this is our chance," Ben said.

"Should we leave her with them?" Nick asked.

"She can turn into a bear if she has any problems," Ben said.

"Understood," Nick said looking at the dark doorway to their left. "My gut tells me that we should be heading that way."

Sniffing the air, Hank said, "That would be my guess, as well."

"I'm not questioning your direction, but I am curious what on Earth you can smell that makes you know where to go," Nick said.

"Formaldehyde," Ben said. "And leather."

"Ah. Then we go through that dark door deeper into this collector's house? Sounds like act two breaking into three of a really bad horror movie." Nick headed through the door with Ben and Hank following behind.

"Are you afraid of the dark or something?" Hank asked. "You

sure are a wuss without Mina around."

"I do believe that I am the one at the front of this group of ours," Nick said over his shoulder. "Seriously though, I can't see a damn thing. Did anyone think to bring a flashlight?"

"No, we can both see in the dark," Ben said.

"Figures," Nick stopped in his tracks. "One of you get in the front."

Hank chuckled to himself and walked on ahead. "Gotta get you cursed and maybe you'd be useful for something."

"Thought crossed my mind once or twice when Mina started showing off," Nick said. "Turns out though, I can't be cursed. Side effect of being what I am."

"Learn something new every day," Ben said then sniffed the air. "Can you smell that, Hank?"

"Yes," Hank said. "The leather and formaldehyde were covering it earlier."

"Wait," Nick said. "I can't smell it, but I know something is very wrong behind that door. What do you guys smell?"

"The cursed," Ben said.

"Not like you two though," Nick said. His eyes were used to the dark now. "Whatever is on the other side of that door feels, well, unholy."

"You remember how we were created?" Hank asked.

"Yes, the soul of an animal was crammed down your throat by a witch," Nick said. "And now you have two souls battling it out inside of you."

"On the other side of that door is the result of that happening in the other direction," Ben said. "A human soul has been trapped inside the body of an animal. In this case it's a wolf."

"What does that look like?" Nick reached for the door handle.

"Hold on a second, Nicholas," Ben said. "There is something you need to know. This is not something that happens often. And it only happens when someone is sacrificed."

"So, the person was murdered and then their soul was forced into the animal?" Nick asked.

"Yes," Hank said.

"That sounds pretty horrible," Nick said. "But why would someone do that?"

"Witches cast curses in death or heartbreak," Ben said. "But this is the result of very evil, but very naïve, mortals playing with magic, magic that they don't understand and cannot control."

"I see where this is going," Nick said. "Let's get this over with then."

"You can wait here while we take care of this," Ben said.

"No, I can't," Nick said and opened the door.

The growling was very deep and guttural. Nick could feel it in his chest. And his eyes were adjusted well enough that he could see the animal off to the right, chained to the wall. It was on all fours, head low and staring right into Nick's eyes. Its chain was long enough to make it to the door, but it did not charge them. It waited.

"This would be easier if there was enough room for you to change, Ben," Nick said.

"Yes, but Hank and I will make it quick," Ben said as he and Hank inched toward the creature. Its size was more apparent the closer the two men got to it. It was huge, bigger than both of them combined.

"Easy big fella," Hank said. But the animal had its own agenda and snapped at him. Hank side stepped the beast's head, and got a hold around its neck.

"Hold him," Ben said quietly.

"Trying," Hank said through gritted teeth. The animal was thrashing back and forth, but Hank had it stuck in place. It took every ounce of strength he had, the muscles and ligaments in his neck and arms sticking out - looking as though they would snap - to hold on. His chokehold was also keeping the animal quiet.

Ben moved quickly to the other side of the creature, running a hand over the fur, and said, "Such a waste." He got in front of the giant wolf, looked in its eyes, grabbed onto the side of its head, then twisted as fast and hard as he could.

The snap was loud, but not as loud as Nick expected. He felt it through the floor, in his bones.

The beast was still in Hank's arms, the limp body behind him. He lowered the great big head down on the floor and closed the animal's eyes.

Looking up, Hank said, "I wish we could get it outside to bury it. I would say to burn it right here but that might take out the whole house."

"Find the hat and I'll figure out how to get it out of here," Nick said. "It's in this room though, I know it is."

"That sixth sense of yours tingling, Spidey?" Ben said looking around the room.

"Yes," Nick said as he knelt down and put his hand in the wolf's furry neck.

"This place is like a museum," Ben said as he looked down the corridor. Along one side of the room were cases filled with hats and headdresses from all over the world and every era of human history. The wall across from the cases was covered from floor to ceiling with masks, many of them looking like demons, watching over the hat collection.

Walking slowly down the wide aisle between the cases and the masks, Ben scanned the displays, unblinking. Then he stopped and fell to his knees about a hundred feet from where Nick was sitting with the dead animal.

Hank slowly walked to his friend and stopped at Ben's side. Hank placed a hand on Ben's shoulder and squeezed.

"We found it, Henry," Ben said, tears welling up in his eyes.

"Time to take it home, Benjamin," Hank said and smashed the glass case with his fist.

Jumping to his feet, Nick yelled, "Seriously?"

"Not like the plan matters anymore since we killed the guy's guard dog," Hank yelled back. He pulled Ben to his feet and grabbed the hat. "Let's move, friend"

The two men ran back to Nick, Hank with the hat in hand as the lights all came on at the same time.

"Hope he doesn't have cameras," Hank sad.

"Have you come up with a new plan yet?" Ben asked wiping his eyes.

"Yes and no," Nick said. He had the map open in one hand and the pen down on Kelsey Town. "Hank, wrap both of your arms around the wolf, Ben, you wrap an arm around Hank and hook the other under me."

"Is this gonna work?" Hank said as he did as instructed.

"Maybe," Nick closed his eyes and saw Julie in Hank's living room.

"Where's Penny?" Ben grunted.

A little Penny bird came flapping into the room and landed on Nick's shoulder and tweeted at Ben.

"Oh good," Julie said looking from Mina to Nick. "Did you find it -- whoa, is that a wolf?"

"Yup on both accounts," Nick said.

"Who are you talking to?" Mina asked.

"Nick. I can see him when he's doing the Map Walking trick," Julie said as Nick grabbed onto her, then crashed into the sofa.

The room got a lot more crowded as Hank and Ben both tumbled into the fire place and the carcass of a huge wolf landed on Nick's lap.

Penny the bird flittered off toward the bathroom.

From one of the recliners, sipping a cup of tea, Bruce said, "Interesting."

"Is it dead?" Charles asked.

"Sadly, yes," Nick grunted as he pushed it off of his lap with every ounce of strength he had. The carcass flopped to the ground.

Chapter 18
No Sleep till Brooklyn

Keeping his balance, Nick looked down at the sidewalk as the ball bounced past him into traffic. He closed his eyes as the little girl in the little white sun dress embroidered with whales blew by into the oncoming traffic.

There were no screeching tires.

No sounds of crunching metal.

Or glass shattering.

A few horns blared but those were in anger not warning.

Turning on his heel, Nick headed down the street to the closest subway station, hopped on the G train and out of Greenpoint. Nick switched to the J train a few stops later and was on his way to Manhattan.

On the other side of the East River, Nick hopped off the strain at Delancey/Essex St Station and hit the streets. He headed up to Houston Street. The city streets were packed, as always, but the walk was short to Katz's Deli. Nick's father waited outside of the restaurant. He was leaning against the building with a cigarette hanging from his lips.

"When are you going to quit that disgusting habit?" Nick said as he walked up.

"When I can drink again," Roger said.

"So, never," Nick said.

"Gotta have at least one vice," Nick's father said. "How ya been, son?"

"Doing okay. Hungry," Nick said. "Do they have the Mets game on in here? Didn't hear a word on the train down here of how they're doing."

"Then we met at the right place," Roger opened the door for Nick. "Houston is up 3-0, and they're in the 8th."

"Damn it," Nick said.

The two men put their order in--two Katz's Pastrami sand-wiches and steak fries-- and sat down near the T.V. It was now the top of the ninth and Mookie Wilson had just hit a single sending Lenny Dykstra in from third cutting the Astros lead to 3-1.

"Time to show off that under pressure magic, fellas," Nick's father said and he sipped his ice water.

Father and son sat in silence and watched as Wilson was bat-ted in from a double by Keith Hernandez. This forced the Astros to change out their pitcher, taking a different direction on the mound. The Astros walked Carter and Strawberry in hopes of striking out Ray Knight. But Knight took a sacrificial swing toward right field and sent Hernandez home, bringing the score to 3-3. Danny Heep swung out and brought the ninth to a close.

"Way to pull out a chance to wrap this up in six," Nick said as his food was set down in front of him.

"They thrive under pressure," Roger said as he grabbed the mustard for his sandwich.

Nick needed no extras for his sandwich and dug in. With his mouth full, the Mets took the field for the tenth inning. Nick said, "So good."

"You should come down more, and we can indulge in this tradition more often." Roger bit into his sandwich.

Nick didn't say anything, he just took another bite of his sandwich.

They ate in silence and cleared their plates over the next three scoreless innings. The game was enough to keep them entertained.

As they sat watching the thirteenth inning pass by scoreless, Roger finally broke the silence. "Want desert?"

"Is that really a question?" Nick said.

"The usual then," Roger said. "Make that happen, I gotta hit the head and make some room."

While his father was making room, Nick ordered two pieces of cheesecake and asked that it be brought out when his father got back.

"Did you go home to use the John or something?" Nick asked

when his father returned.

"Should have, would have been more pleasant," Roger laughed as the two pieces of cheesecake found their places on the table.

"Thanks," Nick smiled at the waitress.

"Looks like I missed a bit," Roger pointed at the television.

"Yeah, a bit," Nick picked up his fork and chopped the tip of the cheesecake off. Then he shoveled it into his mouth.

"Three outs away from going to the World Series," Roger said. "It's making me all nervous."

Nick didn't say anything, he just ate his cheesecake slowly. With one out down, Billy Hatcher of the Astros bounced a homer off the left field foul pole to tie up the game. Luckily, they were stopped there and nothing else really happened for another two, silent innings.

Darryl Strawberry got on base with a double. Ray Knight singled sending Strawberry home to give the Mets the lead. Then a wild pitch gave Knight the chance to t0 round home plate and put the Mets ahead by two. With a single from Dykstra, Backman got across home plate as well.

There was no more cheesecake left, and Nick and his father's knuckles were white with their fists clenched so hard as the Mets went into the bottom of the sixteenth inning, leading 7-4.

Houston rallied once again when with one out, Davey Lopes drew a pinch-hit walk, followed by Doran's single. Hatcher then singled in Lopes to make it 7–5, after which Denny Walling hit into a fielder's choice for the second out. Davis followed with a single to centerfield that landed in front of a charging Dykstra, that brought home Doran to cut it to 7–6.

The Mets' pitcher, Jesse Orosco, stood on the mound with the tying run standing on third and the winning run for the Astros standing on first. Without losing focus, Orosco struck out Kevin Bass to secure the Mets place in the 1986 World Series.

Half the people in the deli, including Nick and his Father, launched themselves to their feet and screamed at the top of their lungs. The other half looked mortified and scared out of their minds. Nick and his father hugged, slapped each other on the back, then raised their hands in triumph while on the television the Mets entire squad rushed the field in victory.

Out on the street, Nick and his father stood outside of Katz's Deli watching the traffic fly by.

"I can't believe the Mets are going to the World Series," Nick said.

"A lot of strange things have come about this year," Roger said.

Looking over to his father slowly, Nick said, "Like what else?"

"For one thing your girlfriend's father and I have the same first name, that's pretty odd," Roger said.

"Yes, yes it is," Nick said. "It was the main reason I called him Mr. Medellin for so long."

Laughing, Roger said, "Maybe this is my chance to resurrect my college nickname."

"First off, no," Nick said. "Second, you have little resemblance to James Dean now that you're twice as old as he was when he wrecked his head."

"Jimmy Dean," Roger said. "And I think I have aged quite well."

"Except for all that hard living you did," Nick said. "Then again I guess this is what James Dean would look like if he was still kicking."

Roger turned and looked at his reflection in the window, "That's a little harsh, don't you think?'

"No," Nick said. "Give me a hug, old man, I gotta catch the train."

Hugging his son, Roger said, "Maybe you can come down and watch one of the Series games. I enjoyed this, I'm glad you called."

"Me too," Nick said. "And it depends on school work and Cross County. Luckily this week was kinda light on the home work front."

"I understand," Roger said. "Call me when you get back home,"

"Will do," Nick said, turned on his heel and headed toward Delancey Street. He stepped into an alley way when he was a block away from his dad and pulled out a map of Kelsey Town.

*****

"Where's Nick tonight?" Holly asked while she and Mina were folding green napkins into flowers for their class's Homecoming float. The chicken wire was wrapped around a two by four foot frame that resembled a dragon with patches of green where the napkins had been stuffed into the chicken wire.

"He went to visit his dad in New York," Mina said as she folded the paper over.

The shop class bays were filled with students working on their respective class's floats. Sheets were hung between the classes so the students couldn't see what their competition was building. They had started on Monday and had to have their floats done for the Homecoming Parade two weeks later.

"Cool," Holly said. "They doing anything interesting?"

"Watching the Mets game and going to some place called Katz's Deli," Mina said.

"That place has the best Pastrami sandwiches on the planet," Filomena yelled as he was cutting a piece of chicken wire. He was working with another guy fashioning the tail for the dragon. "And the Mets suck."

"Thanks for the insight, Paul," Mina said. "So helpful."

"Welcome," Filomena smiled and put his head back into the work of
making the wing.

"Have you met his dad?" Holly asked, the pile of flower napkins grown beside her.

"Yeah, we went down to the city and did all the touristy stuff with him back in the spring," Mina said. "Before my little adventure."

"You are gonna have to tell me what you really did one of these days," Holly said.

"I told you about going to my grandma's horse farm in Greece," Mina said.

"Come on Mina, we all know your dad was looking for you

for months. Wouldn't he know if you were at your grandma's?" Filomena said.

"Shush, Paul," Holly said. "She'll tell us when she's ready."

"And to answer your question, Paul, I asked my grandmother not to tell him I was there because I was angry," Mina said.

"Why are you so angry?" Paul said.

"Was," Mina said. "I'm not that angry anymore."

"Just the usual amount of angry of every teenage girl," Filomena said.

"I'm not angry!" Holly growled.

"Only when you're hungry, or not getting your way, or not shopping—" Filomena was cut short by a set of keys smacking him in the side of the head. "Ooooooooooowwwww, were those my own keys?"

"Yes, you jackass," Holly yelled as she stormed off.

"Wow, Paul, you're just so good with the ladies," Mina stood up and followed Holly out into the dark parking lot.

Turning on her heels, Holly said, "I can't stand him sometimes!"

"Sometimes?" Mina smiled.

*****

Game 1 - Saturday, October 18
Boston Red Sox – 1
New York Mets – 0
Shea Stadium

*****

Game 2 - Sunday, October 19
Boston Red Sox – 9
New York Mets – 3

*****

Game 3 - Tuesday, October 21
New York Mets – 7
Boston Red Sox – 1
Fenway Park

*****

Game 4 - Wednesday, October 22
New York Mets – 6, Boston Red Sox – 2
Fenway Park

*****

Game 5 - Thursday, October 23
New York Mets – 2, Boston Red Sox – 4
Fenway Park

Chapter 19
Let's Dance

It was Friday night and it was Homecoming. Kelsey Town was playing their rivals from Madison. The football player Nick had a few run ins with was quarterback for the opposing team and he didn't seem to have the same confidence he once had. He had thrown two interceptions already and gotten sacked four times. Kelsey Town was winning 21-3.

The bleachers on both sides of the field were jam packed and the Kelsey Town crowd roared along with the school band.

Mina was actually smiling and yelling along with Nick, Paul and Holly as they cheered for their school to press on down the field.

It was a chilly October evening, but the sky was clear. The smell of burning leaves, coffee and hot chocolate permitted the air for most of the night until about halfway through the second half.

Going quiet, Mina closed her eyes and breathed in deeply through her nose. She held the breath for a moment, then let it out. Opening her eyes, she turned to Nick and whispered, "Do you smell that?"

Nick nodded, his smile still plastered across his face. "Lavender."

"Where is it coming from?" Mina looked around.

"From our six," Nick said.

Mina looked over her shoulder and could see a figure standing on top of the announcer's booth. It was only there for a second, just long enough for Mina to see, and for it to see Mina looking at it.

"Mosquito," Mina said. "Fast one."

"Does it look thirsty?" Nick asked.

"Not sure," Mina whispered.

"What are you two whispering about?" Holly said.

"Secrets don't make friends," Filomena yelled.

"I gotta pee," Mina said loudly at Filomena. "Happy?"

"Yes," Paul smiled.

"I gotta pee too," Holly said. "Let's go."

Nick and Mina locked eyes, and they smiled. Mina knew how to be careful and Nick knew she had to go check it out.

"Be right back, boys," Mina said. She and Holly headed toward the steps. Nick watched as they walked down the stairs toward the concession stand on the other side of the field.

"Why do they always go in pairs?" Paul asked.

"I think men have been asking that question for millennia," Nick said.

"LET'S GO BLUE!" Filomena yelled.

Sticking a finger in his ear closest to Paul, Nick winced and said, "Thanks."

"If I'm too loud, you're too old," Paul smacked Nick on the back.

"That saying doesn't work like that at all," Nick said. "Especially since you're older than me."

"Your logic is killing my buzz," Paul said.

Over at the concession stand, Mina and Holly waited in line for the restroom. Mina was scanning the darkness all around them for any sign of something out of place.

"Have you ever been to a dance?" Holly asked.

Turing her attention back to the stands, Mina said. "Nope. First one."

"Do you like to dance?" Holly asked.

Smiling, and turning her attention to Holly, Mina said, "Kinda. Usually I only dance when I'm by myself and a song with a quick beat pops on and I'm not really paying attention."

"I knew you had to have a little bit of a love for it, being Hispanic and all," Holly smiled. "Just didn't know if any of the music you listened to had a beat you could shake it to."

"Not everything I listen to is slow or depressing," Mina said. Then her head snapped back to the crowd. The figure from the top of the announcer's booth was standing next to the bleachers looking right at Mina. This time she could see his face. She only got a quick look before the vampire disappeared again, but she recognized the monster from her time in Vegas. It was one of the vampires from Enoch's entourage.

"Like what?" Holly said. "Cause you should totally play one of those songs next time we hang out at your place."

"I'll put a mix together for next time," Mina said while scanning the crowd. Her gaze met only the darkness beyond. "Damn."

"Damn, what?" Holly asked.

"This line is moving so slow," Mina said. "Do you think the restrooms over near the playground, on the other side of the bleachers, are open?"

"Probably not, but it'll take just as long to walk over there as it will for us to get to the front of this line," Holly said as she left the line heading toward the exit of the football field.

It was darker behind the bleachers, the lights for the field not reaching that far. There was still enough to easily make the trek over the baseball field to the playground where the tennis courts and practice wall was. The memory of the first time Nick put the pen on the graffiti rushed into her head. She shook it off as she focused on her senses.

"The stuff you usually listen too is okay for slow dancing," Holly said. "That band, The Cure, has a few choice songs for being pressed up against a boy."

"Most of them are about heart break though, so I suggest not listening to the words," Mina said. The scent of lavender was faint, but Mina knew it had come this way. It had moved very fast through the field.

At the building with the restrooms, Mina pulled on the door handle. It was locked. She pulled a bit harder and there was a loud metal crunch.

"Is it open?" Holly asked.

"Yup," Mina swung the door open and turned on the light.

Quickly using the facilities, the girls walked back to the bleachers and joined the crowd in a roar of excitement as Kelsey Town High got another touchdown.

"Any luck?" Nick asked as he clapped.

"Negative," Mina said then whistled. "The bat has left the belfry. But there's a bit of a problem. It really likes to gamble."

"Do you think he came to double down on his bet?" Nick asked.

"No doubt he wants to find out if he chose the winning horse," Mina said.

"What the hell are you two talking about?" Filomena asked.

"Bats," Mina said.

"Mosquitos," Nick said.

"Eww, bats are disgusting," Holly said. "And it's too cold now for there to be any mosquitos out."

"There are a few stragglers still buzzing around," Nick said.

"You guys talk about the dumbest stuff," Filomena said.

"And everything that comes out of your mouth is philosophical excrement, Filomena," the guy behind Paul yelled.

"Screw you, Mauro," Paul yelled back.

"You're too pretty for me, Filomena," Mauro said. "I like my men a little less girly. Stanton's more my speed."

"Thanks, Matty," Nick said over his shoulder to Mauro.

"Seriously now, Mina, can I borrow him for the night? Just for the dance?" Matty asked. "I'll return him with his hymen intact."

"Gross," Holly said.

"Sorry Matty, he's gotta suffer through the night as my arm candy," Mina said. "I've barely seen him all week on account of the World Series."

"To bad, I would look dead sexy on his arm," Matty said. He smiled and headed down the bleachers.

"Wait, is he really gay?" Holly asked. "I can't tell since you guys are always smacking each other in the privates and all."

"Totally," Nick said.

"Yeah, whenever he cracks me in the nuts he lingers and calls it the German helmet," Filomena said.

"Wait? What?" Holly said.

"They're just jerkin your chain, Holl," Mina said. "I don't think there's a girl in the senior class he hasn't made out with. He's a bit of a man whore."

"He's made out with quite a few in the sophomore class too," Holly whispered to Mina.

"You floozy," Mina whispered back. "When?"

"Last summer at one of the bonfires out in the power lines," Holly said. "I got a little too buzzed and frisky."

"How frisky?" Mina asked.

"Second base," Holly smiled.

"What about second base?" Filomena said.

"You suck at it," Mina said.

"Whoa, whoa, whoa," Paul said and stood up.

Nick cup checked Paul, and it turned out Paul was not wearing one, "Sit down, fancy pants."

Dropping back to his butt, Paul cupped his groin and growled, "What the hell douchebag!"

"Carry on with your secrets, ladies," Nick said.

"Thank you, kind sir," Mina smiled at her boyfriend.

*****

The music pumped through the gymnasium. Streamers lined the walls and the rafters and hung down within a few feet of the teenager's heads. Balloons were everywhere-hundreds of them tied to the bleachers, taped to the walls and all over the floor and tables.

The local cover band, The One Night Stand, was rocking out to 'Rebel Yell' on the small stage. The bassist was dressed like Evel Knievel, helmet and all, and was air humping his bass violently in front of the stage.

Nick and Mina were dancing innocently enough next to Filomena and Holly who were doing the forbidden dance for every song. Mina proved to have some rhythm while Nick basically flailed his arms about while shuffling his feet.

"Watch my feet and my hips," Mina said.

"I am and that's making it even harder to concentrate," Nick said. "I've never seen you in a dress let alone something that looks that hot."

The guys were both wearing shirts and ties with their black

pants. Mina was wearing a figure hugging red dress with only one shoulder strap and Holly had on a blue halter dress that left her shoulders and arms bare, not that anyone could really see because of how close she was pressed against Filomena.

"Thank you, I guess," Mina looked down at Nick's feet. "You clean up pretty well yourself."

Nick pulled her into him quickly and buried a kiss against her lips. She arched back slightly, curving into him and the kiss.

"Thanks," Nick said when he pulled away.

A scream cut through the music.

Mina and Nick's heads turned toward the sound.

"What the hell was that?" Nick said.

Smelling the air, Mina said, "No way!"

More screams followed and the music stopped as the power went out and the lights were cut. The sound of fancy shoes on the gym floor shuffling towards the doors filled the room.

The emergency lights came on, then the sound of the bulbs being smashed echoed throughout the gym.

"What is going on?" Holly said, hanging onto Paul as hard as she could.

"Zombies," Mina said as she reached down into her cleavage and pulled out the necklace tucked down into her dress. She pulled the knife out of the sheath, but let it remained small.

"What do you plan on doing with that?" Filomena said, his raised eyebrow going unnoticed by everyone in the darkness except Mina.

"I'm gonna kill the dead," Mina started toward the main entrance where the first scream had come from.

The doors shook from the inside as the frantic whispers asked panicked questions. Then the doors rattled harder as shoulders were slammed into them.

"Let's hit the doors over to the back hallway, those are probably open," Filomena said.

"No," Nick said. "Stay right where you are."

Paul and Holly stood still holding onto each other.

"Everyone, stay right where you are," Nick yelled over the

crowd. "Don't move!"

Most of the other kids stood exactly where they were. A scream and horrible moaning made a group of students suddenly scramble away.

Letting her sword out to its full size, Mina brought it up over her head and cut a zombie in half as it tried to bite a screaming girl in a white dress. Mina's arms came around to cut two more in half. The zombies disintegrated into dust as the sword sliced through them.

"These guys are a little different," Mina said as she looked around for more. She found a few of them standing in front of the same figure from the homecoming game. The one that had moved too fast for anyone else to see. The one that had been watching Mina.

Another scream came from behind Mina. She jumped up into the air, flipped backwards and came down on a zombie just before it snapped its rotting jaws into a freshman boy wearing a bow tie. Mina sliced the corpse in half, kept the boy on his feet, then launched herself at the vampire and his dead entourage.

The vampire smiled as Mina came at him and hit a wall of zombies she hadn't seen before. She cut through the zombies as fast as she could, but the mosquito had enough time to disappear into the crowd of teenagers. The zombies all turned to dust when Mina cut into them.

A teacher yelled over the crowd, "Everyone calm down and please walk toward one of the exits, they will be open soon!"

"DO NOT MOVE! EVERYONE GET DOWN ON A KNEE!" Nick screamed. "AND NO ONE SAY ANOTHER WORD!"

Everyone stopped moving, the doors stopped rattling, the whispers and the clamoring stopped.

"You're stronger than you were in Vegas, Melia," A hiss came from among the crowd.

"Why don't we step outside and you can see just how right you are, mosquito," Mina said as she cut everything she could find without a pulse in half. The dead didn't follow Nick's lead very well and turned to dust for their insubordination.

"Pretty silly of you to bring my master's property here with you," the vampire hissed. "Thought you would have been smarter than that."

"What?" Mina said.

"The little bird," the vampire hissed from the darkness. "Our master might be dead, but she's tasted his blood, which means I can track her. Not well, since she had only a drop, but enough. Hope she's well fed because I've always wanted to drain a shape shifter. I've heard they change uncontrollably as you drink them dead and it's one of the best highs ever experienced."

Jumping up into the air, Mina came down where the last hiss had come from, but there were only cowering students - some of them crying.

The exit door that lead out to the sidewalk on the side of the building slammed open, and Mina was through it a second later. She chased as hard as she could, following the lavender that wafted through the air, but when she hit the river behind the building the smell vanished.

"Damn it!" Mina yelled. She listened as hard as she could for any odd splashing or branches breaking, or any sign of something out of the ordinary moving through the woods but heard nothing, not even the crunch of leaves made by an animal moving on the forest floor. She turned and ran back to the gym door where students poured out onto the sidewalk amidst cries and screams.

Going through the school's main entrance, Mina kicked in the gym door to the left. By the time she walked into the gym, her sword was nothing more than a small knife hidden behind her back. When students saw the light from the main lobby, they rushed toward the door. Mina quickly side stepped towards the wall to let them pass and headed toward Nick.

"Did you catch him?" Nick asked.

"No," Mina said.

"What the hell just happened?" Filomena said. His arms were around Holly who sobbed against his chest.

"No idea," Nick said and hugged Mina. Into her ear, he whispered, "What kind of damage control are we looking at?"

"I don't think anyone saw anything," Mina said quietly. "I

think this was all to test me."

"What?" Nick kept his cheek against Mina's.

"That mosquito knew me from Vegas," Mina said. "And he knows about Penny. I need to go find her, and I might find him."

"Go, I'll take care of what I can here," Nick kissed her and pushed her toward the door.

"Where the hell is she going?" Paul said. "And what the hell was she yammering about zombies for?"

"Horribly timed joke. It's her coping mechanism when she gets scared," Nick said. "But she knows first aid so I sent her out to the sidewalk to help if anyone needs it."

"Okay everyone, try and file out the door a little slower," a teacher yelled as the lights flipped back on.

Looking around expecting to see a bunch of corpses, Nick cocked his head in confusion. There was some grey dust here and there but no blood and no bodies. "Interesting."

"We should get her outside too," Paul said looking down at Holly and hugging her harder.

"Yeah, this way," Nick lead the three of them out to the sidewalk where people were milling about, leaning against the building or sitting on the curb whispering to each other trying to get any information on what happened. Looking over all the faces and reading their lips Nick could tell no one knew anything. They heard moaning and screaming but saw nothing. No one was bitten. A few twisted ankles and sore shoulders from trying to bust down the doors, but Nick could see in their faces the stories they were telling and would tell about that night.

"We should get to my car and get out of here," Filomena said.

The Cross Country Coach Mr. Brucella yelled over the crowd, "Is anyone hurt? If so please go to the nurse's office immediately. If you are not hurt, please stay where you are. If you have a car here, please do not leave."

"We're leaving," Paul said.

"No, stay here," Nick said. Sirens could be heard screaming toward the school in the distance.

"EVERYONE, BREATH AND TRY AND RELAX!" Nick

yelled over the crown. "STAY PUT!"

"Thanks, Stanton, for your support," Coach Brucella yelled.

"My pleasure, Coach," Nick forced a smile then turned to his friends. "Sit her down over here."

Nick and Paul got Holly sitting down on a bench. Paul knelt down on the end, with his arm around her as she cried softly into his shoulder.

As the police cruiser pulled into the parking lot, Nick whispered, "This should be interesting."

Nick stayed within ear shot of Officer Stevenson as he talked to the teachers and select students. Two more officers showed up along with a rescue truck and an ambulance, but no one said a word about zombies. No one mentioned what Mina had said or what was said to her.

She was right.

Then the parents started showing up to either pick up their kids as scheduled or because they'd heard that something had happened at the school. They had quite a few questions too, but the police brushed them off as they grilled the students.

Everyone described the lights going out, girls screaming, the doors rattling, a few mentioned the moaning, which Nick knew was coming from the walking dead, but the cops brushed it off as kids moaning in fear or pain after falling down.

The parents murmured with their kids or with each other while they waited.

Then Stevenson saw Nick out of the corner of his eye. "Stanton, front and center."

"Yeah," Nick said as he walked up.

"Where's Mina?" Stevenson asked.

"In the nurse's room helping calm people down," Nick said.

"No, she isn't," Stevenson said.

"Then, she's wandering around here somewhere," Nick said.

"You two are always attached at the hip so excuse me for not buying that you don't know exactly where she is," Stevenson said.

"Shouldn't you be more worried about why the power went out and the gym doors went all HAL on us locking us in that Homecoming nightmare?" Nick said.

"If someone would tell me the truth that would help," Stevenson said.

"You think these kids are lying about the lights going out, hearing some weird noises and being locked in the dance?" Nick asked.

"I don't think the rest of these kids know anything more than that," Stevenson said. "But you, you know something more, I'm sure of it."

"You give me a lot more credit than I deserve," Nick said. At that moment Hank walked up.

"You done with this kid, Stevenson?" Hank said.

"Hello, Hank. I am for now," Stevenson said. Then he yelled over the crowd, "Okay everyone. You can start heading home. Thank you for your patience and please get home safely."

"Is Penny alright?" Nick asked as he and Hank headed toward the Nova in the parking lot.

"She's fine, no sign of the mosquito," Hank said as he opened the driver's side door. The other students and their parents shuffled to their cars and trucks.

"Should we wait a few more minutes just to make sure it doesn't show up here for the last few minutes of the buffet?" Nick asked looking around the parking lot.

"Might as well wait until the parking lot clears out," Hank said and leaned on the car, his arms resting on the blue top.

"It was testing Mina, it was at the tournament in Vegas. It knows who she is." Nick leaned sideways against the passenger's side door.

"What do you think it plans to do with that information?" Hank asked as the cars started to line up at the exit.

"I think we don't have much time before we are knee deep in supernatural creatures who aren't as friendly as you and Ben," Nick said.

"You think it will tell Stone?" Hank asked.

"At the very least it might sell or trade him that info," Nick said. "She pissed Stone and a lot of other creatures off by breaking their tournament rules."

"What do we do then?" Hank asked.

"We can either strap in and wait for Stone to come find us..." Nick said then looked down at the ground.

"Or we can what?" Hank asked.

"We can ask Stone to come meet with us," Nick said.

"Ask him to come meet with us? Are you insane?" Hank said.

"Hear me out. If I tell him exactly where and when to meet us and he accepts we will at least have that in our favor," Nick said.

"Oh yeah great big advantage on our side," Nick said.

"We already have some of the plan in place," Nick said. "Penny plays the bait, we force Stone to lose his cool, and we strike," Nick said.

"The bait? That means we still have to kidnap the cripple," Hank said.

"Seriously, could you be a little more compassionate?" Nick said.

"You're the one who wants to kidnap a kid who can't walk," Hank said. "Get in the car. Nothing is going to happen around here tonight."

Nick opened the door and slipped into the passenger seat.

Chapter 20 - Breaking Glass

Nick didn't tell Mina what he was about to do. He had Hank drop him off at home and told Hank to keep his mouth shut. By the time Nick finished what he planned on doing it would be too late for Mina to stop him. She would have to go along with his plan.

With an atlas opened to Great Britain on the desk, Nick put the pen to the Orkney Islands and looked around the inside of Frank Stone's Castle inside his head. He was getting much better at Map Walking exactly where he wanted to be.

Opening his mind's eye to see a dragon was still a bit of a shock and he had to steady his hand, reminding himself that the dragon could not see him. Nick breathed deeply, then headed for the stairs to the next floor. He had already written the note to Stone, explaining who Nick and Mina were, where to meet them, and their willingness to negotiate.

"Now, just to find that idiot ghost," Nick said as he walked through the door into the study.

But the room wasn't empty.

Valen Tine sat at the desk, with a leather journal opened in front of her.

Slowly, Nick moved over to the side of the desk where he could see the journal better.

The writing ended at the bottom of the left hand page and the book was only half full. It was the newest journal entry from Stone.

Tears welled up in Tine's eyes but she didn't let them fall. Her face changed to one of anger and she tore a blank page from the journal, grabbed a pen and started writing.

Nick watched as she wrote across the page.

"If you are watching me, and you are who I think you are, I need your help. Stone   knows you exist, but he doesn't know exactly who you are yet. But he will find out   sooner or later. He will use every creature he can to find you. Use them the way he has used me. Like a puppet to win the tournament and bare his child. I   understand who and what my husband is. I've always known but the power was   so   intoxicating, to be young and invincible, I lost myself to it, for a very long time.   But... but I can't live this way any longer. I can't let my son grow up to this ..."

Just as she was about to write the next word, the Scottish ghost came blaring through the wall yelling, "Ungrateful swine!"

Tine jumped to her feet and screamed at the ghost, "If only I could get an exorcist into this castle!"

Seizing his moment of opportunity, Nick touched the ghost and braced himself as hard as he could against the blow. Somehow, he kept his footing and pulled the map of Kelsey Town out of his pocket with his left hand, and placed the tip of the pen right where Hank's property was with his right.

"Do you truly want a second chance?" Nick said looking Tine directly in the eyes.

Tine stood stone still, looking right back at Nick. She took a breath, then said, "I can kill you before you can pull that little disappearing trick again."

"Maybe, but you won't. You're going to sit down and answer my question," Nick said, not breaking eye contact.

Slowly, Tine sat down in the chair. "I don't think I deserve a second chance."

"Luckily, you're wrong," Nick said.

"I don't want to be a killer anymore, I don't want to hurt anyone ever again. But it…it just takes a hold of you, the power. And when you go too long without it, it hurts, deep in here," Tine pointed to her head.

"It's like any other drug," Nick said. "But you have a reason to stop."

Leaning back in the chair, Tine said, "I can't help but think that my son is the way he is because of what his father and I are, what we did to make me."

"You can blame yourself from here to the grave, but that doesn't give your son a better life," Nick said.

"He would be better off as an orphan," Tine said.

"I don't think so but that is an option," Nick said.

"Wow, that was cold," Tine said.

"You will get a second chance if you want one, but you are a killer, and you've probably killed more than your fair share of everyday Jane's and Joe's, so execution isn't totally off the table," Nick said.

"How would you even be able to kill me?" Tine said. "Or my husband? I've seen him bathe in dragon's fire and heal with little more than a new scar no one would ever notice among the thousands of other scars."

"Cut off your heads," Nick said. "And make sure they never came near your bodies ever again."

"Straight shooter," Tine smiled slightly. "I like that."

"You sound like Gert," Nick said.

"Ah, Gertrude, how is that old witch?" Tine asked.

"Dead," Nick said.

"Did she fall off the wagon and squander her second chance?

Did you take her head?" Tine asked.

"She died saving Mina, the girl you call Melia," Nick said. "Mina had to cut her in half to destroy Enoch."

"I wondered where that old bloodsucker had been," Tine said.

"So, why do you need my help? Can't you and your son just leave?" Nick asked.

"Do you really think that's an option?" Tine asked.

"What do you want me to do then?" Nick asked.

"I want to be done with this life, and to raise my son to have as normal a life as he can have with his... his illness," Tine said. "Can you help me do that?"

"Then I have a plan," Nick said. "But I need your son as insurance."

"Excuse me?" Tine leaned forward in the chair.

"My plan involves using your son as bait, to make your husband lose his cool, become so enraged that he is not in control of his emotions, then strike," Nick said.

"I have only seen him lose control once. And that was because he thought I was dead," Tine said.

"How do you think he would react if he thought your son's life was in danger?" Nick said.

"His name is Nathaniel," Tine said. "And my husband would go berserk and kill you."

"He would try to kill me," Nick said. "But what if I had not only Mina on my side but you as well?"

"It's not power, you have to outwit him too," Tine said. "That's his true power."

"By threatening Nathaniel's life, I think the playing field will be equaled," Nick said.

"You put a lot of stock in his love for my son," Tine said.

"Am I wrong?" Nick asked.

"My son never leaves this enchanted castle and I only get to leave when there's a Great Comet streaking across the sky."

"You could have just said no," Nick said.

"You joke far too much about things that are so serious," Tine said.

"It's a coping mechanism so I can handle a level of fear that would reduce a normal man to tears," Nick smiled.

"So what is your plan?" Tine asked.

"Come with me if you want to live," Nick said.

"Did you just quote that stupid movie about robot assassins from the future?" Tine said.

"Yes, and first, that movie was awesome. B, I thought you didn't get out much," Nick said.

"One of the advantages to being under house wife arrest and being extremely wealthily is having your very own personal theatre in your enchanted castle," Tine said.

"That sounds absolutely horrible," Nick said.

"Living the dream. Too bad it's built from thousand's nightmares," Tine said. "So, where are we going?"

"Well, we need to get this plan as solid as we can, and that requires my shapeshifting friend to meet your son. And it also requires that Mina trust you. If she doesn't she will kill you. I'm actually a little afraid we might not get to the explanation part before she tries to do that, but I'm a gambling man, and have no other idea how to prove to her that you are going to help us."

"So, what do we do?" Tine said.

"First, get Nate."

"What is your name," Tine asked.

"Nick."

Tine stood up and walked out of the study. Nick waited a few minutes. Then the boy moved slowly into the room on his crutches with Tine right behind him.

"Nathaniel, this is the boy I wanted you to meet," Tine said. "His name is Nick."

Walking over to Nick, Nathaniel extended his hand, "Nice to meet you, Nick. Were you the ghost that's been freaking my mom out for the past few weeks?"

"That I was, Nate," Nick said.

"What now?" Tine asked.

"Hold onto your son with one arm and my shoulder with the

other," Nick said.

"What are we doing?" Nathaniel asked.

"It's called Map Walking," Nick said as Tine pulled her son close to her. "I can look through a map at another place, and if I touch a ghost in that place I appear there instantly."

"Like the teleporter in Star Trek?" Nathaniel asked.

"Kinda, but a bit more violent," Nick said. "So brace your-selves."

"How violent?" Tine asked.

"You should be able to keep the two of you steady because you're much stronger than I am," Nick said. "I, however, tend to land upside down against the least soft thing in the room."

Reaching up, Tine placed her hand on Nick's shoulder. Even from that light grip she had on him, Nick could feel how strong she was. But he knew that she would not hurt him, that he had the last piece of his plan, and even though he was willing to kidnap, and possibly kill a child to stop Stone, he would have to do neither.

"Ready?" Nick asked.

"As I will ever be," Tine said.

"Yup," Nate said.

In his head, Nick was looking at Hank's living room. As he had feared, Mina was there with Penny. Nick could see through the door into the kitchen where Ben and Hank played backgammon at the table. Nick had asked Hank to make sure Julie was there and just as he had wished, she was talking with Mina and Penny.

"Hi Julie," Nick said as he touched her arm.

Julie shrieked and went completely invisible.

Landing next to the fireplace, upside down, Nick laughed.

From his vantage point, Nick watched as Mina jumped from the couch to her feet and onto the coffee table. Her sword came up faster than Nick could register.

Almost as fast as Mina, Valen Tine positioned herself in front of her son - one hand behind herself to shield the boy the other clenched into a fist in front of her.

"What the hell is going on Nick?" Mina yelled.

Not as fast as Mina, Penny the grizzly towered over Mina

from behind. The couch crushed under the weight of the enormous bear. The sound of wood cracking and crunching and splintering echoed through the living room.

Laughing from the kitchen, Hank said, "That was not part of your plan, you dumbass."

"What is Hank talking about, Nick?" Mina said, ready to strike.

Jumping to his feet, Nick got between Mina and Tine.

"You owe me a couch now, too, boy," Hank said as he walked into the room eating a carrot. Ben was right behind him.

"She is going to help us," Nick said. "She wants a second chance."

"Calm down, sweetie, she's not here to hurt you, or any of us," Ben said to Penny as he placed a hand on her enormous furry arm. She looked down at Ben, then shrunk back down to her normal Penny the child state.

"Then why is she here?" Mina asked, not dropping her sword.

"I want a better life for my son," Tine said. "And you are the only ones who can help me make that happen."

Looking to Nick, who nodded and smiled, Mina lowered the sword. She kept it at her side, though, at full size.

"I would say sit down and relax, but I am now a little short on places to sit in my living room," Hank said looking at Nick, not blinking.

"Didn't think Penny would go all grizzly on the sofa on us," Nick said.

"Seriously, you need to start explaining what is going on," Mina said. "And for the record I'm a little more than pissed you scared Penny like that."

"I'm fine, Mina, I like getting spooked and changing spontaneously," Penny said. "It's really fun. And what happened to the couch was hilarious."

"Of course," Nick said. "But I would first like to introduce everyone to Nate."

Peeking out from behind his mother, Nate Stone said, "You guys are intense."

Chapter 21
 Dancing In the Street

It was sunny at 11:30 when Nick woke up. Well, woke up was too gentle a word for it. The recliner he had passed out on was kicked out from underneath him and Nick tumbled violently to the floor.

After Nick showed up with Tine and her son, Bruce and Charles joined them so Nick could explain the plan. Around five in the morning Nick brought Tine and Nate back to their castle in Scotland. Stone never knew they were gone, and Nick crashed on the recliner as soon as he got back.

Mina spent the night at Hank's as well, had cuddled with Penny all night in her room - the sword within reach, right next to the bed leaning against the wall.

"Time to get moving," Hank said eating a bowl of oatmeal looking down at Nick.

"Where are we going?" Nick asked.

"You owe me a new couch," Hank said as he turned and headed back into the kitchen.

"Are you serious," Nick got to his feet and followed Hank. "With everything going on you're gonna make me replace the couch Penny crushed cause she turned into an 800 pound grizzly?"

"Yes," Hank said as he washed the bowl and spoon.

"Can I shower first?" Nick asked.

Hank sniffed the air, then said, "Yes, you stink."

"Is anyone else going with us?" Nick asked.

"Ben, but he's finishing up feeding the animals. Use the downstairs shower so you don't wake up the girls." Hank dried his hands off on a dish towel.

A few minutes later, Nick was drying off in the bathroom.

Through the door, Hank said, "Even though I told you to

stop leaving your crap here, I have a clean pair of jeans and a shirt for you."

Nick wrapped his towel around his waist, then opened the door.

"Here," Hank tossed the clothes at Nick.

"Good thing I don't listen to you," Nick said catching the clothes. He got dressed and headed back out to the kitchen.

"Morning, Nick," Ben said as he washed his hands.

"Is it still morning?" Nick asked.

"Ten minutes left," Ben said. "I think Hank has every intention of bringing us to every furniture store on the shoreline."

"What a waste of a Saturday," Nick said as Hank walked into the room.

"I had planned on hitting every antique store between here and Mystic, but we have a problem," Hank said. "Ben, I need you to wake up the girls."

"Penny is going to be a nightmare if I do," Ben said.

"Then just get Mina," Hank said.

Ben left and got Mina up. Hank poured four cups of coffee and put them on the table.

"Thanks," Nick said as he reached for his cup.

"You're going to need a lot of that, gonna be a long weekend I think," Hank sat down, pick up his cup and took a sip.

"What's going on?" Mina asked as she stretched and yawned.

"One of the students from the high school was found dead last night," Hank said.

"Let me guess, he was a few pints low?" Mina sat down and picked up a mug.

"About ten give or take," Hank said.

"Who was it?" Nick asked.

"Boy named Mathew Mauro," Hank said.

"What a shame. He worked at Hay & Grain, saw him almost every Saturday when I would get the weeks supplies for the animals," Ben said.

"He's been a staple there for the past three years," Hank said and slammed his cup down on the table, accidentally shattering the ceramic mug. "Damn it."

"Do we think there were other mosquitos wandering around last night, or just the one?" Nick asked.

"No idea," Mina said. "I lost its trail a few miles from the school, then headed straight here to talk to the guys and Penny."

"I think we should go down to the police station and do some snooping," Nick said.

"You really think they're gonna tell you anything?" Ben asked.

"No, but Stevenson will certainly talk with Mina," Nick said.

"Does he have interests in Mina?" Ben asked.

"I grew up next to him and he's always treaded the line between pseudo big brother and Lolita chaser," Mina said.

"If you think you can find out something useful then by all means go talk to him," Hank said. "Ben, Penny and I will go hunting."

"Where was the boy found?" Ben asked.

"Middle of the football field," Hank said.

"Screams 'message for Mina' if I've ever heard one before," Nick said.

"Why?" Hank asked.

"We saw the mosquito at the game, it eyeballed Mina, then showed up at the dance with Zombies, she destroyed them, then chased after him. It was testing her, and then dropped one dead body in the middle of the field where it recognized her from the tournament in Vegas. I think you're very right about this weekend. It's gonna be a long one," Nick stood up. "I think we need to get prepared for something big coming our way."

"You did just put into motion a plan for Stone to come have a powwow with us, pretend to threaten the life of his kid and demand he take a death sentence," Mina said. "Are you trying to tell me there's something bigger than that?"

"When you put it like that," Nick said. "I mean we have no idea what that blood sucker is doing with that info right now. He could be gathering a small army to come and try and take you on, or he might be going to Stone and telling him he found you. Or he might be doing a million other things that soulless mosquitos might be into. I just want to be prepared in case we have to fight. So I want to get my bat, and then we can go talk to Stevenson."

"Your bat?" Mina asked.

"Yup," Nick said. "Let's roll."

"Don't I get to finish my coffee?" Mina asked.

"Nope," Nick said.

"Actually, she should eat, and eat a lot," Ben stood up and walked to the fridge.

"Yeah, Nick, I need to eat, a lot," Mina stuck her tongue out at Nick.

"I have a bat in the closet in my room," Hank said. "And a .45. I think it's time you learn how to shoot."

"Really?" Nick said.

Ben got to work making eggs and bacon and sausage and pancakes.

"Yes," Hanks stood up and walked out of the room.

"I could go for some food too now actually," Nick breathed in the smell of the bacon and sausage sizzling on the skillet.

Looking out the window, Ben said, "I think you'll have to wait for Mina's leftovers, Hank's outside on the back porch waiting for you."

"You better leave me some eggs, woman," Nick smiled, then kissed her on the top of her head as he rushed past her to the back door.

"Have you ever used a firearm before?" Hank asked over his shoulder. He was walking away from Nick, carrying a pistol case in his right hand.

"Negative, Ke-mo sah-bee," Nick said as he ran out to catch up to Hank who was already heading into the woods directly behind his house.

"First lesson, only point it at things you want dead," Hank said.

"What are we gonna kill?" Nick asked.

"I have some bottles out here in a trash can next to a log for target practice," Hank said as they walked into the tree line.

"Cool," Nick said. They walked in silence for a few minutes

and came to a clearing Nick had never been to.

"Go over there and set up some bottles on the log," Hanks said.

Nick did as he was told.

Hank opened the pistol case and pulled out a Colt M1911 Pistol and a full clip. There were three more full clips in the case.

Nick jogged back to Hank's side. He was looking at the bottles lined up on the tree trunk.

"Stand with your feet shoulder width apart," Hank said as he slid the clip out of the handgun.

"Is that an original issue to the Navy?" Nick asked

"Yes," Hank said. "You take the clip like this, and slid it into the handle.

"I've seen that a thousand times in movies," Nick said. "Were you in the Navy back then, or just buy it from someone?"

"It was issued to me in 1914 when I joined the Marines to fight in the Great War," Hank said.

"Wait, you were a Jarhead and a werepig?" Nick chuckled.

"Yes," Hank said and handed Nick the pistol. "And if you crack one more stupid joke, I'm not gonna give you the clip."

"Okay, okay, okay, but in all seriousness," Nick said. "How did you deal with the whole being a werepig and full moons when you were at war?"

"What better place for a monstrous killing machine is there to be than on a battlefield?" Hank said then handed Nick the clip. "Slide that into the butt of the handle."

Doing as he was instructed, Nick kept the gun pointed down and slid the clip into place. He smacked it with the palm of his hand, clicking it into place. He had his finger on the trigger.

"Second lesson, only have your finger inside the trigger guard when you intend to fire the weapon," Hank said.

Nick slid pulled his finger out of the trigger and rested along the side of the pistol.

"To cock a semi-automatic weapon, you pull back on the slide," Hank said and Nick did as instructed.

"Now, hold the gun up in front of you, resting the butt of the gun in your left hand, with your arms slightly bent," Hank said and Nick raised the weapon and aimed at the bottles.

"Now, line the sights up on a bottle and squeeze the trigger with even pressure," Hank said.

BANG!

The bottle in the center of the lineup disintegrated as the bullet tore through it.

"Of course you would be a natural at this," Hank said.

"I do have excellent hand-eye coordination," Nick said. "But I'm gonna stand this way cause the box stance doesn't feel right."

Nick staggered his feet and dropped his right shoulder back, and bent his left arm more.

"Fire away since you don't want to wait for me to instruct you on the different standing positions," Hanks said.

Smiling, Nick took aim at the rest of the bottles and destroyed the other ten, emptying the clip. On the last shot, the slide slipped back and Nick caught the discharged casing in his left hand as it arched through the air.

Looking at him with a stone face, Hank said, "Is that burning your hand?"

"Yup," Nick squealed tossing the shell to the ground then shook his hand to move air over the burned spot on his palm.

"Moron," Hank said.

"It looked cool when I did it and that's what matters. But I do have a question. Will this stop a vampire or a were creature, or do we need silver bullets or soak them in holy water or something?" Nick said.

"Silver and holy water won't help too much, so just aim for the head of whatever you're shooting at. That will give you the chance to run. Hand me the pistol and go set up eleven more bottles."

*****

"Why didn't you show me how to do that a long time ago?" Nick asked as he and Hank walked into the kitchen.

"A long time ago is relative," Hank said. "I'm 285 years old and there are a lot of things I won't be able to teach you in your limited lifespan."

"Ouch," Nick said as he sat back at the table and grabbed a plate. "I was just joking."

Hank walked to his room.

"I wanna shoot a gun," Mina said then shoved a breakfast sausage in her mouth.

"It's awesome, you gotta come with us next time," Nick said as he took the last of the bacon and eggs from their respective dishes on the table.

Hank came back into the room with the Colt .45 in a holster that could be concealed under a jacket or in the back of a pair of pants. He placed it on the table in front of Nick along with a belt pouch with two full clips in it.

"What's this?" Nick asked.

"It's not a baseball bat," Hank grabbed his coffee cup and filled it. "You'll leave it here while you and Mina go to the police station and speak with Officer Stevenson. Ben, Penny and I will go hunting. You come back here wearing that black bomber jacket you have, and keep that on you for the rest of the weekend. And the baseball bat."

"Awesome," Nick said and dug into his food.

*****

The police station was quiet when Nick and Mina walked in. The small waiting room had three chairs, a door and a narrow window with thick bulletproof glass.

"Can we talk to Officer Stevenson?" Nick yelled through the small opening at the bottom of the window. The thick glass sat level with the counter, and the only access to the other side was a metal gutter deep enough to slide through identification or paperwork.

"You don't need to yell, I can hear you just fine," the woman on the other side of the glass said. "Who are you and what is this concerning?"

"Well, now we know," Nick said. "I'm Colonel Mustard and

this is Miss Scarlet. I can prove she did it in the study with the candlestick."

Smacking Nick on the shoulder, Mina shoved him aside and said, "Excuse my moron of a boyfriend. My name is Mina, Paul is my neighbor and I need to talk with him.

"Take a seat and I'll let him know you're here," the woman picked up the phone and dialed a single number. Her eyes narrowly focused on Nick.

"Sit down, jackass," Mina pushed him toward the three plastic chairs.

"Come on, how many chances in life will I have to say that to an actual cop?" Nick said as he sat down in the chair in the center.

"I'm sure you're going to try it at least three times before Christmas," Mina plopped down in the chair on Nick's right.

"You need to quit joking around, things are starting to get really serious," Mina whispered. "Another one of our friends was killed by one of these monsters."

"I think it's the best time to joke, a lot of bad shit is going to go down, and if I can make one person smile or even laugh during all of that, cool. Even if that's only me." Nick said.

"It was a little funny," Mina smiled.

"That's right!" Nick said as the door to the main part of the station buzzed and opened. Stevenson walked out.

"Oh look, the invisible woman has appeared," Stevenson said.

"What?" Mina asked.

"Oh right, he kept asking where you were last night and I kept telling him you were helping in the nurses office or wherever," Nick said.

"I know you left the school before I got there, Mina," Stevenson said. "I don't know where you were, but you certainly weren't there when I was questioning everyone else."

"Well, if you have something you want to ask, I'm sitting here right now," Mina said.

"Come outside," Stevenson walked out the front door.

Nick and Mina stood up and followed him. Stevenson headed around the back of the building toward the river. There was a small dock back behind the police station.

Leaning on the railing of the dock, looking out over the water, Stevenson said, "I need you guys to level with me. Some weird crap has been going on and I know the two of you know something about it."

"We're just some dumb kids. You really think we know something the cops don't know?" Nick laughed.

"Yes, I do," Stevenson turned toward Nick. "I'm not much older than you, and the other officers would rather try and force logical explanations on everything, or brush it under the rug, but there's more going on than anyone wants to talk about. And you two are almost always there or involved peripherally," Stevenson said.

"How do you spell peripherally?" Nick asked.

"Stop being a wise ass," Stevenson said.

"She just said the same thing to me and I told her no to that request and I like her," Nick said. "So bite me."

"Stop it, both of you," Mina said. "Paul, you're right. This is not a normal town. Nick and I are not normal teenagers. But we can't tell you more than that. You have to figure it out yourself."

"Why did you come down here today?" Stevenson asked.

"To ask you about Matty Mauro," Mina said.

"What about him?" Stevenson asked and looked out over the water again.

"Is it true that he had bled out?" Mina asked.

"In a way. We didn't find any blood at the scene though," Stevenson said. "Like those other bodies we found in the spring. The supposed bear attacks."

"Hank Kelsey tracked that animal down," Nick said. "The police confirmed that it was the animal that killed those kids."

"My superiors said it was the animal because Kelsey brought them the most logical conclusion to the case," Stevenson turned to Nick again.

"What do you think happened then?" Mina asked.

"I'm not saying that out loud for fear that I will sound like a psycho even to myself," Stevenson looked Mina in the eye.

"They were all drained of blood. With none of it pooled around them, looking as though they were attacked by an animal, but not eaten as though they were prey," Nick said.

"You're right there, Paul, but not everyone wants to accept it," Mina said. "But we do. We know very well that these things exist, that at a lot of things exist. It doesn't matter how, it only matters that we are trying to stop them from hurting anyone else."

"How?" Stevenson said.

"Hunting them," Nick said.

"How do you hunt monsters like that?" Stevenson asked.

"Carefully," Mina smiled. "And thoroughly. The more we know, the better chance we have."

"What else do you want to know then?" Stevenson looked out over the water again.

"Just one last thing. Was anyone found alive with him? Or is anyone else missing?" Nick asked.

"No one was with him, and no one else has been reported missing. The last person to see him alive was Craig Delecke. He dropped Matty off at home after the incident last night at the dance." Stevenson said. "As far as we can tell he died alone."

"You've talked with Delecke?" Nick asked.

"I did, he was the first lead we had," Stevenson said.

Nick and Mina looked at each other.

"Why?" Stevenson asked.

"These monsters tend to leave eyes and ears behind. And those eyes and ears blend in almost perfectly," Mina said.

"I can have Delecke brought in if that would help," Stevenson said.

"No, we'll pay him a visit," Nick said. "But I suspect that this particular mosquito is planning on coming back very soon and didn't bother leaving a henchman behind."

*****

There was no answer at Craig Delecke's house when Mina banged on the door so she and Nick headed over to Jackie Schoen's.

The couple was sitting on the front porch, drinking out of red plastic cups.

"What's up Stanton? You hear that you and I have something in common now?" Craig mumbled. He was slumped back in one of the lounge chairs. His eyes were red and puffy.

"Don't mind him, he jumped right into his stash the minute the cops left after telling him what happened to Matty," Jackie said. She forced a smile but her eyes were just as red and puffy as Craig's. "Sit down for a minute and take a load off."

"Matty was a great guy," Nick said as he sat down with Mina on the two seater swing.

"He will be missed very much," Mina said.

"We just wanted to stop by and see if you need anything?" Nick said. "Even if it's just to talk."

"We should call Filomena over here and the three of us can talk about our best friends getting mauled by bears," Craig held his cup up. "Sounds grand."

"Craig, that's really not nice," Jackie said. "Their offer is very kind."

Looking down at his chest, tears started pouring from Craig's eyes. "Sorry."

"Not really much to do right now, I'll start diluting his drinks and keep him mellow," Jackie said. "But if I need anything you're the first two I'm gonna call."

"Please do, if you need anything at all," Nick said. "Even if you just need someone to punch in the face, Mina can take a punch like no one I've ever seen."

Mina shot an evil look at Nick, but Craig and Jackie both chuckled. Snot shot out of Craig's nose, and he wiped it off on his sleeve.

"Wow," Jackie said. "And I'm sure he's not even joking."

"Not even a little bit I'm afraid," Mina smiled.

"Thanks for stopping by," Craig said. "But I don't really wanna talk anymore."

"Understood," Nick said and stood up with Mina.

"Call me later," Mina smiled at Jackie.

Nick and Mina were on the last step when Craig yelled down, "One question, Stanton. Do you really think they were all killed by a bear?"

From the walkway, Nick turned and said, "No, Craig, I don't." Then he turned and headed over to the scooter. He and Mina put on their helmets, hopped on and took off down the road.

*****

After talking with Craig and Jackie, Nick and Mina grabbed his bomber jacket and headed back to Hank's house.

"Anything?" Hank asked when they found him. Ben and Julie sat around the fire pit in the backyard.

"Paul Stevenson is wiser than we gave him credit for," Mina sat down next to the fire.

"He knows there's more to the last round of dead bodies and to this one than just animal attacks," Nick plopped down next to Mina and leaned against a log that served as a bench most nights.

"So the police are going to blame this on another animal," Hank said. "I'm not hunting down another bear to make this all look legit this time."

"Where's Penny?" Mina asked.

"Running in the woods with Bruce," Ben said.

"And Charles?" Nick asked.

"I was getting hot dogs," Charles said as he walked out into the yard from the house.

"I miss hot dogs," Julie said as she floated near Hank. "I wonder if you can bring them into the Ethereal Plane, or whatever it's called that you go into in the maps, Nick."

"We'll have to try that one of these days," Nick replied.

Mina took a pack out of Charles's hands. She looked around the fire pit for a stick to cook with but didn't see any, so in the blink of an eye she raced off to the tree line, grabbed a thin fallen branch and jumped back to her seat near the fire.

"Thanks," Ben said as Charles handed him the other three packages of hotdogs.

"I need to go call Montreal. Mind if I use your phone, Hank?" Charles said.

"Tell that Jinn to kiss my ass," Hank said. "And you could have gotten a few sticks for the rest of us, Mina."

"Uggggghhhh," Mina jumped up again and shot off to the trees.

"Will do," Charles said.

"I'm gonna grab something to drink," Nick stood up. "Anyone need anything?"

"No," Hank said.

"No thank you, Nick," Ben pointed with the beer in his hand to six pack sitting between he and Hank. "We're good."

Following Charles inside, Nick opened the fridge and pulled out a pitcher of iced tea.

"So, Charles, wanna check in with your boss in person?" Nick asked as Charles picked up the phone.

"Not really," Charles said. "But I suspect that you would like to."

"You would suspect right," Nick smiled. "Remember that little problem of yours I want to help you with?"

"You figured it out?" Charles asked softly putting down the phone.

"I did, but I need to see that fart monster in person," Nick said. "Care to take a quick trip up to Montreal?"

"Do I have to go with you?" Charles asked.

"I need a witness," Nick said.

"A witness for what?" Charles asked.

"You can ask me a thousand questions that I will answer vaguely, or we can go together and you can see and hear exactly what I'm gonna do and we can be back here in a half hour roasting weenies by the fire with some of our favorite people as we wait for the biggest battle of at least my life to start."

"Should we let them know we're going?" Charles asked.

"Negative. They will just bog us down with questions," Nick said.

"You don't like questions do you?" Charles said.

Nick just smiled and shook his head. He pulled his pen out of one pocket, walked into the living room and pulled the Atlas off of the book shelf.

Charles followed him.

"Having you come with me helps too because you know where all the ghosts are near your bar," Nick said.

"Ah yes, there's a particularly annoying fellow who haunts the building across from the club," Charles said.

"Perfect," Nick placed the tip of the pen on the area of Montreal where the Jinn's bar was, and closed his eyes. "Put your hand on my shoulder and close your eyes."

*****

"Where the hell did the two of you go?" Mina yelled as Nick and Charles tumbled across the grass near the fire.

"I totally touched that hot dog!" Julie squealed. "I gotta try biting it next time!"

"That was very weird," Ben said.

Rolling onto his back, the front of Nick's shirt was covered in ketchup and mustard. A hot dog was smooshed into the grass where he had landed.

"The great white north," Nick said.

"Seriously, you need to stop listening to those stupid Bob and Doug McKenzie tapes," Hank said. "How much more trouble have you piled on the crap pile now?"

"First, both of their albums are hilarious," Nick said as he pushed himself to his feet. "And B, I only got myself into trouble if we lose."

"What did you do?" Mina stood up, her eyes narrowed at Nick and her fists on her hips.

"I tricked a very powerful Jinn into showing up to our little battlefield to make us look as though we have more numbers than we do," Nick said.

"What?" Julie said.

"I didn't even think of that as you were talking with him,"

Charles said.

"Did you make another bet with that crap phantom?" Hank said.

"When did you make a bet with that demon?" Bruce said as he walked up to the fire from the forest.

"When Hank spent a night in the cage at the Jinn's bar," Nick said. "I bet that Hank would win, and since I knew he would it was a no brainer."

"Why do I have the feeling this is not a no brainer?" Ben said.

"Because things are a lot more complicated than Hank in a cage fighting against a blood sucker. And it doesn't matter how many times you ask me, you'll have to wait until tomorrow to find out what the bet is. You only find out if we win. If we lose we're dead so it won't matter."

"I'm not even remotely happy with you right now," Mina walked into the house.

"Smooth," Hank said. "Real smooth."

"I would go after her, Nick, and maybe try and work some of the kinks out of this little relationship of yours," Ben said.

"Fine," Nick said as he stood up. He slouched dramatically and made a pouty face as he walked into the house.

Inside, Nick looked around for Mina but she wasn't in kitchen or the living room. The bathroom was empty too. He headed up stairs and found her sitting on the end of the bed in the guest room, her head in her hands.

Nick sat down next to her.

Mina lifted her head up and her hands were smeared with tears and mascara, and so was her face.

"Um, just so you know, I am doing my best not to laugh cause your makeup is all over the place," Nick said.

"Why do you have to keep making jokes when everything is so heavy and complicated?" Mina said and wiped as much of the makeup from around her eyes as she could with her shirt sleeve.

"It's my thing," Nick said.

"Will you please tell me your whole plan? I can't do this knowing so little. And every time you go off and do something without telling me drives makes me more nuts. How am I supposed to protect you if I don't know where you are and I'm in the dark about so much of this?"

Putting his arm around her, Nick said, "If things go to shit, I'm going to be the first to die. You understand that right?"

"What?" Mina whispered and looked into his eyes.

"I am the only one who will be there who is not super strong, or super fast, or magically immortal," Nick smiled. "And I will die first. I will be closest to Stone, most likely across from him at a picnic table, with you fighting with Valen Tine in the moonlight on the beach. And if you don't do your part perfectly, then he will be able to grab me and tear me in half."

"Now I'm even more against this plan," Mina wiped at her eyes again.

"But it won't work unless I'm sitting with him, being the physically weakest. We need him to feel as confident as possible, as though he is better than all of us at everything. Then we take away some of the pillars holding up his huge ego. First, I tell him I infiltrated his home. Then I show him we took the most important thing from him, his son. Then we show him that his closest ally has been turned against him, as he has done to my family," Nick said.

"That last part sounds like you're out for revenge or something," Mina said.

"I am," Nick said. "But it's also our job to stop him from hurting anyone else."

"I still don't understand what keeping the plan a secret and you being the first to die if this goes to hell has to do with one another?" Mina said.

"If you don't know the backup plan, then he can't torture it out of you, or any of the others," Nick said. "Not that I don't have complete confidence that you will destroy him if he kills me."

"You also have a backup plan?" Mina said.

"A half assed backup plan, but yes," Nick said.

"And you're not going to let me in on that either?" Mina said.

"Nope," Nick said.

"I don't know what I would do if you died, Nick," Mina said.

"Whether it's tonight or in eighty years, you and I will both die Mina," Nick said. "None of us get out of this life alive."

"That doesn't help, Nicholas," Mina said. "Game Six is on now isn't it?"

"Started a few minutes ago, yes," Nick said.

"Wanna grab some snacks and hunker down here for the night?" Mina said.

"Yes, yes I do," Nick smiled, then kissed Mina on the forehead.

Nick and Mina spent the rest of the night on the couch watching the Mets force a game seven even after being behind the entire game against the Red Sox. The game was as serious and nerve wracking as it gets, except when some guy dropped in using a parachute to Shea Stadium with a sign reading 'Let's Go Mets.' That did little to help Nick relax the entire four hours of game play, but when Knight leapt on the plate for the winning run, Nick's blood pressure finally dropped and he slept like a baby that night.

*****

Mina hadn't closed her eyes the entire night. But her arm fell asleep not long after Nick passed out leaning on her. Hank, Ben and Bruce patrolled the yard in pairs while one of them got some shut eye.

But it was a quiet night.

When the sun came up, Nick stood up and stumbled to the bathroom.

"Did you get any rest?" Ben asked Mina as he came down the stairs.

"Nope," Mina stood and stretched.

"Are you hungry?" Ben asked as he walked into the kitchen.

"Is that a serious question?" Mina followed Ben into the kitchen.

The door opened and Hank walked in carrying a basket full of eggs.

"If only you were wearing a pink apron with flowers all over it," Mina said as she grabbed the coffee pot. "I could die happy if I saw that just once."

"You'll die sad then," Hank set the basket down on the counter for Ben and headed back outside.

"Has he always been so serious?" Mina asked as Ben dropped some butter into a skillet and she filled the coffee filter with grounds.

"He used to be way worse," Ben said as he grabbed some peppers from the refrigerator. "The time he has spent with Nick has been good for him."

"How has it been good for him?" Mina dropped the filter into the coffee maker. "All they do is fight."

"Not exactly," Ben grabbed a knife and cutting board. "Hank never had any sons, and this time with Nick, teaching him, has given Hank a little bit of what he never got to have with a son of his own."

"But Hank had daughters right?" Mina hit the brew button on the coffee maker. "What about them? He certainly taught them something."

"Not the same, Mina," Ben said as he cut up the peppers. "And Hank was cursed before he could have any more children."

"You can't have kids after you get cursed?" Mina asked.

"We cannot, it is part of the curse," Ben said as he grabbed a bowl to crack the eggs into.

"Did you have any kids before you were cursed?" Mina said as she sat down at the table.

"I had three sons. My wife passed away from a fever when they were still young. That's when I met the witch who cursed me. I found some comfort with her, but then I discovered what she was. I had to think of my sons, and ended the relationship. She obviously did not take that very well." Ben whipped up the eggs in a bowl and mixed in the chopped up peppers.

"Whatever happened to your sons?" Mina asked.

"My brother raised them, as I could not trust myself around them," Ben said as he poured the egg mix into the skillet.

"Did you ever find out what they did with their lives?" Mina asked.

"I checked in every so often. They all married, had children and died old men," Ben said. "And yes, some of my descendants are still living."

"Have you ever thought about contacting them?" Mina asked.

"Of course," Ben said. "But what would I ever be able to say to a great, great, great, great grandson?"

"Gotcha," Mina said.

"But back to Hank," Ben flipped over the eggs. "He and Nick are a better influence on each other. Hank has had the chance to tap into more of his humanity than ever before, and Nick has gotten to learn some very small points to what it is to be a man, to make decisions."

"Oh," Mina said. "Wait, Penny is helping you tap into your humanity by giving you the chance to raise daughter."

"And here they keep saying that Nick is the smart one," Ben smiled.

"Who's saying I'm the smart one?" Nick walked into the room and sat down. "Cause I would sure as hell like to meet them. Any bacon floating around here?"

"No," Ben said pointing to the skillet with the wooden spatula he was using. "Just a pepper and egg omelet."

A police siren blared as a cop car came screaming down the long driveway. Nick, Mina and Ben all looked to each other.

"What the hell?" Mina said as she stood. Nick jumped to his feet and headed out the back door.

Tossing the skillet onto a cold burner, Ben followed Nick and Mina out the door.

Standing on the edge of his driveway, Hank watched as the cruiser screeched to a stop a few feet in front of him. Mina, Nick and Ben stopped in their tracks right next to him. Stevenson jumped out of the driver's side, wearing sweats and covered in blood.

The Living

Chapter 22
Scary Monsters

"Thank God you're here. There's no way I could have called into the station with what just happened?" Stephenson paced in front of his cruiser.

"What happened, Paul?" Mina asked.

"I shot a bunch of zombies," Stevenson stopped and looked directly at Nick.

"How many?" Hank asked.

"Five or six," Stevenson said. "I emptied my clip. I usually don't even run with my pistol, but I've been taking it everywhere recently."

"Were there more?" Nick asked.

"Yeah… yeah," Stevenson said. "That's why I came here. We can't just leave them there."

"Where?" Ben asked as he stepped to Officer Stevenson's side. "It's okay, we all know about these things."

Stevenson looked to Mina, who nodded, then he said, "Chatfield Hollow."

"Was there anyone else around?" Nick asked.

"I don't think so, there weren't any other cars in the parking lot when I tore out of there," Stevenson said.

"I'll drive," Hank said as he walked to the cruiser and got in. Stevenson hesitated, but followed as everyone else got in the car. Ben took shotgun.

"Does anyone know where Bruce is?" Nick asked as Hank sped down his driveway to the road.

"Who's Bruce?" Stevenson asked as the car hit the road and headed towards Chatfield Hollow.

"No," Ben said.

Shaking his head, Hank said, "He was still in the woods when

I started my chores this morning."

No one said anything else on the short drive. Hank parked in the lot. Ben and Hank got out, but Nick, Mina and Stevenson were trapped in the back. Officer Stevenson cleared his throat and pointed at the door. Hank shook his head and opened the door.

"There are more here," Ben said as he sniffed the air.

"How can you tell?" Stevenson said as he opened the truck of the cruiser. His uniform was back there and he grabbed his belt that held an extra clip for his pistol.

"We just can," Hank said and started walking toward lake. "This way."

"Do you have a billy club in there?" Nick asked.

"Here," Stevenson grabbed his club and handed it to Nick.

"Thanks," Nick said then jogged ahead to catch up with Hank.

They walked down the access road in silence, Nick and Hank up front, Mina and Stevenson in the middle and Ben bringing up the rear. Stevenson held his pistol in his hands in front of him, pointed towards the ground.

Reaching to the back of her belt, Mina wrapped her fingers around the handle of her sword. She looked at Stevenson and said, "Don't freak out, okay Paul?"

"Little too late for that," Stevenson said.

Smiling and shaking her head, Mina pulled the sword out and as she did it grew to its full size in her hand.

"That's magical, isn't it?" Stevenson asked.

"Yeah, pretty much," Mina said.

"These, these things I shot, are they really zombies?" Stevenson asked.

"Did they look like zombies?" Mina asked.

"Yeah, pretty much," Stevenson said.

"Then probably," Mina said looking over at the officer. Over his shoulder she saw something move out of the brush and head directly for him. "Make that, definitely."

Moving faster than Stevenson could comprehend, Mina circled around him and cut the zombie in half from head to foot. The two halves fell to the ground and turned to dust.

"I really hope that turning them to dust thing works on vampires now too," Mina said as she fell back into step with everyone else.

"What the hell just happened?" Stevenson asked.

"I cut a zombie in half with my sword and it turned to dust," Mina said.

A few steps ahead, Hank and Nick stopped, staring down at the beach.

"How many did you say you shot?" Nick asked.

"Five or six," Stevenson said as he stopped next to Nick.

Looking down at the beach, there were at least twenty zombies shuffling toward them.

"Aim for the head," Hank said as he started down toward the water. Nick followed with the Billy club up in front of him, ready.

Mina and Ben leapt into the air and came down beside Hank and Nick. They all opened up on the walking dead - Mina cutting them down, Nick crushing their skulls and Hank and Ben just tearing them to shreds.

Shrugging, Stevenson, raised his weapon, "When in Rome," and provided cover fire for his comrades. Stevenson knew instinctively that he needed to focus his attention on Nick and dropped one zombie after another when they got too close to Nick.

It all only lasted about a minute. Every one that Mina cut through was dust in the wind, so she took a moment to chop the fallen zombies at least once to clean up the evidence.

"When did that little trick manifest itself?" Hank asked as Mina stabbed her sword down through the skull of a corpse.

"The other night at the Homecoming Dance," Mina pulled her sword out easily from the ground.

"I always wondered how your kind cleaned up after themselves so quickly," Ben said.

"I wish it started happening earlier," Mina brought her sword down on the last of the dead. "Had to make a hobo fire in an alley in New York last summer after running into a mosquito. Wasn't the best smell I've ever encountered."

"Mosquito?" Stevenson asked as he joined the group on the

beach.

"Vampire," Nick said. "Do you guys smell any more rotting crash test dummies?"

Hank, Ben and Mina all sniffed the air.

"No, but I smell something else that will be a problem," Mina said.

"Is that lavender?" Stevenson asked then took another deep breath through his nose.

"It is," Nick said.

"Every story says that vampires can't go out in the sun," Stevenson said.

"They're young," Hank said.

"New blood suckers hide in plain sight, as their former selves, until they are strong enough to live only at night," Ben scanned the tree line. "It's a survival mechanism. It's not easy for a vampire to make another, so the new ones tend to feed only on animals their first few months, unnoticed by people. Helps hone their hunting and hiding skills. When they start feeding mostly on people, they change over to the familiar sun hating blood sucker."

"So, where are they?" Stevenson asked.

"Up there," Mina nodded to the picnic area and the hill beyond it.

"Are we going to go after them?" Stevenson asked.

"Mina and I are. Ben will catch any that get by us so they can't get to the two of you." Hank pointed at Nick and Stevenson.

"Mina, one or more of them up there might be people you know," Hank said.

Scowling, Mina said, "Understood."

"So you're just gonna kill whoever it is?" Stevenson asked.

"Yes," Hank said, and started toward the woods. Mina marched in step with him to the hill.

As they passed the picnic tables, Mina got flashes in her head of watching Halley's Comet and eating hummus with Nick, of their almost first kiss and first clumsy head knock. And she remembered the first time she saw Hank change.

With his clothes shredding, Hank morphed into his enormous, tusked werepig form.

Shaking her head, Mina said, "We don't have any extra pants for you to wear."

Hank looked over at her and shrugged.

The first bloodsucker stepped out from behind a tree.

"Mr. Dower?" Mina whispered.

Her former science teacher stood before them. His face was not the gentle, knowledgeable face she learned from, the one that had introduced her to Nick. It was wild, his teeth were jagged and shark-like, and his eyes were black, the pupils fully dilated and none of the color remained.

"Hello, Ms. Medellin," Mr. Dower hissed.

"Why do you all hiss like that? Does the change fork your tongue or something?" Mina asked.

Hank moved first but the two vampires that were hiding to either side of Mr. Dower moved faster. They got ahold of each of Hank's hands and pulled.

Dropping from the trees, two more mosquitos crashed into Mina, a man and a woman she had never seen, and knocked her backwards. She was not letting them walk away. She cut them down and turned her attention back to Mr. Dower, but he wasn't standing there any longer.

"Damn it!" Mina said as she looked to Hank.

Hank scowled, then yanked his arms back toward himself as hard as he could. The two vampires who had surprised him were no match when all his faculties were firing. The mosquitoes' heads came slamming together so hard that they burst, sending blood and skull fragments flying in every direction.

Dropping the two carcasses, Hank motioned with his head for them to move up the hill. He and Mina moved quickly, and they could hear things moving in the brush.

"I've only read about this pack hunting trick," Mina said. "Where did all these young ones come from anyway?"

Hank didn't say anything, but he pointed up with his snout. Mina nodded, then he launched himself straight up into the branches above. The sound of wood snapping and leaves rustling mixed with the squealing of a vampire as Hank got ahold of it. Hank scuffled with the mosquito in the canopy while Mina listened, waiting.

Then Hank dropped from the branches above, holding the mosquito out in front of him. The vampire clawed at Hank's hands, face and neck. Mina was ready and she brought her sword up through the blood sucker's neck, sending the head tumbling off down the hill.

"Interesting," Stevenson said as the vampire's head rolled past and hit the water. It floated for a few seconds letting Nick, Ben and the officer get a good look at the face before it crumbled to dust.

"That was Fern Crosby," Stevenson said as the ash spread over the surface of the water and rained slowly through the water and to the lake bed below.

The body crumbled to ash in Hank's hands. He clutched the sweatshirt with both of his fists, watching as the pants fell to the leaf covered ground at his feet.

Putting her hand on Hank's shoulder, Mina said, "We had no choice. She's better off."

Grunting, Hank threw the sweatshirt to the ground. His eyes narrowed, and his lips curled back exposing more of his tusks.

"Understood," Mina nodded.

Then, to their left, they heard a cackling followed by extremely fast steps across the dry forest floor.

Hank took off and raced after the sound. Mina followed, but stayed a few steps behind. They came down the hill to see Mr. Dower race toward Nick, Stevenson and Ben. The pack had their backs towards the water.

Hank was almost within reach of Mr. Dower when the sand opened beneath his feet. Mr. Dower was far enough ahead not to lose his footing. Hank tumbled and rolled to a stop, sliding through the sand on a knee. He looked up to see a man-sized scorpion bearing down on him. Growling, Hank focused his attention on the arthropod standing between him and his friends.

Killing the distance between her and Mr. Dower in a second, Mina brought her sword up in both hands. Ben stood ready to grab the mosquito.

Then the sound of rushing water filled the beach. Mr. Dower

cackled, even louder than before, as tentacles reached from the water to pick up Nick, Stevenson and Ben.

"What the hell?" Nick struggled against a tentacle.

"This can't really be happening," Stevenson groaned as the tentacle squeezed him tighter and tighter.

"You have got to be kidding me!" Mina yelled.

Mr. Dower ran straight into the water and disappeared below the surface.

"I've got this Mina, go get the blood sucker," Ben yelled, already changing. His free arm was an enormous red claw that snapped at the tentacle holding him in the air. His claw cut through the meaty wereoctopus's arm. A blood curdling scream reverberated through the water. Nick and Stevenson dropped to the beach gasping for air.

In the chaos of the giant flopping tentacle on the beach - Ben changing into his giant lobster form and Hank wrestling a man sized scorpion - Mina dove into the water.

The water was murky, and Mina could only see a few inches in front of her face. She tried to listen, but the commotion on the beach at the water's edge was making it nearly impossible for her to hear anything under water. Mr. Dower couldn't have gotten very far and he would be suffering from the same distortion of his senses. But Mina had some experience in the water, and she had learned to feel the movements around her. She could feel Mr. Dower swimming toward the beach on the other side of the lake.

Under the water, Mina smiled to herself as she took off like a torpedo. She was smiling because she knew she was faster than the blood sucker. She closed the gap quickly, but the mosquito had broken the surface of the water and was about to hit the sand ahead of her. Mina shot down to the lake bottom and pushed off, launching herself out of the water and over the last twenty feet. She came down on the back of the vampire, slamming it into the sand.

With a quick glance over her shoulder to the beach on the other side of the lake, Mina smiled to see Hank and Ben standing over the defeated bodies of their opponents.

"Why are you smiling, Ms. Medellin? You may have won this little skirmish, but you won't survive the next battle," Mr. Dower hissed.

Mina pulled out her sword and brought it down on the vampire's neck. "No one can see the future."

The head separated a few inches from the body and Mina stood up. She pulled her sword from the sand, and the head and body disintegrated to leave nothing but the clothes of her teacher behind.

The sword shrank down and Mina easily slid it into the sheath on her belt. She took a deep breath, and dove back into the water. A few seconds later she walked out of the bloody water onto the beach.

"Was that Mr. Dower?" Nick asked.

"Was," Mina said and hugged him.

"The science teacher?" Officer Stevenson asked.

"Yup," Mina said still hiding onto Nick. "Are they both dead?"

"The wereock is. That's his blood you're covered with from the water," Hank said.

Pulling away from Nick, Mina took his hand and started toward the parking lot. "Grab the giant sand lobster and bring him with us, I have a few questions for him."

"You want to bring him with us?" Stevenson asked as Hank picked up the bloody naked man from the ground and tossed him over his shoulder. "And we're gonna drive around with three naked guys in a police cruiser?"

Hank looked over at the officer and shook his head.

"Unless you have three pairs of pants in the back of your cruiser, I guess so," Ben laughed.

"Actually, Ben and I will cut through the woods with him," Hank smacked the unconscious, bloody naked man on the rear. "And you can drive the kids home. I suggest you go home, shower and sign in for your shift today until we call you."

"Seriously?" Stevenson said as they walked.

"Please no more questions or blathering," Nick said. "Just try and process what you saw. I need to think."

"See ya at the house," Ben said as he and Hank took off through the woods.

No one spoke again until they were parked in Hank's driveway.

"Tell the dispatcher that if Hank Kelsey calls for you to put him through over the CB," Nick said.

"And then what?" Stevenson asked. "I just show up and shoot a few more zombies or arrest a leprechaun or something?"

"I wouldn't tangle with Conan, he fights really dirty," Mina said as she opened the passenger side door.

"What?" Stevenson said.

"A buddy of ours is a leprechaun named Conan," Nick said. "But never mind that. If we call, bring a bigger gun."

"See ya later, Paul," Mina said as she got out of the car. She opened the door for Nick and he got out.

As Nick was closing the door, Stevenson yelled, "Wait, what are you gonna do with that other guy?"

"Best you don't know," Nick closed the door and walked toward the barn.

Half smiling, Mina turned and followed Nick.

Stevenson sat for a moment, took a deep breath and then headed back down the long driveway.

Inside the barn, Hank had the man wrapped in a thick chain.

"Good idea," Mina said when she caught sight of the man lying on hay, turning red from the blood seeping from his wounds.

"Can you wake him up?" Nick said.

"Hopefully this works," Ben said as he walked into the barn from the side door holding something up in his left hand. "Smelling salts."

Ben held a pair of sweat pants in his other hand and tossed them to Hank.

"Prudes," Hank snatched the sweats out of the air and jumped into them.

"It's the little things that make me like you more than Hank, Ben," Nick smiled as he pointed at Ben's shorts.

Ben snapped open the little packet under the chained man's nose.

Jerking awake, the man screamed.

"No one can hear you, so you might as well shut it," Hank said.

Through clenched teeth the man asked, "Why haven't you killed me?"

"We still might," Mina said. "But that's only two of your three options."

"Wait, we're giving him three options?" Nick asked.

"Everyone deserves a second chance, right?" Mina said.

"What if he already has had a second chance?" Ben asked.

"He hasn't had a second chance with us," Mina looked down at the man's face. "Unless one of you guys have run across him before?"

Hank shook his head and leaned against the barn wall crossing his arms.

"Never seen him before," Ben said.

"That's good news for you," Nick knelt down next to the chained man. "What's your name?"

"What do you want from me?" the chained man said.

"I would like to know your name, your favorite color and what your hobbies are," Nick said.

"Are you putting an ad in the personals for me?" The chained man asked.

"I'm trying to save your life," Nick said.

Mina pulled out her sword and it grew to its full size.

"Is that supposed to scare me?" the chained man said.

"I'm hoping you're at least a little impressed by its size," Mina said. "But it would be an added bonus if you were a bit scared too."

"He'll do worse to me if you let me live," the chained man said. "So you might as well shove that pig sticker through my heart and get it over with."

Hank narrowed his eyes at the chained man, but didn't say anything.

"When you say he, you're referring to whom?" Nick asked.

"My master, you moron!" the chained man said.

"Is your master by chance a mosquito?" Nick asked.

"He'll drain you dry for calling him that," the chained man said.

"So, yes," Nick said. He looked at Mina, then back to the

chained man. "Were you sent here to find us and kill us?"

"I was told to raise the dead and gather my master's children," the chained man said. "Then cause some noise."

"So you didn't even know what you were going to be facing here?" Nick asked. "And what is your name?"

"Donald and I do as I am commanded. I have no choice and no reason to question." He said.

"Are you a slave?" Mina asked.

"We all answer to someone," Donald growled.

"Do you teach philosophy at night school in your free time? Cause if not, you should," Nick said and stood up. "How long will it take for him to bleed out?"

"About an hour," Hank guessed.

"That's not really a fun way to die, right?" Nick asked.

"No, it's not," Ben said.

"Well, it's your barn, so dealer's choice, Hank," Nick said and started for the barn door.

Screaming, "Wait!" the chained man sobbed.

"Are you interested in editing those lines about long walks on the beach and slow dancing the night away in your personal ad in the Pennysaver?" Nick turned back toward the chained man.

"My name is Donald," the chained man said. "Donald With-ington. I was sent here by a vampire named Jacob. She killed his maker."

"Oh," Mina said. "Which one was his maker?"

"Enoch," Donald said.

Hank snapped to attention, and growled.

"Seems you are connected to the death of his best friend, Donny," Nick pointed at Hank.

"What?" Donald asked.

"When I killed Enoch, our friend Gert sacrificed herself so that I could cut him down," Mina said.

"Where is your master?" Nick asked. "Tell us and I'll get you to a doctor."

"I can't tell you where he is," Donald said.

"You know that if we kill him, you stop being a slave right?"

Mina pointed out.

"I am well aware of that, but I do not know where he went to sleep," Donald said. "So you might as well let me die."

"Damn it," Nick said. "Unchain him. Might as well get him fixed up. Not like he's going to be changing into a sand lobster as hurt as he is. Plus it will look more legit for his blood sucking master to see him at their rendezvous point up on the ridge at Chatfield Hollow later - make it easier for us to catch the mosquito."

"I already called in some help, actually," Ben smiled.

"Wait! How did you know that?" Donald asked.

"I'm psychic," Nick said looking down at the chained man.

The side door of the barn opened and Conan walked in. "Hello."

"Ahoy, Conan," Mina said. "Good to see you. What brings you by right at this particular moment?"

"Leprechauns are not only lucky, but exceptionally magical creatures," Hank said.

"Including amazing healing abilities, when paid properly," Conan said.

"I thought your kind weren't going to help us in this little battle," Nick smiled down at his small friend.

"I lied and I was paid very well for my help," Conan said.

"I paid you a ton of money to help me with that chest of gold," Nick said. "Why did you tell me no when I asked you to stand against Stone with us?"

"You didn't offer me what I wanted," Conan walked over to Donald and put his hand on the chained man's forehead. Conan closed his eyes and a white light appeared to glow under his hand.

"A four leaf clover," Nick shook his head. "Takes me a minute to put two and two together sometimes."

Conan pulled his hand away from the chained man's head, and Donald's head fell back to the hay covered ground, unconscious.

"What?" Mina asked.

"This isn't the time for all of this," Ben said pointing down at Donald. "Let's get this squared away then you can explain everything to her, Nick."

"Right," Nick looked down at the chained man.

"He is healed enough so that he will live until the night, as long as no one stabs him," Conan looked at Mina.

"Don't get me wrong, I really want to shank him, but I can control my urges," Mina smiled at everyone.

"He should be out for a few hours, maybe more after I put that much energy through him," Conan said.

"Does anyone else feel like we're playing the most ridiculous game of Dungeons & Dragons?" Nick asked. "Especially since we now have a Dwarf/Elf/Leprechaun Mage?"

"I'm not a dwarf," Conan said as he walked out of the barn.

"I'll stay here for now with our guest," Ben said. "You guys go get cleaned up."

"You sure?" Mina asked.

"You may have the next shift," Ben smiled. "Go figure out a plan to catch this, how did you put it Nick, 'Sand Lobster's' master."

"No offense, Ben," Nick said. "Werescorpion is just way too big of a mouthful."

"None taken," Ben said. "It's a very apt description. Go get cleaned up and get some food."

Outside of the barn, they found Conan talking with Bruce.

"Seems I missed an interesting morning," Bruce said as Nick, Mina and Hank walked out of the barn door.

*****

For the next hour, Nick filled Conan in on how he was going to invite Frank Stone to come to Kelsey Town and meet with him. Nick was confident that the Monster wouldn't turn down this opportunity to, at the very least, hear what Nick had to say, or to kill them all and take what he wanted. But Nick had two aces up his sleeve. First, they were going to trick Stone into thinking that they had kidnapped his son. Second, they had turned someone very close to Stone to their side.

"So, you think by making him this angry he will lose control of his faculties and be vulnerable?" Conan asked.

"Yup," Nick said.

"That's a big gamble," Conan said. "I like it."

"You would," Mina said.

"But you're sure that Valen Tine is going to help you?" Conan asked.

"No doubt," Nick said.

Pointing at herself, Mina said, "I have doubts."

"I believe her as well," Bruce said.

"Why?" Conan asked.

"I didn't know the whole story of what was done to her when I met her before her tournament when the Comet West came in '76," Bruce said. "I stumbled on some of the truth shortly after she won. But I didn't know the whole truth until Mina's tournament. That tournament was Stone's coming out party, in a way. He had kept himself in the shadows, dealing only with the most powerful creatures on the planet in secret. And there were only whispers about what he planned on doing. I believe now, being a mother, Valen understands she was on the wrong side of this plan."

"Exactly," Nick said.

"Either way, we will do everything we can to stop Stone from completing his plans for world domination," Mina said.

"Now we sound like we are in the most awesome James Bond movie ever made," Nick smiled.

"Just to be clear, you expect this Frank Stone to come here just because you ask? You don't see him turning down your offer and coming whenever he wishes with an army of supernatural creatures to take what he wants?" Conan asked.

"That is a fear, but the note I gave to Tine explains that his only option on getting the power we possess is to sell us on his vision of the future," Nick said. "And I am confident that he learned from his previous attempt at taking the power Mina and I possess."

"And he won't suspect that Tine is conspiring against him? Especially if she hands him a letter from you?" Conan asked.

"She is going to leave it on his desk for him to find when he returns tomorrow morning," Nick said. "He is too full of himself to think that anyone would turn against him, especially the person closest to him."

"We were a little worried that this mosquito, Jacob, had run off and told him where I was," Mina said. "But that would only have put the plan into motion sooner."

"Well, I have a few things I need to do," Conan stood up. "I will meet you at Chatfield Hollow around sunset."

"We'll see you there," Nick said as the leprechaun walked out the front door.

"So, what do you want to do with this Jacob when we confront him?" Bruce asked.

"Cut his head off," Nick said.

*****

Everyone was just hanging out watching television in Hank's living room. The weather looked spotty and it was dark and gloomy even for a New England Autumn afternoon. There was a rain delay for the seventh game of the World Series already and it wasn't looking good for the game to be played as scheduled.

"At least I won't miss it if it's raining," Nick said. "But then again I might miss on account of possibly being dead."

"Stop joking about that!" Mina smacked his shoulder.

Nick winced and rubbed where she hit him. "You play too rough when you're worried."

Mina scowled.

"Will you two stop with the incessant flirting," Hank said from his recliner.

"No," Nick said.

The phone rang in the kitchen, and Mina jumped up and sped to answer it on the second ring, "Hello? Yeah, I'll grab him. Nick, it's Filomena."

"Why is he calling me here?" Nick asked as he got up and headed to the kitchen.

"Ask him," Mina handed Nick the phone.

"What's going on man?" Nick asked.

"Where the hell have you been?" Filomena asked.

"Around," Nick said.

"No, seriously, have you heard about Mauro?" Filomena asked.

"Yeah, pretty sad," Nick said. "I always liked him. Wish I had hung out with him more."

"Have you heard what people are saying?" Filomena asked.

"No, what are people saying?" Nick asked.

"That all these deaths, including Adam's, were done by a serial killer dressed up like an animal, not an actual bear," Filomena said.

"That's insane," Nick said. "I know for a fact that that is bull crap."

"Well," Filomena said. "What if you just thought it was a bear when you were attacked? How well do you really remember that night? And what about the fact that your buddy Hank supposedly took down the probable man-killer and yet now we have another dead teenager on our hands? It's all a bit coincidental when you factor in that all the victims have been teenagers."

"Teenagers tend to be more reckless and stupid," Nick said. "Easy targets for a hungry or rabid animal."

"Easy targets for a serial killer," Filomena said.

"I can't really argue with you there," Nick said.

"Anyway, putting aside all the conspiracy theories, are you going to go to the vigil up at Chatfield at sunset?" Filomena asked.

"I believe so," Nick said quickly. "I'll see you there, and we can discuss some of these theories more."

"Or just drink our asses off," Filomena said.

"Or that," Nick laughed. "See ya later."

"Peace out," Filomena said and hung up the phone.

Nick walked back into the living room, "It seems we're going to a vigil for Matty Mauro this evening."

"Don't we have something else to do this evening?" Hank said.

"I think we can squeeze in both since they're in the same place," Nick said.

"No way!" Mina said.

*****

There were well over one hundred students, teachers and parents holding candles on the beach at Chatfield Hollow. About half of the crowd also carried or were leaning on umbrellas in case the clouds over head opened up again.

"Let's hope the mosquito isn't really, really hungry when it gets here," Mina said.

"It would be better if you just kill it really, really fast," Nick said. "Luckily it will be harder for it to pick us out with all these people here."

"That's comforting," Mina said. "Hank, Ben and Bruce should be in place by now. You think this Donald character will start quacking to his master the moment he shows up?"

"Either way you'll be there," Nick smiled and pointed down near the water. "There's Holly and Paul. Let's say hi and then head up on the ridge."

"Hey guys," Holly forced a smile.

"Hey," Mina said.

"How is everything going out here?" Nick asked.

"Pretty easy going," Filomena said. "Everyone is pretty quiet."

"That is to be expected. Are Delecke or Jackie around?" Mina asked.

"Haven't seen either of them, I don't think this is something they are up for," Holly said.

Popping out of thin air, Julie said, "They're at Jackie's house, physically comforting each other."

"Oh Jesus," Nick grabbed his chest and bowed his head.

"You okay?" Holly asked.

"Yeah, yeah, I'm fine," Nick said.

"I think he might be in need of some comforting," Julie laughed.

Mina shot Julie a look of death.

"You two are party poopers," Julie said. "These are the only kind of social events I can crash anymore and not feel like a leper. But to answer the question in your eyes, Hank is ready."

"What are you two doing after this?" Filomena asked. "Might grab a movie over at Westbrook Video and hunker down at my house with some snacks, since game seven is postponed until tomorrow and all."

"I think that sounds like a great idea," Mina smiled.

"Really?" Nick raised an eyebrow.

"Yeah, I think it would be relaxing to sit down and watch a movie," Mina put her hand on Nicks face, "after such a trying week-end."

"You on the scooter?" Holly asked.

"We got a ride over with Hank," Mina said. "He, Penny and Ben are around here somewhere."

"Oh, I love Penny!" Holly squealed. "Where is she?"

"I think they are over near the picnic area," Nick said.

"Let's go say hi!" Holly grabbed Filomena's hand and started toward the picnic tables.

"You comin?" Filomena said over his shoulder.

"We're gonna say hi to a few more people," Mina said.

"Meet you at your house later," Nick said.

"Cool," Filomena said.

"How long do you think she'll look for Penny?" Nick said quietly.

"At least fifteen minutes," Mina said. They turned and walked into the crowd. They were each handed a lit, small, white candle with a paper guard to catch spent wax. They nodded to a few friends as they walked through the crowd, and headed toward the ridge trail head.

Walking along, holding their candles, Nick and Mina looked like any other pair of teenagers searching for a quiet spot to relax and take their minds off the events of the past few days. They held hands as they walked.

Then, Nick was yanked from his feet up into a tree.

It wasn't Hank.

It wasn't Ben.

And Mina didn't let go of his hand.

But she did drop the candle, and smashed the blood sucker

holding Nick in the face with her fist, then her elbow.

The vampire let go of Nick, and he fell fifteen feet toward the rocky path below but was caught by what he thought was a bear.

"Gotcha," Bruce said then put Nick on his feet.

"You were a little hungry, weren't you?" Mina said as she held the blood sucker by the collar and kneed him in the stomach. The force of her blow sent the blood sucker sailing off the branch and crashing into the rock ledge where they had been heading. Donald, the man who had been chained up in Hank's barn, looked down as his master tumbled down the rocks.

The mosquito got ahold of the ledge, righted himself, then turned toward Mina and bared his fangs. It screamed a blood curdling scream. Its face was monstrous, and its eyes were black.

"I made him angry," Mina said as she came down next to Nick.

"I think he's hungry," Nick said. "Maybe you should make him dead as soon as possible."

"Don't rush me," Mina jumped up into the air, pulling her sword from the sheath at her waist.

Ben came crashing down the ridge, knees first, into the mosquito's face, knocking it from its perch. It hit the brush at the bottom of the ridge, hard.

With her sword at full size, Mina came down on the mosquito's neck. The blood sucker wasn't beaten yet, and commando rolled out of the way. Mina cut deep into the Earth. The vampire turned on her so fast she didn't have time to pull her blade from the dirt. But before it could get its hands on her, Hank speared the blood sucker in the ribs with his enormous pink shoulder. They both slammed into the rock ledge and bounced off.

Mina had her sword free and rushed Jacob, looking to cut him in two, but he still had gas in his tank and took off for the beach. Mina slid to a stop in the wet leaves and brush, looking to Hank. Hank rolled to his feet and grunted. He pointed in the direction of the beach with his chin, and tusks, then shook his head.

"Can't stop now," Ben said as he fell noiselessly to Mina's side. "We need to take him before he gets to that crowd."

All three nodded and took off.

"You guys run too fast," Nick said. A little sparrow flittered down and landed on his shoulder. "I was wondering where you were, Penny."

The little Penny-sparrow chirped then hopped off his shoulder, landing next to Nick in her familiar little girl form.

"We need to get you some super powers," Penny said. "You're too slow."

"That's what I've been saying all along," Nick said.

"That is a horrible idea," Bruce said stepping next to Nick and Penny as they headed down the trail.

Heading down at a good pace, Nick didn't want to miss the action. Luckily for him, the vampire was not going down easily. Off in the distance, someone had either hit or tossed the blood sucker in Nick, Ben and Penny's direction because the vampire crashed onto the trail right in front of Nick. Bruce grabbed him by the shoulders and spun him so that Nick was standing behind the Sasquatch.

"Your fur stinks," Nick said.

The vampire rose slowly, and Bruce brought both of his fists down on the vampire's head like a hammer. The blood sucker hit the ground again, but rolled away out of reach. Penny had flittered off as the sparrow, chirping and whistling.

Out of the darkness to Nick's left, Ben slammed into the vampire. He wrapped his arms around the mosquito's waist, and growled, "Now Mina!"

Mina came down out of the sky with her sword over her head. Having learned from the past, she shrunk the size of the sword down at the last second so that when it cut throughout the mosquito it only scratched Ben's torso lightly.

The vampire fell from Ben's arms in two pieces. The head and left arm went in one direction and the right arm, most of the torso and legs went the other.

Ben's shirt fell open, cut cleanly from the collar to the bottom, and the scratch from Mina's sword glistened with blood.

"Is it dead?" Nick asked.

The vampire laid in two pieces on the forest floor at Ben's feet.

Then its left hand twitched.

"Nope," Hank said as he walked up naked and stood next to Nick.

Mina hacked the left arm off, cut the head off, then carved the larger portion into three pieces.

"Why isn't it turning to dust?" Penny asked as she popped up next to Mina.

"Maybe that only works on weaker creatures," Mina said.

"Weird," Penny said.

"You okay, Ben?" Nick looked at Ben.

"Not really," Ben said then fell to his butt in the wet leaves. He touched the wound on his chest, then looked at his fingers.

Penny fell to her knees at his side, and looked over the cut. "It's not healing. He's not healing."

"That's not good," Ben said and laid back. "This is a very strange feeling indeed. Been a while since something has hurt this much."

"No," Penny cried. "Do something, Mina!"

"I…I," Mina sheathed her sword and fell to her knees on Ben's other side. "I don't know what to do."

"Don't worry, I can take care of this," Conan said as he walked up slowly. "Don't you know that vampire blood is poisonous to werecreatures? And I'm sure that a cut from your sword can't be good for any of us, Mina."

"Kinda forgot with everything going on," Ben said and coughed a laugh.

"Forgot about that, too," Hank said.

"Is it lethal?" Penny asked.

"No, just hurts real bad and makes one weak," Conan said. "But I can help if you give me some room."

Penny and Mina stood and backed up so Conan could put his hands on Ben's chest.

"There," Conan said. "Still gonna hurt for a bit, but you'll heal in a minute of two.

"Thanks," Ben sat up, "Yup still stings."

Penny helped Ben to his feet, "Don't scare me like that again, okay?"

"Sorry, sweetheart, I'll do better next time," Ben smiled, keeping his arm around Penny. He looked around, then said. "Where's Bruce?"

Everyone looked around, then the sound of giant feet, quietly crunching leaves came down the trail along with the sound of someone struggling to get free of a larger creature's grasp.

"Figured we should say a proper goodbye to our new friend Donald here," Bruce said. Donald was trapped in the Bigfoot's grasp, his mouth covered by Bruce's enormous hand.

Nick smiled, "Maybe a nice bonfire to take care of the leftover pieces of his former master to send him off."

Pointing down, Ben said, "I don't think that will be necessary."

"Interesting," Nick said as he looked down at the pieces of Jacob that were slowly turning to ash, flaking and disappearing into the leaves and sticks and dirt.

"Do you think anyone heard all that racket?" Nick asked and looked over his shoulder in the direction of the beach.

"Maybe we should go find out?" Mina said.

"We'll take Donald here back to my house," Hank said.

Nick stepped closer to Bruce and Donald, who was suspended in the air with his mouth still covered. Nick looked into Donald's eyes and said "I have an idea and I think that Donny here will be more than cooperative in giving us a hand later."

Donald nodded.

"Good," Nick said and turned on his heel and headed down the trail with Mina at his side.

Ben, Bruce, Hank and Penny escorted Donald back to Hank's barn through the woods.

The beach was empty now, except for fifty or so umbrellas. Julie floated around the sand and umbrellas shaking her head and smiling.

"Maybe we were louder than I thought," Mina said.

"Yeah, everyone freaked out as you were cutting that vamp apart in the woods," Julia smiled. "It was hilarious as everyone scrambled to their cars."

"I wonder if Filomena has a skid mark or two in his drawers," Nick laughed.

A siren screamed in the distance, then the lights of the police cruiser lit up the access road and the parking area next to the beach. Officer Stephenson jumped out of the car and ran down the beach, gun drawn, "How did I know you two would be down here? And what the hell is going on?"

"Couple of coyotes fighting over a choice bit of deer, I suspect," Nick said.

"You can put that away," Mina said.

Holstering his weapon, Officer Stevenson said, "I thought you were going to call me if something was going down?"

"We said we would get in touch of we needed you," Nick said. "We didn't."

"What did you two do?" Stevenson asked.

"Killed Donald's blood sucking master," Nick said. "And now I'm really hungry."

"You're hungry?" Mina said. "You barely did anything."

"Leading troops into battle is hard work too," Nick said.

"Who's Donald?" Stevenson asked.

"The werescorpion," Nick said

"He's back at Hank's house," Julie disappeared.

"She thinks he can hear her, how cute," Nick said. "Hank and Ben brought him back to the barn."

"Who is this 'she' you just referred to?" Stevenson asked.

"Our ghost friend, Julie," Mina said. "And yes, the one who was killed on the beach last spring."

"Seriously?" Stevenson asked as Mina and Nick walked toward his cruiser. "Wait, where are you going?"

"Will you give us a lift over to Hank's?" Mina said as she stopped next to the police car. "I don't feel like walking back there."

"I would suggest bringing you to your respective homes," Stevenson said as he walked to the driver's side door. "But I don't think you'll even entertain my advice."

"We might go home tonight," Nick said. "But probably not

since our families are safer with us not being under the same roofs as them. Or within miles of them, for that matter."

"Oh," Stevenson said as they all got into the cruiser. "Gotcha."

"What are we gonna do about ol' Donnie, anyway?" Mina asked as they pulled out of the parking lot.

"I've been wondering if he would like a little vacation to Scotland," Nick said.

"Wait, what?" Mina asked.

"If a note shows up on Stone's desk, then he will know I can get into his castle, and that could be seen as a little aggressive on our part," Nick said. "But if I leave a present on his doorstep, with a nice little invitation, that might be less threatening."

"But Tine is already set to leave the note for Stone on his desk," Mina said.

"I'll let her know the plan has changed," Nick said looking out the window at the darkness on the side of the road.

"And you think that Stone won't kill Donnie the minute he sees him?" Mina asked.

"Stone will still read the note either way," Nick said.

Stevenson and Mina both tensed up and slowly looked to each other, then back to the road ahead.

"Fine, I'll bring him straight to Tine, with a message from Jacob about finding us," Nick said. "And she can let him go before Stone even sees him."

Mina and Stevenson relaxed, a little.

A few moments later, they pulled into Hank's driveway. Nick and Mina headed inside and got to the task of amending their plans.

*****

Ghost Walking didn't even faze Donald in the slightest. In his time as a slave with Jacob he had seen so many weird and horrible things that his only comment was that it was a neat trick.

They found Valen Tine easily, and she promised to get Donald out safely after he explained that Jacob had found the pen and the sword, that the one's in possession of these items wanted to talk with Stone, civilly, and try and come to an understanding and make a compromise. And Donald was to tell Stone when and where Nick and Mina would be waiting.

Nick knew Stone would come, but the monster wouldn't be coming to compromise, he would be coming to take what he wanted.

*****

"Where did the two of you end up hiding out after all that racket at Chatfield?" Filomena slapped Nick on his back while Nick changed out books between his locker and backpack.

"Ended up taking off with everyone else," Nick said. "What do you think all of that was, anyway?"

"Probably two coyotes humping or something," Filomena said. "I tried to go investigate but Holly was being such a rag about it."

"That sounded like coyotes to you? Of all people, you don't think that was something a little bit more, sinister than coyotes?" Nick slammed his locker shut and threw his bag over his shoulder.

Looking around, Filomena leaned in and put his arm around Nick's shoulder and whispered, "I think there's another dead kid and they're not telling us about it. I think we should go investigate."

"I heard the cops already combed through the woods and found squat," Nick said.

"You think for a minute that if they did find something they would have told any of us about it?" Filomena said.

"Yeah, they seemed to have no problem the past ten times," Nick said. "Why would they suddenly get shy now?"

"Cause there were so many of us down there, all at the scene of the crime," Filomena said as they walked toward their geography class. He looked around at all the students that littered the halls and raced toward their classes. "It was probably one of the kids, teachers or parents that's been killing all these kids."

"What if it was a mix of all of them?" Nick said quietly as they walked ingot hero class.

"Holy Hell, I didn't think about it that way," Filomena said as they sat down at their desks.

"Nick," Mina said from the doorway.

Nick stood up and headed over to the door, "What's up?"

"I'm freaking out," Mina said.

"Why?" Nick asked.

"Why do you think?" Mina said and pulled Nick out into the hall.

"What do you want me to do?" Nick said.

"Ditch school with me," Mina said.

"And do what?" Nick said.

"Anything, everything, nothing," Mina said. "The waiting is killing me. My heart and my head won't stop racing."

"Do you want to go for a run with Penny or Bruce?" Nick asked.

Taking Nick's hand, Mina said, "No, I just want to be around you."

"Then let's go on an adventure," Nick smiled and headed toward the nearest exit dragging Mina behind him.

Sticking his head out from the doorway, Filomena yelled, "I wanna go on an adventure too?"

"Sorry, friend-o, you have to stay and take notes," Nick yelled over his shoulder. "And make sure they're legible."

Chapter 23
Ashes to Ashes

Nick and Mina spent the day riding around town, getting lunch at 9 East Main, getting ice cream at Friendly's, then spent a little bit of time alone in the barn behind Nick's house.

His mother and grandmother were out when Nick and Mina got to his house. It was a little after four when Sue and Trudy pulled into the driveway in a pickup with something large wrapped in moving blankets in the bed. Nick and Mina stood in the driveway.

"Hey, guys," Trudy said as she opened the driver's side door.

"Give us a hand getting this into the barn," Sue said as she got out of the passenger's seat.

"What is it?" Nick asked as he opened the tailgate. He jumped up into the bed of the truck.

"It is an antique curio cabinet from one of the Kelsey houses Hank bought. He thought it would look perfect in the living room here," Trudy said.

"How did you two get this in here," Nick grunted as he lifted up one end of the cabinet.

"Seemed pretty light when Ben and Hank put it up there," Sue said.

"I'll help you," Mina jumped up onto the side of the truck, balancing easily on the thin rail.

"Really, Mina?" Nick looked from Mina to the cabinet.

Losing her balance, Mina dropped down into the bed of the truck, "Would have stuck that landing if you hadn't rushed me."

"Sure," Nick said.

"I'll get the barn door," Trudy said.

"Be careful, that thing is handmade and sturdy, but really can't use anymore bumps or bruises," Trudy said. "It has enough character as it is."

"I was more worried about the glass," Mina said.

"We took the doors off and left them in my car for that very reason," Trudy said.

"Smart," Nick said as he jumped off of the tailgate. "Let's get it closer to the edge, and then we can pick it off the tailgate."

"Okay," Mina pushed it gently toward Nick and it slid easily on the blanket toward him. They got it positioned long ways on the tailgate.

Mina jumped off the truck landing right next to Nick. She grabbed one side and picked it up easily. "Ready?"

"Maybe," Nick put his hands under the other side and slid it off slowly.

"I'll go backwards," Mina said and they started with small steps toward the barn. Twenty feet later Mina gently placed her side on the ground inside the barn.

"You're a strong little minx," Sue said as Mina helped Nick tip the cabinet up onto its feet.

Nick was sweating profusely.

Mina was not.

"Nick had the heavy end," Mina smiled.

"Smart girl," Trudy laughed.

"We're going to head over to grab my car at the Kelsey house we got this sucker at," Trudy said. "Then drop this back off at Mike Valenti's house. Probably going to make him some dinner as well to thank him for letting us borrow his truck."

"Poor man doesn't look like he's had a good meal since his wife passed. Been about a year now. Surprised he hasn't starved to death," Sue said as she closed the barn door.

"Hank said he had some work he needed help with over at his place," Trudy said as she opened the driver's side door. "I volunteered the both of you."

"Both of us?" Mina asked.

"Yes, both of you," Sue said as she got into the truck. She leaned out the open window a bit. "Don't forget to bring a jacket Nick, it's been getting chilly these past few nights."

"Yes, ma'am," Nick said and cocked his head to the side.

"See you two later," Trudy yelled out the window then fired the truck up.

Nick and Mina waved as his mother and grandmother backed out of the driveway.

"Grab your jacket, and let's roll," Mina smacked Nick on the butt.

"OOOOOOOOWWWWWW," Nick yelled through clenched teeth. "Too hard!"

"Wuss," Mina shook her head and walked over to her scooter as Nick headed into the house.

When Nick came out Mina's scooter was already purring and she handed him his helmet.

"Are you packing heat?" Mina said.

"Yes," Nick said.

"Kinda weird that your grandma reminded you to take your jacket," Mina said as she got on the scooter.

"Yeah, kinda threw me for a loop for a moment," Nick said. "But she is a grandma, and that is the kind of stuff they worry about."

"Very true," Mina said as she opened up the throttle and took off into the street.

The beach was only a few minutes away from Nick's house, and the sun was already going down. The days had become much shorter as the fall had begun to take hold of New England, and the changing leaves were falling in reds, yellows, oranges and browns. They parked, stowed their helmets and held hands as they walked over to the beach.

"I hate the waiting part," Mina said. "The anxiety and the anticipation are killing me."

"Yeah, the whole 'not knowing if you're gonna be dead or alive at sunrise' is pretty nerve-racking." Nick said as they sat down on the covered swing overlooking the beach and water.

"Not funny," Mina said and leaned into him.

"False," Nick smiled and kissed Mina on the top of her head.

"Are we gonna make it through this?" Mina asked.

"Honestly, this has all been way less chaotic so far than I imagined. Kinda anti-climactic so far," Nick said. "So I've got no idea what might happen."

"That's not very reassuring," Mina said.

"Well, I hope you're ready," Nick said. "You're my ace in the hole. And they're here."

Walking down the beach from the small marina next door were Valen Tine and Frank Stone.

"They came by boat?" Mina asked.

"Ghost ship actually, young lady," Frank Stone said from right behind Nick and Mina.

Valen Tine appeared in front of them holding a sword, her face like granite - showing no emotion, no fear, no recognition.

Mina pulled her sword from the sheath on her belt and kicked Tine backwards in one motion.

Stone didn't move.

"You guys are fast," Nick said, keeping his attention on Mina and Tine, who were now sword fighting on the beach. The moon was close to full and even though it wasn't very high in the sky yet, it made for an exhilarating view. The two women went back and forth, only silhouettes against the sand and water.

"The two of you are very brave, coming here alone to meet with me," Frank Stone said stepping beside the swing, watching Mina and Tine as well.

"I wouldn't say we are alone," Nick said.

Charles's master, the Jinn, rose from a puff of smoke and red flame on the opposite side of the swing as Stone. "I thought you'd be bigger."

"Oh, you brought a Jinn," Stone said.

"He came mostly to watch," Nick said.

"And what, pray tell, is he here to watch?" Stone asked looking over to Nick with his one brown eye and one blue eye.

"A fight it seems," Nick said. "I know you can easily snap my little mortal neck, but I have another idea."

"And what is that?" Stone asked.

"We talk for a few minutes while the ladies work off some nervous energy," Nick stood up. "Walk with me?"

"I'll entertain this for a few moments," Stone smiled and

stepped slowly in the sand next to Nick. They kept their focus on the two women fighting in the moonlight.

"You can't take the pen or the sword from us," Nick said and pulled out the pen. "You don't seem to grasp the fact that these items are just what help us tap into our power."

"Then give them to me," Stone said.

Nick stopped, turned toward Stone and held the pen out. "Here."

Stone stopped and his lips parted ever so slightly. He looked at the pen, then to Nick and back to the pen.

"What do you think you will be able to do once you have the pen and the sword?" Nick asked, still holding the pen out.

"There are legends," Stone said, "that suggest the people who wield the power of these can write their own destiny."

"You think if you have these two pieces of the puzzle your plan for dominating the mortal world and the supernatural world will be unstoppable?" Nick asked.

"More or less," Stone said.

"Then take it," Nick said again. Then he turned toward the two women fighting on the beach and yelled, "Mina, give Valen Tine your sword."

Mina had been in the air coming down with a powerful blow with her sword when Nick yelled to her. She was able to pull back enough to merely send Valen Tine sliding back in the sand as she blocked with her weapon.

"Okay," Mina said and held out her sword to the Tine could take it by the handle.

"What kind of game is this?" Tine asked.

"No game," Nick said. "Take the items you came for and leave. Or we will have to kill you."

Throwing his head back, Stone let out a laugh that rumbled in Nick's belly. Then Stone said, "Kill us? How would you possibly be able to do that? Nothing can kill me. I was resurrected and do not suffer the weakness of the mortal coil. I have burned and I have bled, and I have drowned and been cut and shot and nothing has ever caused me more than a few moments of pain."

"Nothing on this beach is immortal. Well, maybe that stink monster over there is," Nick pointed to the Jinn. The Jinn crossed his arms and scowled.

"Do you understand who and what I am?" Stone said. "I am something that has only been accomplished once. I am the dead reborn, not just a lifeless husk reanimated for a moment. I have spent most of my time gathering the strongest magic this world has ever seen and made myself more powerful with each new spell, with each new item I acquired. Because mortals felt they had to experiment with life and death they got more than they bargained for."

"Was it one of Giovanni Aldini's students who created you or was it he who did this to you?" Nick asked, still holding the pen out for Stone.

"What?" Stone said, his eyes fixed on the pen.

"You didn't think that once I figured out what you were I wouldn't find out who might have created you or how, or where? Mary Shelley based her story on real events, events that some people knew about because of the newspaper's coverage of the George Forster execution in 1803, and Aldini's experiments on the murderer's corpse. But I know that you aren't Forster, at least most of you isn't him, because there is a description of him from before the execution. But you could have his heart or brain or something," Nick said. "And are you going to take this thing? My arm is getting tired."

"How do I know it is the real pen?" Stone said collecting himself slightly.

Mina was still holding her sword out for Tine, motioning for Tine to take it.

Valen Tine looked to Stone who was now looking to her, then looked to the sword and reached for it slowly. Tine wrapped her fingers around the handle slowly, tightening her grip and took the sword from Mina. The sword changed size in Tine's hand, becoming smaller and then back to its full size. Tine smiled, looked to Stone and nodded.

Stone snatched the pen out of Nick's hand. He looked it over and closed his eyes.

"Kill them," Stone said and turned on his heels in the sand.

"You don't get it do you?" Nick said.

"I have what I want," Stone said.

"When you killed my uncle and his protector, how long did you search for the pen and sword after she threw them into the sky?" Nick asked.

"I hadn't stopped until today," Stone said.

"Please put it together so I don't have to explain everything to you like I'm some Bond villain," Nick said.

"Wait, that would make him James Bond, Nick," Mina said.

"Damn it," Nick said. "Anyway, don't you get it Stone? We die and the pen and the sword go bye-bye too."

Stopping in the sand, Stone turned slowly back toward Nick, "Then you come with us."

"Not without a fight," Nick said.

A smile crept across Stone's scarred face, "Really?"

"And there's the monster I expected to see tonight," Nick said. And at that exact moment, the blue Nova came screaming into the beach parking lot and screeched to a stop.

The driver's side door opened first and Hank got out. The passenger's side door opened and Ben got out holding Nate Stone in his arms.

"Nathaniel?" Frank Stone whispered. "What is the meaning of this?"

"I gave you the option of taking the pen and the sword and leaving, but you had to be greedy," Nick said. "And you will never stop because you will never be satisfied."

"Let go of my son or I will kill all of you," Stone said.

"We are all prepared to die, but he will die too," Nick said looking to the boy.

"I will kill all of your families if a single hair is out of place on his head," Stone screamed.

Mina took that moment to kick the sword that was lying in the sand into the air where she grabbed it.

"You wish to give me a reason to burn every living thing on this planet to ash?" Stone said.

"There would be nothing left for you to rule," Nick said. "So you would lose either way."

"Do you expect me to get on my knees and let you execute me?" Stone said.

"That would make it much easier on us, yes," Mina said.

"The other option is to see if you are fast enough to stop them from tearing your son in half," Nick said.

Stone moved so fast that it looked as though he had teleported to Nick. Luckily, Bruce had been hiding under the sand near where Nick was standing and got ahold of Stone's leg before he got to Nick. Stone tumbled onto the beach and Nick ran for the water. Stone was up before Nick got more than four steps away.

Bruce slammed Stone across the face with both fists, and the monster spit blood into the sand. He smiled, then kicked Bruce in the gut so hard the Sasquatch sailed off over the parking lot, over the grass, and into the marsh on the other side.

But Mina was between them, ready. She cut Stone deep in the belly but it did not seem to affect him. Stone brought his fists down at Mina. She was able to get her own arms up to block him, but the blow buried her hip deep in the sand.

This gave Nick the chance to get a few more steps toward the water. But Mina was stuck giving Stone the chance to get by her.

Stone did not go after Nick. Instead he turned and headed toward the two holding his son.

"Valen!" Stone screamed as he slammed into Hank.

Tumbling backward Hank slammed into the blacktop of the parking lot and bounced off into the tall grass.

Tossing the boy into the air, Ben began to turn. His clothes shredded from his changing body.

As Stone set his attention on Ben, the boy was well over head. Stone roared, searching the sky for his son but saw nothing but empty sky.

Now Ben was in his full were form, thousands of pounds of claw and shell and tail. He grabbed Stone with a giant claw. Ben squeezed and Stone struggled against the vice grip. He pounded at the shell, over and over so fast and so hard the shell cracked and it echoed over the beach and water.

Mina was now free and searched the beach for Nick. He had run to the water where he faced Valen Tine.

Mina jumped up into the air and came down between Tine and Nick, her sword raised.

"We were just discussing what comes next," Nick said.

"I hope that doesn't involve double crossing us," Mina said. "I would be a shame for me to kill her with her own sword."

"No, the next step is we cut him," Tine pointed toward Stone who was struggling against Ben's claw, "to pieces, burn him down and spread his ashes around the world."

"That could be fun too," Mina said. "But it looks like Ben will get to that before we do."

Ben reached up with his other claw to get a double hold on Stone. But Stone kept beating on the cracking shell of Ben's claw, no matter how hard Ben squeezed. The pain the crack caused Ben made him lose his grip and Stone was able to kick free of the other claw and fell to the blacktop.

Stone turned and grabbed Hank who had rushed up behind him and tossed him through the air, slamming into the werelobster form of Ben. Ben's cracked claw was laying on the ground, oozing, and the added blow of an eight hundred pound werepig made him lose his form and he tumbled into the sand as a man.

Hank sprung straight up from the collision and sprinted toward Stone.

Ben pushed himself up with his good arm and got to his feet. He stumbled a few steps as he watched Hank lower his shoulder and slam into Frank Stone.

Stone did not move. Instead, he grabbed Hank by the back of the head, then kneed Hank directly in the face and sent him up into the air and down onto his back.

Smiling, Stone turned around and picked up the powder blue 1970 Chevy Nova. He turned back to where Hank lay on his back, stunned. Stone brought the car down as though it were a hammer toward Hank.

"NOOOOOOOOOO!" Ben screamed and launched himself at Stone.

With lighting fast reflexes, Stone was able to redirect his swing of the car at Ben, but as it connected, Stone lost his grip. Ben and the car sailed off into the grass on the other side of the parking lot.

"BEN?!?" Penny screamed as she landed next to where the car lay on top of Ben's broken body.

"Penny," Ben whispered. Blood oozed from his mouth, nose, eyes and ears. "Run, please. Save yourself."

"I'm not leaving you, Ben," Penny cried, tears streaming down her face. "I can get you out of here. I can get you help."

There was no answer from Ben.

Penny screamed. Then she exploded in fire and launched herself into the air.

Mina, Tine and Nick ran toward the parking lot. Nick slid down next to Hank to check him out while Mina and Tine took guard in front of them.

"You okay, man?" Nick asked Hank who was bloody.

"No," Hank said.

"Lame," Nick said.

"Where is my son?" Stone yelled looked around frantically. "Nathaniel?!? NATHANIEL!?!"

"Where's Penny?" Mina asked.

"Did she run off?" Nick asked. "And where's Ben?"

"He's under the car," Hank said quietly.

Stone roared again.

"That doesn't sound good," Nick said.

Then there was the sound of beating wings, enormous beating wings. Then the woosh of fire as a dragon came swooping down, lighting up Frank Stone.

"You think fire can hurt me?" Stone yelled as he reached for the tail of the dragon. He got his fist wrapped around the end of the tail and yanked the dragon down hard, slamming it into Mina and the pavement. Stone's clothes burned away leaving him smoking and charred, but still moving and fighting.

The blow knocked the wind out of the beast and stunned it enough to force it back into its familiar form of Penny the little girl.

"PENNY!" Nick screamed and rushed past Valen toward

Mina and Penny. He slid in next to them and checked both girls for a pulse. Luckily, it was there, but faint. But Mina had absorbed most of the blow, and laid unconscious with her arms wrapped around Penny. Blood ran from Mina's nose, mouth, eyes and ears.

"No, no, no no, no," Nick growled and took Mina's hand in both of his and willed his strength to her, all that he had and more.

Stone stood over them, his fists raised, and said, "You are all dead."

Nick looked up at the monster, and said, "To the death."

But before Stone could bring his fists down, Hank speared the monster with a shoulder tackle knocking him backwards a few steps.

With a great roar, Frank Stone wrapped his hands around Hank's neck. Stone pulled Hank's arms lose and lifted the werepig into the air, strangling him. Bruce rushed from the marsh toward Stone, but the monster brought his leg up, slammed Bruce in the chest with his massive foot, and pinned the Sasquatch to the ground.

Hank reached his hands out and wrapped his fingers around the monster's neck and squeezed as hard as he could.

Stone smiled.

Mina's eyes flew open, she let go of Penny, and hurled herself onto Stone's back. She wrapped her arms around Stone's head and yanked toward the sky.

"Cut deep, Valen," Mina screamed. "NOW!"

With no hesitation, Valen Tine kicked Hank out of Frank Stone's grasp and plunged Mina's sword into the monster's chest. It was like slamming the blade into granite, but Tine had used every ounce of strength she had to sink that blade into his chest. Right through his heart, out his back and right through Mina.

Mina's eyes widened.

Her sword was buried to the hilt in Stone's chest, and the blade angled up through the monster, into Mina's stomach and out of her back.

Stone looked down at his wife and whispered, "What have you done, Valen?"

Valen's eyes welled up with tears, but she said nothing.

"MINA?" Nick yelled as he stood.

Mina snapped to attention and screamed. And as she screamed she yanked on Frank Stone's head as hard as she could. A great and terrible ripping sound came from the flesh at Stone's neck, and he screamed in pain. He tried to bring his arms up to grab Mina but she was too fast and tore his head from his body as she pushed herself off of Frank Stone's back with her legs. She slid up the blade of the sword and tumbled to the ground.

Frank Stone's massive head rolled from Mina's grasp and came to a stop at Nick's feet.

Nick looked to Mina, who was bleeding profusely on the ground, then to Frank Stone's head. His massive body crumpled to the ground.

Nick looked back to Mina and was about to run to her when she whispered, "Go, this is our chance."

Grimacing, Nick turned to Frank Stone's head and picked it up. It was heavy and blood dripped down from the wound to the blacktop. He didn't know where the pen was and didn't have a map, but as he had told Stone earlier, he was the pen, and all the power was within him. He closed his eyes and saw Julie floating next to a volcano. Steam and smoke and sulfur filled the air as Julie touched Nick, knocking him to his rear on the rocky path next to a lava flow at the Hawaii Volcano Observatory. Nick no longer needed a map, or the pen, to ghost walk.

Nick looked over at Frank Stone's head and smiled. He stood up, pulled the .45 from under his jacket and put a bullet right between Franks Stone's eyes. "At least now I can say I've shot someone between the eyes."

Frank Stone's head looked up at Nick, then spoke in a low raspy tone, "You have not won yet."

"Pretty sure I have," Nick grabbed the head by the hair, then flung it into the lava flow. The lava swallowed it easily, hissing and spitting as it did.

"That was rather anticlimactic, I was expecting an —," Julia said but was interrupted by an explosion from under the lava that shot a plume of magma a hundred feet into the air. "Wow, you might want to get out of here before that lands on your head."

Looking up Nick coughed through the smoke and the sulfur, "Thanks, Captain Obvious." Closing his eyes Nick pictured Mina's house. Inside, the small children who played in the dining room were all sitting there, going about their usual games, and Nick placed his hand on one of their shoulders. The ghost boy looked up at Nick in horror as Nick fell into a chair at the dining room table.

In the other room, Mr. Medellin got up slowly from his chair and looked into the dining room. He reached in and flicked the light switch on.

"Nicholas?" Mr. Medellin said. "Why are you covered in soot and stink like Hell?"

"I was just standing next to an active lava flow at Hawaii's Kilauea Volcano," Nick said and coughed. "May I have some water please?"

"Of course," Rogelio said and went into the kitchen.

Nick stood up and walked into the living room, and looked up at the television. Game seven of the 1986 World Series was on and it was the bottom of the ninth.

Mr. Medellin came into the room and handed Nick the water. Nick drank the entire thing down then pointed at the television. His voice was low and course as he said, "The Mets are really that far ahead?"

"Si, mijo, they are," Rogelio smiled.

Nick smiled, then fell unconscious on the couch.

The empty glass in his hand didn't fare so well. It slipped from his fingers and shattered on the hardwood floor.

"Oh boy," Mr. Medellin said and ran to the phone.

*****

"Holy crap!" Nick yelled as he sat bolt upright. "Where the hell am I?"

"Mina's house," Sue said putting her right hand on Nick's chest. She pushed lightly, and said, "I used smelling salts to wake you up. Lie back for a few minutes and get your baring."

Following the instructions, Nick put his head back on the couch pillow.

"I'm fine," Nick said. His voice still raspy from the smoke at the volcano.

"I don't know if you're fine Nicholas, you passed out right before the Mets won the World Series and Rogelio called your mother and me to come check on you," Sue said.

"Been an emotional roller coaster of an evening. The Mets doing the impossible just kinda pushed me over the edge," Nick said looking up at his grandmother.

"I bet, after what you just did," Sue smiled. "I knew you could do it."

"Thanks for the vote of confidence Grandm--, wait what?" Nick sat back up and spun his feet to the floor.

"Silly boy," Sue picked up a glass of water and handed it to him. "Drink this."

Nick took the glass and sipped. Then he gulped the rest of it down.

"Please explain what you meant, Grandma," Nick said. "And where's mom?"

"Your mother is with Hank and Penny right now upstairs. The poor child was hysterical after what happened," Sue said.

"What happened?" Nick growled.

Sue took her grandson's hand and whispered, "Ben didn't make it."

Stunned, Nick looked his grandmother in the eye.

"Nicholas, you really thought I didn't know what you are or what you were capable of?" Sue smiled. "You think the women of this family are naive and don't have our own place in all of this?"

"I never knew what to think because there was no one around to teach me," Nick said. "I didn't know how to bring it up either."

"I did what I could, Nicholas," Sue said. "But the men in our family have always employed a trial by fire method of training. It's a tradition. Even more so in this case, it was a necessity."

"Why the hell was it a necessity?" Nick yelled. "How many times have we almost died over the past few months, and how many of our friends are now dead because of this?"

"Please calm down, Nicholas," Trudy said as she walked down the stairs.

Trudy motioned Nick over to her.

Nick stood up and went to his mother. She wrapped her arms around him and squeezed him as hard as she could.

Sue sat down on the couch.

"You have no idea how hard all of this has been on me," Trudy said. "Your grandmother is the only one who understands how hard it was. When my brother died, I knew I would have a son that I would have to send into war against the strongest, most vicious creatures on the planet. For what you had to do, we knew that your abilities would manifest faster and stronger."

"A lesson learned is far more powerful than a lesson taught," Sue said.

"So you knew about everything we did?" Nick asked, still hugging his mother.

"Not everything," Trudy said. "But the big stuff. And we're sorry about the people you have lost. We both loved Gertrude, but she knew exactly what she was doing. And Ben turned out to be an amazing man in the end. His time with Penny changed his life and he was also well aware of what could happen by helping you."

"And they would both die for you again if given the choice, as all of us would," Sue said.

"I never wanted anyone to die for me though," Nick said. "I would rather they were both here, to take care of Penny and teach Mina more about who she is and what she can do than sit here myself."

"And that is why you are a leader, Nicholas," Sue said.

"Where's Mina?" Nick asked.

"She's upstairs Nick, but she was a little worse off than you when Hank and Bruce got her back here. She hasn't fully healed yet or woken up," Sue said.

"What?" Nick said and rushed passed his mother up the stairs.

Mr. Medellin was sitting in a chair next to Mina's bed, holding her limp hand. Nick stayed in the doorway as Roger looked slowly over his shoulder at a Nick.

Mina's sheets and blanket were bloody, and her breathing was shallow.

"Why isn't she healing?" Nick asked. "And why haven't you brought her to an emergency room?"

"Not sure exactly, and no doctor can do anything I didn't try," Conan said as he appeared next to Nick. "Probably a mixture of Stone's blood, the amount energy it took to tear his head off and her own sword being stabbed through her gut. Only God knows what sort of curses he may have had on his blood."

Nick stepped into the room and stood beside the bed looking down at Mina. Mr. Medellin's eyes were red and puffy.

Trudy had come up the stairs and leaned in the doorway.

"Whenever she's been run down or hurt before, she came to me and got better," Nick said.

Mr. Medellin held Mina's hand out to Nick and nodded. He took her hand gently and looked down at her in the bed. He looked to his mother, who smiled, then to Mina again. Then he lay down next to her and wrapped his arms around her.

Nick kissed her forehead and held her gently.

Trudy walked over and pulled the blanket back, exposing the bandage that was on Mina's stomach. Pulling the bandage back, Trudy looked over the wound.

"The bleeding has stopped," Trudy said as she covered it back up.

"The bleeding would have stopped one way or another," Conan said and walked out of the room.

"Leprechauns have the worst bedside manner," Trudy said as she walked to the door. "Let's let them get some rest, Roger. You look like you could use some shut eye yourself."

"I think a night cap is in order first," Roger said as he closed the door.

*****

The sun was up and the wound on Mina's stomach was healed shut.

She was still unconscious.

Nick had not left her once all night.

The Living

*****

Darkness had come and gone as the sun and moon chased each other round the world.

Mina would have a scar on her stomach and back the rest of her life.

She had not woken up.

Nick had not eaten or left her side for more than a few moments.

The Living

*****

As the light trickled in through the thinning trees, Nick squeezed Mina a little tighter than he had been all night.

"Too tight," Mina mumbled softly.

"Oh good, neither of us are dead," Nick whispered.

"Not funny," Mina groaned.

The Living

*****

The sun was high in the sky and Nick, Valen Tine, Nathaniel Stone, Charles, the Jinn and Bruce were standing on the beach at Chatfield Hollow.

Nick had gone to Stone's castle on the Orkney Islands, gotten Nathaniel, and come back to fulfill his promise and collect his prize from the Jinn.

"So you won. What do you want, mud bag?" the Jinn said.

"Hold your horses, stinkbug," Nick said.

"I still think this is a bad idea, Nick," Charles said.

"I hope you have thought this out very thoroughly, Nicholas," Bruce said, arms crossed.

"Wait," Tine said. "What isn't a good idea?"

"I want Nathaniel Stone to be cured of his disease, to live life as a healthy boy, and grow up naturally."

The Jinn narrowed his eyes at Nick then said, "Done."

"No!" Tine screamed and reached for Nate. "There's always a consequence with these demons."

"Not this time," Nick said. "They can't manipulate my commands for their own amusement, a fringe benefit of putting my neck on the line all the time."

Tine dropped to her knees, looking at her boy, "Are you okay?"

The boy looked more relaxed than Nick had ever seen him.

"I think so. I feel a bit different," Nate said. He was leaning on his crutches. He shifted his weight from foot to foot, then lifted one foot off the ground, balanced on it, then did the same with the other foot. "My legs feel stronger and the muscles are loose. I don't remember ever feeling like this."

"Does anything hurt?" Tine looked him over frantically.

"The exact opposite," Nate smiled and handed his crutches to his mother. He stepped away from her, taking slow steps. He got ten feet away when he took off down the beach at a full sprint. About twenty yards out, he slid to a stop in the sand, turned and ran back to his mother, jumping up and hugging her. "Did you see that mom? Did you seem me running? I never thought I would do that!"

"I saw it, baby," Tine smiled and hugged her son.

"What else do you want?" The Jinn asked.

Nick looked at Valen Tine, then back to the Jinn, "I want Valen Tine to be free of all of her added gifts. I want her to be a healthy, young mother, and to grow and age naturally as a person."

"Wait, what are you doing?" Tine asked quietly.

"It's for the best, Valen," Nick said.

"NO!" Valen dropped her boy to his feet and lunged for Nick. Nick dodged her fist easily and caught her in his arms, and held her tight as she tried to squirm and flail out of the stronger young man's grasp.

"You were never supposed to be that powerful, and you made it clear to me you would rather have never had those powers or hurt all of those people. This is your second chance, Valen, to live a good life. Everyone deserves a second chance. And that's what I'm giving you."

Valen Tine stopped struggling, and sobbed into Nick's shoulder, hugging him back. "What am I supposed to do now? I have only known that life."

"You can do anything you want. Have you ever thought about going to college?" Nick said.

Valen leaned back from Nick, still holding onto his arms, "Have I ever thought about going to college? Are you out of your mind? I've spent over a decade with a monster set on conquering the world, so no, college hadn't ever really crossed my mind."

"Think of it as an adventure, ma," Nate smiled. "We can literally do anything now that we are free."

Tine let go of Nick and turned back to her son. She knelt down in front of him, and looked him in the eyes. "I'm sorry we had to go through all of this."

"Life has not been very fair to us, Ma, but this is a whole lot better than being prisoners. He may have been my father, but even I knew he was a monster. No matter how hard you tried to act like he wasn't."

"I tried to protect you from all of that," Tine said.

"That was impossible, Ma. I grew up trapped in a castle guarded by vampires and a dragon. And I had a lot of time to sneak around and read. I knew what my father was a long time ago." Nate kissed his mother on the forehead. "Tag you're it," he said, then ran off down the beach.

"Oh, it's like that huh?" Tine yelled and chased after him. She stumbled on her third step, over extending herself, but recovered and ran at a reasonable pace after the boy.

"That leaves one more," Charles said, who had been patiently watching everything unfold.

"Yeah, what else do you want?" The Jinn asked and crossed his arms.

Nick looked to Bruce, and the Sasquatch nodded.

Pulling out a brass Zippo Lighter, Nick looked it over in his hand. Then he held it up for the Jinn to see and said, "I want you trapped in this Zippo for the next ten thousand years."

With that request, the Jinn disappeared.

Charles's eyes widened and he looked from the lighter to Nick, to Bruce, and back to the lighter. His mouth fell open when he looked back at Nick.

"For the next ten thousand years, this will be that fart phantom's prison. He may be able to torment someone unlucky enough to stumble onto this Zippo, but I am going to do my best to hide this where it will be nearly impossible to find." Nick slid the lighter into his pocket. "And do you know what this means, Charles?"

"I'm free," Charles whispered. He pulled out a pocket knife, opened it, wrapped his left hand around the blade, and yanked it down with his right hand. He opened his hand to see a slice through his palm. Blood pooled in his hand as he watched. After a few moments, he looked up at Nick and said, "I'm not healing. I'm not healing!"

Charles jumped up and down and screamed it again, "I'm not healing! I'm free!"

Right then, Mina, Penny and Hank dropped to the beach from the sky.

"Thanks for leaving a note telling us where you were," Mina said shaking her head. "It's not like we haven't been fighting off monsters from every direction the past few days so it's totally cool if you go gallivanting wherever."

"I had to tie up a few loose ends," Nick smiled and looked down the beach at Nate running in circles around his mother who still hadn't tagged him. "And Bruce was with me."

"I thought he was crippled?" Hank said.

"Not anymore," Nick said. "And she's going to have a bit of a tougher time keeping up with him now that she doesn't have super powers."

"Excuse me?" Mina asked.

"Now that it's over, the bet I made with the Jinn to get three wishes if we defeated Stone," Nick said. "We won, so I made Nate a healthy young man and Valen a regular old single mom. And for my third trick, Charles is now free and will grow old just like the rest of us."

"Really?! That's awesome," Mina hugged Charles. "What are you gonna do with your newfound freedom?"

"I'm going to find Ishmael," Charles said. "And do whatever I have to free him."

"Why is your hand bleeding so profusely?" Mina asked.

"Yeah, so I cut my own hand to see if it would heal like I did before," Charles had his hand held up in front of him, and he was squeezing it with his other hand trying to stay the flow of blood. "May have been a bad idea."

"Bit dramatic, don't you think?" Nick said pulling off his sweatshirt and wrapping it around Charles's hand. "Penny, could you turn into a bird large enough to fly Charles back to the house so we can take care of his hand?"

"No problemo," Penny smiled and turned into an eagle the size of a Volkswagen.

"Hopefully only blind people live between here and Hank's house," Nick said.

"No one lives between here and my house," Hank said.

"Okay, that's good to know, Hank," Nick said. "Can you

head back with them, and take care of Charles's hand?"

"Yeah, sure," Hank said and launched himself into the air.

Penny the eagle motioned Charles to climb onto her back, and he did clumsily with the sweatshirt tied around his hand. She took off into the sky.

"I'll head back with them. Charles and I have plans to make," Bruce said and took off into the woods.

"Am I carrying you back?" Mina smiled.

"I think we can walk with Valen and Nate. I'm sure he won't mind stretching his legs," Nick said, took Mina's hand and they headed down the beach toward where Valen Tine and Nate Stone where playing tag.

Nate was now it.

The Living

Epilogue

Nick and Mina stood side by side holding hands in their blue robes, tassels dangling in their faces. Filomena and Holly stood behind them, also holding hands.

There were two sets of students ahead of them, and the front pair was called onto the stage, handed diplomas, and shook the hands of the Vice Principal, Principal, and Superintendent of the town.

Filomena smacked Nick on the rear, and giggled, "I'm nekked under this thing!"

"We know, you have told us about a million times," Nick said.

"I wonder if people can tell?" Filomena grinned ear to ear.

"Why don't you tell them instead of annoying us with this info over and over again?" Mina said.

"What should I do when I get on stage?" Filomena said. "Should I moon everyone?"

"I will murder you if you do that!" Holly smacked him on the shoulder.

The next pair were called onto the stage, got their diplomas and shook the line of hands.

"I don't think you have the balls to do that," Nick said smiling, looking ahead as his name was called. He stepped up onto the stage and a huge roar came from his mother and grandmother. A ridiculously loud clapping rang over everyone else's from Hank's giant hands. Nick took his diploma, shook the hands and turned just as they read Mina's name.

Nick put his fingers in his mouth and whistled as loud as he could, the noise piercing the clapping and hollering from the crowd.

Mina's grandmother and two of her cousins clapped alongside Nick's mother, grandmother and Penny.

But the hoots and hollers from Mr. Medellin still rose above all the clamor.

Mina took her diploma, shook the line of hands as fast as she could while still hiding the fact that she was possibly the fastest woman on Earth and ran for Nick. She jumped into his arms and squeezed him.

"Too hard," Nick gasped.

"False," Mina smiled. "You're still breathing."

The Living

To all my friends - thank you, thank you, thank you.

Jennifer, you have no idea how much you inspire me. Thank you for being such an amazing sister.

Joanna, seriously, nothing I can write even comes close to how much you have helped and inspired me to write this story down. Thank you so much. And Pete, I thank you for your support and I hope that I can shake your hand and thank you in person soon.

Jake, your turn. And thank you for being a great man and a great friend.

Nick, there are many reasons why I started to write, but you're the reason I finish.

Bryan, thanks for talking through the wall with me. Literally and figuratively.

Nod, thank you for reading and seeing what I could't see. *

Paul, I still miss your smile.

And Claire, every day is more wonderful than the last because of you.

*Except for this mistake, Bryan found this one.

The Living

Author Photograph by Bryan Capri

Jonathon Wolfer grew up in a small town on the shoreline of Connecticut. He's lived in New York, Los Angeles, and Las Vegas. He loves Harleys, loves telling stories, loves hearing them and he loves the great outdoors.

For more about his work and what else he is up to visit
www.thelonewolfer.com

The Living

www.ingramcontent.com/pod-product-compliance
Lightning Source LLC
Chambersburg PA
CBHW020738250626
47155CB00003B/811